MISSING

A gripping thriller full of stunning twists

CHARLIE
GALLAGHER

Published 2017 by Joffe Books, London.

www.joffebooks.com

This book is a work of fiction. Names, characters, businesses, organizations, places and events are either the product of the author's imagination or are used fictitiously. Any resemblance to actual persons, living or dead, events or locales is entirely coincidental. The spelling is British English.

ISBN-13: 978-1-912106-75-2

Dedicated to the team at Joffe Books. Let's see where this goes.

Author's Note

I am inspired by what I do and see in my day job as a front-line police detective, though my books are entirely fictional. I am aware that the police officers in my novels are not always shown positively. They are human and they make mistakes. This is sometimes the case in real life too, but the vast majority of officers are honest and do a good job in trying circumstances. From what I see on a daily basis, the men and women who wear the uniform are among the very finest, and I am proud to be part of one of the best police forces in the world.

Charlie Gallagher

Chapter 1

When the carnage began, the High Street still bustled, the shops had an hour left of trading and the fashion outlets and coffee shops still sucked in passing trade from Canterbury's ancient, cobbled streets.

The street vendor was at his usual prime pitch opposite the entrance to Mercery Lane, the short and narrow thoroughfare that led to the city's iconic cathedral and the surrounding square with its pubs and cafés thronged with shoppers and tourists. Just a few minutes earlier he had started packing up for the day. A warm Sunday afternoon, he should have known better.

As he stood behind his hot plate cooking crepes and doing his best to smile at the teenage couple joining the queue, his attention was snatched to the squeal of a car tyre turned sharply on the shiny cobbles. A big blue SUV was hurtling towards them. Pedestrians shrieked as they jumped out of the way, some pulling others with them.

'Look out!' the vendor shouted — just in time for the group queuing in front of him to leap back out of the way. The car now banked hard left, the offside clipping his cart as it swung left into Sun Street. The engine revved and it picked up speed. The vendor had time to flinch but not to move. He'd been narrowly missed; his cart lay on its side with frothy batter running into the city's drains. He could hear cries of pain and screams in the direction from which the car had come.

He watched the car as it sped towards the cathedral square and past a pub with chairs out the front where patrons swigged drinks in the last of the sunshine. Its nearside thumped into the kerb, it was now half on the pavement. It made token efforts to swerve from people who leapt out of its way. A middle-aged man didn't quite make it and took a glancing blow to his right hip — enough to throw him into a solid flint wall. The car pushed into the square, the noise of screams and shouts combining with screeching tyres as it pulled up harshly. Then it jerked right and out of the vendor's sight.

* * *

The woman followed the boy to a table by the window. Despite the shopping hanging from her arms, she was just about able to balance the items on the tray: cake and a latte in a tall, elegant glass for her and a bottle of water with a straw for him. A young waitress walked behind with the boy's toasted sandwich that wouldn't fit on the tray. Before he'd even sat down, the boy tore eagerly at the new pack of football cards she had bought for him. It had been a good day for them both, she reflected.

As she laid down the tray and hung her bags gently from the back of an empty chair, the woman was alerted to a high-pitched whine and the squeal of tyres just outside. She turned to see a big blue car reversing at speed. Less than twenty metres away, it stopped with a screeching of brakes and crunching of gears — then it surged forward. She saw passers-by flinch around it as it quickly picked up speed. It was coming right at them.

It all happened so fast and there was no time for reaction. No time for warning. The kerb outside was low and did nothing to slow the car's momentum and it crashed into the coffee shop window a split second later, shattering the glass like thin ice. The car bucked and bounced, plunging into the interior, where it dropped off the raised pavement. The next table — even closer to the window — was hurled aside. Chairs spilt backwards, the occupants falling under the wheels and screams of pain and panic mingled with the revving engine and splintering wood. All the while, the woman and the boy remained rooted to the spot.

The car came to a rest against the metal railing to a staircase that led to more table space in the basement. The engine stalled and the driver's door pushed open. Shards of glass popped beneath a black boot as a man stood up out of the car. He was tall, of strong build and dressed all in black — including the balaclava that covered his face. He levelled a black handgun and swept it around the café.

The commotion stopped in an instant. The only sounds now were shards of glass sliding off the car's bonnet and a terrible moaning from under its front wheels. Someone had to be trapped. The man scanned the interior of the coffee shop. He stopped when he faced the woman who pulled the young boy close to her. She could almost reach out and touch the car. Her panic increased as she realised she couldn't see the young waitress. She scanned the shop quickly. She found her. She was sat up against the counter on the other side of the shop. Her eyes were open but were motionless, glossy and transfixed. Blood pooled steadily from where she sat. The woman took a quick breath and sucked in the dry dust that now filled the air. The man levelled the gun at the boy. Her head snapped back to the movement as she fought the urge to cough.

'You!'

It was directed right at her. She pulled the boy around so that he was behind her and she felt him grip her waist tightly. She jerked her eyes towards the shriek of a second car coming to a hard stop on the street just outside. This car was black and smaller than the one that had crashed into the café. There was movement within — maybe two more men. She heard doors pulled open. The man stood in front of her still held her attention.

'You!' he shouted again, and gestured with the gun to the car outside. 'Get in!'

She couldn't move, could summon no response at all. She felt the boy push his head into her lower back. The man now moved the gun to point right into her eyes. She could almost feel it. She stared right back, testing him. She could still hear someone moaning from under the car. Suddenly the gun went off with a terrific BANG! Her eyes slammed shut to the noise but she heard a thump into the ceiling above her. She felt pieces of debris fall into her hair.

'What do you want from me?' she croaked, but managed to stand her ground.

'I won't ask you again. Get in the car! Now!'

She made a decision. She reached down and took a firm hold of the boy's arm and peeled it away.

'I've got to go, honey. But I'll be right back, okay?'

'No! Don't go!' The boy squealed and sprang to her side. She held her arm straight to keep him back.

'He comes too!' the man barked.

The woman's eyes snapped back to him. She still wasn't moving.

'Now. Or I shoot one of you and take whoever is left.' He stepped towards her. Still she held firm. He lifted his boot and drove the heel into her thigh. The pain was excruciating and she stumbled backwards, trying her best to stifle a gasp for the boy's sake. The boy held her up. She was grabbed from behind by the shoulders and, feeling suddenly hopeless, she did nothing to resist.

She took the boy's hand firmly but gently. 'Get in the car. We'll be okay.' She managed to hold on to him as she was dragged outside and pushed roughly into the back seat. The armed man followed them in and the door was slammed shut. It was so cramped she could barely move. She had landed on her side and had to wriggle to get sat back up. Suddenly the car moved off and she was able to right herself, banging her head on the solid door rim. As she looked out towards the shocked faces of onlookers, she held the boy as close as she could. The car picked up speed, making for the back streets of the city.

Chapter 2

Sergeant Shaun Carter stepped out into the bright sunshine. It was not as warm as it had been down among the tall buildings where the air didn't move. Up here his hair, swept over to one side and held in place by a pinch of product and a layer of sweat, still shuddered gently in the cool breeze that drifted around him.

The man was right where the witness had said he would be: stood on the edge of the viaduct whose brick walls had a layer of black filth for each of its 170 years. It ran high over the town of Langthorne, its square legs stepping carefully over the rows of terraced houses and giving elevated views of the town to the ever-evolving rail stock. It was a hundred feet back down to the tarmac. And this was the fourth call to a jumper this year.

The sergeant liked to take time to scan the area and see what was to be seen. No one else was around and he had been assured by the British Transport Police that the live track running along the centre was switched off. He would still have preferred to have been further away. It was a tight space, two sets of metal train tracks and two brick walls either side. It looked barely wide enough for two trains to pass. The only sound was his feet crunching on the grey gravel. He liked a quiet area in which to work. It was 3.30 p.m. on a Sunday afternoon. The man stood still at the edge, his arms by his sides and his feet shoulders' width apart. His head was raised slightly as if he was letting the sun warm his face. It was a pleasant day in the middle of March. The sort of day where the seaside town of Langthorne might be fooled into thinking that spring had arrived.

'Control, I've located the male. I am now going to approach.' He received confirmation into his left earpiece and made his way forwards. He waited until he was some twenty metres from the man before he called out.

'Hey. It's cooler up here than I thought. Do you want your jacket?' It was close enough to start a conversation, far enough away for everyone to be comfortable — as comfortable as he could be this close to the edge and with that drop on the other side of the low wall. Beyond the man he could see what looked like a coat. The man took his time, but turned eventually towards Shaun.

'You came!' A nervous smile flickered on the man's face.

'Of course I came. We're all worried about you down there.'

'But you remember me? Right?'

Shaun used the question as an excuse to edge a little closer. Slowly and deliberately, he closed the gap to ten metres, ostensibly shading the worst of the sun from his eyes. As he got a little closer he found he was shaded.

'Ah yes! I didn't recognise you from back there. Of course! It's Bobby, right?'

A month ago. Shakespeare Cliff in Dover, the next town. Another popular place for jumpers. Shaun had been called out just like today; it had been a Sunday — just like today. He had found Bobby Leonard stood up on the edge, contemplating his life.

Déjà vu.

Shaun could usually tell in the first minutes of a conversation whether he was talking to someone who was serious or not. He had known that Bobby was serious right from the start, even before he had heard his reasons. It had been a victory when he had walked him away from the edge and back to his waiting family. Such outcomes were rare, and Shaun was acutely aware of the lengthened odds of a repeat performance.

'You talked me down, Sergeant. You made me think that it was the wrong thing to do, that I could still have some sort of life.'

'I was right too, Bobby. I even got you a brew, didn't I? Not everyone gets a brew you know. We can talk again, Bobby, but can you come away from the edge a little? I'm not going to come any closer to you — I just don't want anything bad to happen.'

'Bad? You mean like falling off?'

'That's exactly what I mean, Bobby.' Shaun had a bottle of water in each hand. He held one out.

'Do you want a drink? I brought you some water. I reckoned you might have been up here a little while.'

Bobby shook his head. Thick hanks of long, greasy hair fell about his face and he had to keep raising a hand to sweep them from his eyes. He wore a checked shirt and jeans, the shirt untucked over a pot belly, and a battered leather bowler-style hat that, like the rest of his outfit, looked like it had accompanied him for most of his life. 'I'm sorry, Sarge. I'm sorry you have to go through all this again. I told you, didn't I? About me?'

'You did.'

'Early-onset dementia.'

'Yeah, I remember.'

'Don't take that for granted, Sergeant.'

Shaun attempted his best warm smile. 'Fair point. I promise I won't. Now what about that bottle of water? You've been up here a little while from what I've been told.'

'I have. You can't rush these things, Sergeant.'

'No one's rushing you, Bobby. Just as long as we're working towards walking you back down to your family, I can stand here all night.'

'Can't do that, Sarge. Not this time.'

Shaun adjusted his stance and the stones crunched underfoot. There would be no sneaking forward up here. 'Sure you can. And it's Shaun. You know that. We had this exact same conversation the last time we met.'

'We did. But I respect you lot. I never used to, but you grow up don't you?'

'I've seen your record, Bobby. You were a right handful once.'

Bobby offered a fleeting smile. 'I was a lot of things once.'

'There's plenty left in you, Bobby. You've not had the news long right? Once you've got your head round it, once you're thinking clearly—'

'They can slow it down,' Bobby cut in. He produced a polished metal hip flask and took a swig. Shaun could make out the crest of Millwall FC on its side.

'Well, okay, so that's a positive.'

Bobby chuckled drily and then smacked his lips a little. 'If you were told that you were going to die confused, in pain and lonely, would you ask to slow it down?'

'You're a long way from lonely, Bobby. We talked about your family — your grandson. The one who adores you so much he even started supporting Millwall! I know he'll take every minute he can get with you.'

'I was about his age, Sarge — a couple of years older I suppose. Twelve years old. I watched my uncle die. He was a young man too. Young for *this*.' Bobby took another swig then immediately sucked in air. Whatever the drink was, it was harsh. 'Older than me, though. He was a bit of a loner, no one was really close to him, but we visited a lot when he got ill. At first at least. Early-onset dementia. Of course, it meant nothing to me then. It got worse quick. I couldn't understand why he didn't seem to know me no more. And we'd talk about the Millwall score and then have the same conversation over again. They all took the piss out of him, you know. Even I did. Then he became a burden. My dad would get calls in the middle of the night about how his brother had been found walking up the motorway in his pyjamas, or sat at a train station not knowing where he was or why he was there. Who knew this sort of shit could run in a family, eh?'

'You're nothing like that. You're loved. You've got family around you.'

'I have. But you know what they said about my uncle, at the time? That at least he didn't have any kids to see it — to watch him go downhill. My boy — he's my daughter's kid, but she lost her own battle with this world . . . Lord knows that kid has seen enough suffering and sorrow for one lifetime already. He's ten years old.'

'So you have him full time?'

'Yeah. My Lizzy was murdered — found stabbed up in some drug dealer's hovel.' Shaun remembered Bobby had told him this before, but he wasn't about to point it out.

'Jesus, Bobby! The boy needs you all the more then.'

Bobby's face twisted suddenly as if he might cry. He swigged at the flask and it seemed to pass. 'He needs a version of me that I can't ever be. Not now. He needs me to be strong and smart. To take him to football . . . to teach him how to hit from his core if a bully starts. He don't need me to fall apart, to forget who he is. To forget who I am. I gotta go, Sarge, before I forget how much I fucking love them.' Bobby did now break. He sagged forward, his tears dropped over the edge. Shaun considered rushing Bobby and taking hold, thinking this might be the time, but Bobby straightened himself up and he lifted his face back to the sun.

'I knew it would be you. You said you was the only one who did Sundays.'

Shaun cursed silently to himself. He could remember saying it. He had been a little annoyed and had vented. In his training he had been told that it was okay to talk about yourself a little: it was apparently a way of sounding natural, of forming bonds. But perhaps the fact that he had been stitched up with two months of weekends on the negotiators' rota hadn't been the best topic of choice. He had made Bobby smile at least, joked that Bobby thought *he* had problems. He should definitely have kept that to himself. Now Bobby was timing his cries for help around his shifts. Shaun put both bottles of water on the ground at his feet.

'You told me that you worked on your own too,' Bobby continued. 'You said that you lot normally pair up but you always keep the second one back until you've struck up a bit of a dialogue like. You don't like to make anyone feel like they're getting surrounded.'

'Your memory is sharp as a tack right there, Bobby. I forgot I even told you any of that.'

'I'm right though, aren't I?'

'Yeah, you're right. Sometimes I don't get a choice anyway. We're all on the end of a phone and we come from all over the county to where we're needed. I've got someone else coming but they're from a lot further away. Lucky for me, I'm kinda local.'

Bobby turned to face Shaun, a sudden intensity in his gaze. 'Tell them to stay away! It's just you and me up here.'

Shaun nodded. 'Okay, Bobby, no problem. I don't need anyone else up here anyway. I know you're a man who can see what he has. There's a future for you, Bobby, and I don't reckon you're the sort to give up because it's getting a bit tricky.'

'I'm old, Sarge, you know? Not old compared to some — fifty ain't fuck all these days. But I've been around a bit. Seen a lot in that time. I've learnt a bit too, and I've learnt that you got to pick your battles. I can't win this one, Sarge. That's just the truth.'

'Maybe not, but there's never been a fight more worthy. I didn't have you down as the sort to chuck in the towel first sign of trouble.'

Bobby let his eyes drop towards the gravel. He shook his head.

'I'm so sorry it had to be you.'

'Don't do it on a Sunday then! I get the impression this was always meant to be me!'

'I don't mean like that. I knew you would come out today. But so did they.'

'They? Who's they?'

'I don't know, Sarge. You gotta believe me when I say I don't know. But they know all about you — everything.'

'What are you talking about, Bobby?'

'They've got your kid. It's Tyler, right? Your ex-wife too — I don't think they had a choice. They were together like.'

Shaun felt as if he had been kicked in the chest. It took several seconds to compose himself just enough to ask the question. 'Who has? Bobby, what are you talking about? How do you know my son's name?'

'You gonna need to do some things for them, Sarge. I've got some instructions — some stuff you need to do and then you get them back. They're gonna be fine . . . but you do need to do what they want.'

Shaun could hear his own pulse singing in his ears. His mouth was suddenly dry, opening and shutting; he couldn't find words. It was his feet that moved first, slowly backwards, edging away.

'Yeah, you go for now, Sarge,' Bobby said. 'Do some checking, some calling around. It's a bit of a change of pace. You don't believe me, I know. But when you come back, make sure it's still only you. I see anyone else and you won't get another word from me. And no word to anyone about what we talked about. They'll know. I'll see you in a minute, okay?' He turned and faced out over the drop.

Shaun spun away. He strode back quickly towards where the sides of the viaduct met with a steep bank. He'd walked up this way via a hole already cut in the chain fence and a winding footpath shaded by trees. He stopped where he could keep Bobby in sight. He dialled his ex-wife and put the phone to his ear. Their son was with her. He used to have his boy most weekends but the on-call rota had scuppered that, too. They were probably out and about in Canterbury right now.

The phone rang and rang. No one answered.

Chapter 3

'What do you want from me?' Shaun moved back over to where Bobby was stood up straight, still looking out over the town, facing the sea. Shaun could just make it out in the far distance as a glittering line of bluey grey with big container ships hanging in mid-air where the horizon furred the sea with the sky.

Bobby was still stood up on the thin wall — three bricks wide and hip height. He paced along the edge, jittery and uneasy. Far below, looking ant-like, a crowd of jeering urchins had gathered. Shaun heard one of them shout, 'Jump, ya cunt!'

Bobby Leonard's demeanour had changed; he was a lot more agitated now and it had nothing to do with the shouting. But then, Shaun was agitated too.

Bobby turned to face Shaun. 'Look, this isn't me right . . . Fuck! Okay, okay . . . They've been watching you a while, Sarge. Like I said, I don't know who — so don't even bother. They sent me out on this ledge to get you isolated. To get you in the picture. They want you scared.'

'Who? Why?'

'I already fucking said, Sarge! Fuck . . . You got to get better mate — do you understand? These people . . . I know their sort. They're fucking ruthless, but they don't want to hurt people. Causes too much of a mess, like . . . makes a real noise. You just have to play by the rules.'

'What rules Bobby? What is this all about?'

Bobby slumped to a sit on the wall. His legs hung towards Shaun, his back facing out. 'The rules are simple, Sarge. You will stay up here on this level until you are told otherwise. You don't speak to anyone out of my earshot again and you make it clear to your police buddies that no one else comes up here. Is that clear?'

'Or what? You hurt my boy?'

Bobby shook his head. '*I* don't, Sarge.' His voice was now meek, his whole persona had weakened, and it made Shaun all the more angry. Bobby's chin dropped and his lank hair fell forward. It covered his face and wafted in the breeze. He might have been sobbing.

'So who does?'

'I told you already, Sarge. I don't know! And, let's be honest, right now, does it really matter? Does it make a jot of difference? Probably not, really. You are where you are and you can't leave and you can't tell anyone either.'

'So what do I have to do?'

'What you're told. Follow the rules. Don't come any closer either, Sarge. You have to realise that I'm all you have if you want to get back to your kid. If I jump, then you're starting from nowhere.'

'You're not going to jump. This is all a ruse to get me out here and isolated. You said it yourself.'

Bobby rubbed his face. Pulling his lips into a distorted smile, he became more animated.

'Fucking THINK, Sarge! You have to start thinking. You have to be better than this or you are going to lose. And losing means everything. These people identified you as being right for the job. Fit for purpose, as they say. They worked out that you would respond to a call today and they knew you would work alone. You told me last time that you don't like bringing two people out straight away. It could have been anyone walking out here today and waiting for you to rock up. Could it not?'

'Okay, Bobby. Okay. So you told them all about us meeting.'

'They chose me just like they chose you. Because I'm fit for purpose, too. I want to die, Sarge — have no illusions about that. I've been dealt a shit hand, I know how I'm supposed to die and it ain't something I relish. Well, I reckon fuck that. I reckon it can be on my terms — how I want and when I want — that's how I've always been. Some shitty disease that's been sneaking up on me my whole life ain't gonna take someone like me out. I want some control of my life and I want it to be for *something*.'

'So your something is to deliver a message to me? To take part in the kidnap of a ten-year-old boy? That makes you worth something does it?'

'Maybe not, Sarge. But maybe I can help. I didn't take no willing part at the start, but maybe I can make you see that you have to listen . . . that you have to follow the rules and we can get this all sorted. Maybe if it was someone else up here they wouldn't be able to do that. This was always going to happen and maybe I can be a part of putting it right.'

'Without you this wouldn't be happening, Bobby. Jesus! Who are you kidding?'

'Wrong! You're wrong, Sarge. They would have found someone else. They found me. Fuck, I wish they hadn't.'

'Tell me what you know.'

'I can't.'

'Who found you?'

'I can't.'

'They ain't here, Bobby, that's for sure.'

'They'll know.'

'I'll be clever. I just want to know what there is. I can still act like I don't. I've done it before.'

'They'll *know*, Sarge!'

'And you'll be dead anyway! What the fuck do you care?'

'I care because all I have to do is get you to play by the rules. Second guessing these cunts and then chasing them with your arse on fire, now that ain't playing by the rules is it? Then it gets all fucked up and you don't get your boy back or your happily-ever-after. They will know and you will pay for it.'

'Like hell they will! Trust me. You put me here. Now you can trust me to get us out of this.'

'They were very clear, Sarge. I need to give you a very strict set of instructions and I have to convince you to follow them.'

'What instructions?'

'Are you ready to listen Shaun? No more questions. Just listen.'

Shaun reached down for one of the bottles, his throat suddenly running dry. 'Tell me what you have.'

Bobby took a second, his eyes to the ground. Then he started. 'You have a contact at the port. Your girlfriend. They need you to call her and you need to get her help. Right now, there's a lorry on a passenger ferry bound for Dover. She needs to make sure it gets through the customs people. It might already be marked up for a stop.'

'What makes you think she can—'

'Don't even bother, Sarge! I told you, these people — they know it all mate. They know you, they know her, they know she runs the show down there when it comes to what goes through and what don't. This is nice and simple for her, and that's a good thing, right?'

'Nice and simple? How is it nice and simple when I call her out of the blue and suddenly ask her to start letting traffic through or my boy gets hurt. What do you think she does from there? I can't control her any more than you can.'

'You can't tell her that, Sarge. You can't tell her nothing about your boy, about me — about any of this.'

'This won't work. This doesn't work. You don't know her — she's a clever girl.'

'You need to be cleverer, Sarge. You need to make this happen. Call your girlfriend . . . get that lorry through.'

Shaun took a few seconds to try to digest the information. It wasn't making much sense to him. Who were these people? How could they know about his personal relationships — *his boy*?

'So you know my boy's name. It caught me out a little. And you challenge me to call my ex and she isn't picking up her phone. That doesn't mean you've got him or her. If you're messing with me, Bobby, you will wish you had just come up here and jumped silently to your death. Now, how about you tell me what is really going on?'

Bobby had been swigging at his flask. He lifted his eyes. They streamed with tears, his face flushed red. He looked exhausted and terrified all at the same time.

'I have to make you believe me, Shaun. It's all I have to do. I thought you would have called up on that thing.' Bobby gestured at the radio that was gripped in Shaun's right hand. 'I thought you would have done some checks? Do your checks, please! They were in Canterbury — they got them from there. They always go into the city on a Sunday, right? It wasn't a quiet snatch, Sarge. They wanted to be sure that your people knew it had happened — so *you* would know it had happened. Just don't go any further away. If you talk to someone else I need to know.' Bobby's eyes lingered on Shaun. They still streamed with tears and he did nothing to wipe them away.

Shaun lifted the radio to his mouth. 'Control from Alpha One.' It was a croak; his lips and mouth still felt so dry.

'Go ahead Alpha One.'

'Control, do you have an eye on the Canterbury area? Is there an abduction job running over there? Or anything like it?'

The controller took a few seconds to come back.

'Canterbury are running a major incident in the city centre, which may involve an abduction. Are you away from the suicide risk at Langthorne? I didn't get an update is all.'

'I can't hear it!' Bobby interjected. 'That's one of the rules, Sarge.'

Obediently, Shaun pulled the headphone jack out so the radio could be heard through the speakers and then spoke back into his radio.

'No, no, control. I'm not away. I was just getting an update. Do you know the names for the persons abducted?'

Another pause.

'No, no. I can only see a description on the log at the moment. A female and a young boy. Witnesses are saying he was around eight to ten years old, brown hair. Not much on there at the moment. There's no suggestion on here of anybody making contact or any request for a negotiator. I'll let you know if that changes but for now you are free to deal with your Langthorne job.'

'All received.'

He pushed the radio back into its clip on the side of his belt. He twisted the bezel to turn it down. He took a moment to steady himself, his eyes scrunched tightly shut.

'I'm telling the truth. You're going to have to do what I ask you, Sarge. We both know it. Get in touch with your girlfriend down the port. She'll have access to the customs manifest for the *Spirit of Britain* passenger ferry. There's a lorry that'll show as being registered to a company called Manesco. It's refrigerated. The manifest will show as if it's carrying pallets of tomatoes from Spain. You need to make sure they get through the port without any issues.'

'This is a lot of bother for tomatoes,' Shaun said quietly.

'You need to make the call where you stand. And, Sarge . . . I'm sure I don't need to say it, but a big part of your job is to make it clear that she can't be telling anyone else what she's been asked to do.'

'She might not be at work today. I don't know her—'

'She went on at three. Handover takes around half an hour. Now's the perfect time, Shaun. I still don't think you understand your situation fully . . . how much these people have got stuff worked out.'

'What if this Manesco lorry is already marked? What happens then? If the lorry has been marked to be stopped then it *will* be stopped from what I know.'

'She'll need to find a way.'

'And I can't tell her why?'

'No. Let's hope she trusts you, Sarge. She's going to need to.'

Chapter 4

As she walked into the rest area, Jess Norris rolled her eyes at Alice Young. Alice responded with a wry smile; she was being regaled by their work colleague Simon Johnstone, and he was in full flow.

'So, I dropped it on the new springs — it's just about as low as it can go,' Simon enthused.

Alice was filling a large teapot. Jess raised an eyebrow at her.

'Simon dropped his Volkswagen yesterday, Jess.' Alice said.

Jess looked over at Simon. He looked very pleased with himself.

'Careless,' she offered.

'Golf Anniversary,' Simon said. 'Brilliant red. Absolute mint it is.'

Jess sat down at the table and thanked Alice for the tea. 'Simon, these are all words that I know and understand — just not in that order. Don't be offended. If I had the remotest idea of what you're talking about, I'm sure I would be very impressed.'

Simon was leaning against the work surface with his arms crossed. 'Well, your boyfriend would be. Trust me, anybody who knows their cars would want her.'

'Oh it's a car!' Jess exclaimed. 'Shaun's not into cars, actually.'

'Not into cars! What do you see in someone like that?'

'Well, the fact that he's not into cars for starters. So I don't have to hear him describing lumps of metal as a *her*.'

Simon grinned. 'I'm glad you didn't make me a tea now.' He walked towards the door. 'I cannot take the blatant rudeness any longer.'

'I don't make tea for the early shift!' Alice called after him. 'You people get to go home!'

Jess pressed her mug against her lips. 'He definitely fancies you, you know.'

Alice blushed a little. 'Well, it's all harmless. We both know I'm taken.'

Jess remembered suddenly. 'Oh, yeah! How was the night away with Dean?'

Alice bit her bottom lip and stretched her left hand towards Jess. A diamond engagement ring sparkled under the strip light.

'Oh my god! He didn't?'

'He did.'

'Six months together! You don't mess about, do you?'

'Nope. If it's right, it's right. We haven't finished unpacking the house yet!'

'Good Lord. How did he do it? Tell me everything.'

Alice chuckled behind her mug. 'It was lovely actually. He was just a little unlucky. We had a delightful lunch, a bit of a walk around a few shops and that, and then he suddenly said that he wanted to go on the London Eye. You know . . . the big wheel over the Thames.'

Jess laughed out loud, 'I've not heard it called that before!'

'Anyway, we turn up and he's already sorted tickets, he must have booked ahead because he just scanned his phone and we got into a pod with loads of other people. It was really lovely. I've not done it before, but it takes off and we're moving. Is *takes off* the right way to describe it?'

Jess was still laughing, 'I know what you mean. So, yeah.'

'So, we get nearly to the top and then suddenly we stop and there's an announcement over the speakers that someone wants to ask a special question.'

'Oh wow! He really did the business, didn't he?'

'Well, yes *and* no.'

'What do you mean?'

'The next pod along. Some fella had obviously booked out the whole thing. I suddenly see everyone was gawping over at the pod at the very top, and it was just this couple and another fella who was dressed like a fancy waiter. He had some champagne and he poured it into two glasses while the bloke was down on one knee. It was all very lovely.'

'Oh. So that wasn't Dean's plan.'

Alice started laughing and took a few moments to compose herself again. 'Well, yeah it was, but he didn't know you could do the book out the whole pod thing. At least that's what he said. Anyway, I said how lovely it was and when I turned to speak to him he was down on one knee too. He said that they had kind of stolen his thunder a little bit, but he wanted to ask a very similar question.'

'Oh no! Oh poor Dean! So he had the top of the London Eye all planned out and then you watch a better version of it just as he's about to do it!'

'Yeah! And he was well nervous!" Both girls laughed hard.

'Great recovery though!' Jess managed. Her laughter fell away a little and she gripped the ring while it was still on Alice's finger. 'And this is beautiful.'

'Isn't it. I couldn't have chosen a better one and he didn't ask me at all. I really didn't have any idea.'

'Must be a goodun, see? Well, after all that, you still said *yes.*'

'Exactly. So he got his happy ending.'

'Well, I guess a happy ending is the least you could give him after he'd spent all of that money!' Jess laughed so hard she had to cover her mouth.

'You dirty bitch!'

'Well, you did though didn't you?'

'It *was* a special occasion! Anyway, never mind me . . . When is your man going to pop the question? Your turn next. Maybe we could do a joint hen!'

'Ah, well you see this is the benefit of maturity. We've only been together nine months and, while I appreciate that is a lifetime for you teenagers, with age comes a bit of a measured approach.'

'Fuck measured. And I'm twenty now — me and Dean both are. We're not kids anymore.'

'You're certainly old enough to make your own decisions. I hope it works out perfectly for you, Alice. I'm sure it will.'

'*You're* sure, maybe. We spoke to my parents last night. My mum said something similar, except she said we were old enough to make our own *mistakes.*'

'Well, that's true too. It's natural for parents to be cautious.'

'Well, she doesn't have to worry about me. I think she sees all the world's men as being like Jake.'

'Is he still giving your sister issues?'

'He gives her hell more like. I've given up trying to see her now. I've started going to the supermarket near her a lot, just to try and bump into her. It's the only place he lets her go alone.'

'Has it worked?'

'Not yet.'

'It's all down to him that you don't see each other is it? I remember you said she was upset with you after your talk.'

'Ah yeah. We never really sorted that. The Becks I once knew, you could sit down with. Tell her that her new boyfriend was a shitbag who tried to get in her sister's pants and she would listen. Then she'd get angry, but she would be angry at *him*. She would know that I wouldn't just make shit up like that. She'd know that I was telling the truth, no question, and by the end we'd probably be plotting his slow death together. And having a right laugh doing it.'

Jess nodded. 'Blokes can change a girl. I've seen it happen.'

'I never thought anyone would change Becks though. I don't recognise her anymore. I can't see how she got mixed up with someone like Jake.'

'You really don't like him do you?'

'No. But it seems the world does. He's got his claw's in my beautiful sister. He flashes his money about. A nice car. He thinks he's a footballer or a pop star or something.'

'What does he do for money?'

'Who knows? Not much from what I've seen. He's got contacts though. He got me here — I owe him for that. And he makes sure he tells me enough.'

'He got you an intel admin role with customs and excise! It's not like he got you a part in Holby City! This is the booby prize surely?'

'Hey! Don't go mugging off my lack of importance or I'll tell him that what I really want is my boss's job!'

'Do it,' Jess smiled. 'I'm bored of it anyway. Speaking of which I'd better go do it. At least show some willing.'

They walked through to where the building opened up into a large office space. The early shift had now vacated completely with the exception of Jess's opposite number, who was waiting to give a handover before he could leave his station. Sunday afternoon was an anomaly in the shift pattern as there was no overlap, just the late team taking over from the early. Her early turn counterpart stood ready to greet her just as her pocket buzzed. She recognised Shaun's ring tone.

'Shit! Anything I need to know?' She still held the ringing phone.

'Nah, standard Sunday.'

'You get off then, I don't need you. No offence,' she grinned.

'None taken!'

Jess waved cheerily as she answered her phone. 'Sorry, Shaun, just starting here. You okay?' He never called her when she was at work.

'I got called in. A negotiator job.'

'Oh right. Nothing serious I hope.' Jess felt ruffled; his tone was straight-to-business.

'Nah. One of those that should resolve itself. I'm not calling about *this* job, Jess. I've got wind of some intelligence that's linked to the port.'

'Oh really? So what do you know?'

'I know what you're like, Jess . . . please don't go off half-cocked.'

'Stop being a dick, Shaun.' Jess chuckled. 'What's going on.' She had made her way across the floor to a side room. She pushed the door shut behind her with her elbow.

'I'm not being a dick. I know what you're like for a job, Jess, and I know you're going to want all the answers. I don't have much detail. There is a ferry due to dock at three forty-five this afternoon. There is a lorry on there and I need you to make sure that it gets through without being stopped. I'm sure it would anyway — there shouldn't be anything conspicuous or unusual about it — but I need you to be sure.'

'Why would I do that?' This was starting to irritate her. 'You know we've had this before with police operations. Your lot calling through and talking to me like you're in charge of my port. Well, you're not. We have total jurisdiction down here and we stop what we want.'

'I know that, Jess. Jesus . . . I know that. I wouldn't even make this call unless it was critically important. This isn't pre-planned. This isn't us leaving you out of the loop and throwing our weight around. This is my reaction to live intelligence. There aren't the resources to assist you with the stop down there and, *trust* me, if you try and stop this vehicle you'll need a lot more people.'

'Why? What do you know?'

'I can't go into it, Jess. You know I'd—'

'There you are, just like the rest. We're not important enough to know what the police are planning. Tell me what you know or you get no promises from me.'

'I shouldn't even be calling you at all. This isn't about a police operation — I don't give a shit about that — this is about you not putting yourself or your people at risk. We don't know enough. You need to let them run so we can have a little bit of time to do something further up the line. And I promise I will tell you everything I know when I can.'

'The best way for me to keep my people safe is for me to be aware of everything you are.'

'Look, Jess, take the details of the lorry. Check that they're not on any list to be stopped and I'll try and find out some more information for you. You know about as much as I know and we don't have time to be discussing it. Do you want these details or not?'

'Fine. Give me the details. But I'll be running my own checks down here. I don't like not knowing.'

'Nor do I, Jess. Do what you can on the quiet. Just make sure that vehicle gets through.'

'Look, I got to go. Text the details through.' Jess didn't give Shaun the opportunity to reply before she pressed to end the call. She opened the door and peered out onto the floor. She had four customs officers, six immigration officers and Alice, her civilian intelligence officer. Hardly a SWAT team, but she wasn't one to walk away from anything.

Chapter 5

Alice was smiling at something on her smartphone as Jess approached her desk.

'Alice? Have you reviewed the manifest for the 15.45?'

Alice jumped at Jess's urgent tone. 'I had a look. It was reviewed by early turn and there was nothing highlighted.'

'Is there a stop list?'

'There's always a stop list, Jess. If your question was *is there anything interesting on the stop list?* I would be able to give you a very definite *no*. What are you after?'

'Can you send it to me please?'

'What do you want that for?'

'Can you just send it please, Alice!' Jess snapped, and then took a breath. 'Sorry, Alice. I just want to run my eyes over it is all.'

The document was attached to an email by the time she got back to her own desk. The HGV quota wasn't full: the *Spirit of Britain* could hold 180 full-size lorries before the health and safety people got twitchy. On this Sunday afternoon in late March, they were running with just under ninety. Ten lorries were marked with a stop. These were auto-generated using a computer algorithm, but they would sometimes have manual marks against them if there was specific intelligence. The algorithm usually picked out a sample of around 10% of the vehicles and the team were expected to stop and report on each of these. Jess also knew that they could pick different ones if they wanted to; sometimes her officers would stop something based on the driving style or a reaction to their uniform. She ran her eyes down the list. She could see that someone had manually marked one lorry for a run through the X-Ray machine, but none for a full stop and search.

Jess's phone beeped to announce an incoming text. It was from Shaun, and it carried the details of the lorry that needed to roll through.

'Tomatoes,' she said out loud. Well, it wasn't going to be carrying tomatoes. She went back to her list. The details from Shaun were for a Spanish registered lorry, it was the same vehicle that had been marked up for a run through the X-Ray. She made her way back over to Alice's desk.

'Hey, Alice.'

'Everything okay?' Alice looked up from her monitor.

'Yeah, of course. Did you mark a Spanish registered lorry up to be ran through the X-Ray or was it the early turn? It's the only one with a manual mark. I was just wondering if there is any specific intel?'

Alice shrugged. 'That was me yeah. I had a quick look. Tomatoes, right? No specific intel — I keep an eye on the stats and patterns. That company always come through in a convoy, never less than four lorries. It just stood out being on its own. Pretty thin I know, but I gotta justify my existence somehow!' Alice chuckled,

Jess smiled back. 'Understood. I don't think it warrants it. We're just generating work. I'm not saying you're wrong, Alice, but it's a Sunday afternoon, you know. Let's not over stretch.'

Alice still smiled. 'Sure thing, boss. They've printed the list though. There's no point taking it off. I'll go out and tell them.'

Jess checked her watch. It was 15:35. She took in the office and saw that most of her staff had already slipped on their hi-vis jackets and headed out to their stations. They would have the printed list with them.

'Don't worry. I fancy the fresh air anyway.' Jess pushed her way out of the door and startled two uniformed police officers on their way in.

PC Alan Hayward and PC Matt Eaves both fixed wide grins and held their ground. They wore the navy-blue uniform of firearms patrols and were regulars at the office. A spotless police SUV dripped water from its panels onto the double yellow lines directly outside of the office block.

'Ah! The lovely Jess!' Alan said. 'How are you this fine evening?'

'Suspicious,' Jess replied immediately.

'Good to hear. Everyone should be more suspicious in my opinion. The ABC of policing . . . Assume nothing, believe no one, check everything.'

'So I shouldn't *assume* your visit coincides with the phone call I just took two minutes ago then?'

The men exchanged looks. Jess couldn't tell if it was surprise, perplexity or the fear of being caught out.

'Our visit, Jess, is nothing more than a quick go on your jet-wash and in the hope of a lovely cup of sunshine,' Matt said. 'And with even lovelier company!'

Jess still eye-balled them. Dropping in for a cup of tea was not at all unusual. This was a natural tea stop for firearms patrols who gathered in the middle of the county and were then sent to each compass point to ensure coverage. The southern patrol would sometimes base itself at the port for an entire shift. But their timing today seemed too much of a coincidence.

'Well, you'll have to wait for your tea if you want your tomato lorry to get through my port. Don't ask me to be happy about it though. I guess I could do without the bother on a Sunday afternoon.'

There was an awkward pause. Alan stepped forward to puncture it. 'The people of the UK are in your debt, Jess. We are a nation of tomato lovers after all!'

'Yeah. So you don't have to be here to check on me.'

'Deal! Can we be here to drink your tea though?'

'After I watch it through. And if you give me an inkling as to what this is all about then I might just think about it.'

Matt's smile dropped away as his attention was caught by his radio. He spoke into it. 'Foxtrot One, go ahead.'

Jess held her ground, stood still with her arms crossed.

'Received that, we'll make a start towards that location.' Matt let go of the radio on his chest. 'Sorry, Jess. Seems like the tea's going to have to wait. We'll try and drop back in later in the shift. Duty calls!'

Jess huffed as she pulled the door closed behind her and stepped into the dull roar of one of Europe's busiest ports. Her team were already in position. The ferry was finishing its docking procedure. Soon the huge doors would drop to form a bridge over the water for the steady exit of cars and lorries. She made her way towards the front two officers who would be directing the traffic.

* * *

Alan waited until Matt pulled the door shut on their police SUV before he spoke. 'What was all that about? The tomato thing?'

'I know! No idea, mate, it must be them intel boys holding back the juicy stuff again.'

'This shout's probably a load of nothing. I've a good mind to sit up and give one of the lorries a tug. Routine traffic stop.'

'That's because you don't care who you piss off!'

Alan guided the SUV onto the one-way system that led from the port. He pushed the screen on the phone suckered to the windscreen in front of him. 'I'll at least give Rachel the heads up. I don't think she's being pulled away for this job and she's in the unmarked. She might be able to keep tabs on the lorry and we can get involved a bit later.'

Matt shook his head. 'We don't even know what lorry she's talking about!'

'Tomatoes. You can spot them a mile off, right?'

Both men shared a chuckle.

Chapter 6

'That was risky, Sarge.' Bobby looked genuinely worried.

'What else was I supposed to tell her? I can't tell her the truth.'

'You've stoked her interest. We need to hope that she doesn't go too far in her investigations.'

Shaun shrugged. 'She isn't the sort of woman you can tell what to do. Not without a damned good reason why.'

Bobby checked his watch. 'I guess in ten minutes or so we will find out just what sort of a woman she is.'

'So this happens, the lorries get away from the port, and what? My kid just gets released?'

'Your kid, your ex. Like I said, these people don't want no mess around them and snatching kids — that's some messy shit right there.'

'It's a lot of risk just to be sure some lorry doesn't get stopped. What's on that lorry?'

Bobby swigged back at his flask. His eyes were glazing over, his pupils losing their focus a little. Shaun could tell the liquid was starting to have some effect. Then Bobby shrugged. 'Tomatoes.'

'It's not going to be something wholesome, now is it? Someone went to a lot of trouble to get it through and you expect me to believe that you're just going to release your only assets as soon as they are in the country? What's to stop me going after that lorry the second they hit the road network?'

'Common sense, Sarge. Think about it, man . . . Do you really need all this shit? It's no skin off your nose, is it? So some bad man gets a lorry into the country carrying some contraband. He might get richer on it or whatever, but it happens every day, right? I see it in the news. You hear about a load of coke washing up on the coast down at Dungeness, right? And you people talk about how it's a big hit against the criminals. But that isn't the first time they've tried it now is it, Sarge? You and me both know they've landed a hundred loads before they fuck up and lose one. Pocket change. They might even give you one every now and then just to keep you sweet or to get you patrolling the wrong area.'

'There's more to this than some contraband. There has to be. This *had* to get through.'

Bobby checked his watch. 'Yeah it did. For your sake.'

Shaun also checked the time. It was 3:47 p.m.

'Can you listen in to what they're doing in Canterbury?' Bobby asked.

'You what?'

'Canterbury. Where they're talking about the snatch. Can you listen to that on your radio?'

Shaun grabbed the radio from his belt. 'Yeah.' He switched to the channel covering Canterbury. The operator was talking about a road traffic collision in the city centre. A major job like the abduction would probably have its own channel assigned by now.

'As soon as the lorries are clear there should be an update.'

Almost as Bobby stopped talking the tone of the operator on the radio changed.

'Zulu Three, are you available for an immediate call?'

'Go ahead, Control.'

'Zulu Three, we are receiving a call that might be linked to the abduction job in the city centre. A female caller who says she and her son were forced into a car earlier today and have been kept locked in a room. She says someone just threw a phone into the room. She's called 999, but doesn't know if there are still people with her.'

'Received, Control — show us en route.'

Shaun bit his lip as the control room updated with the location. It was a cider farm just outside of Canterbury. A lot of other patrols also called up and confirmed they would make their way. Someone with local knowledge called up to confirm that the farm was no longer in use.

'Shouldn't be long now, Sarge.' Bobby had his flask in his hand, he tipped it right back, catching the last few drips on his tongue. 'And perfect timing . . . I'm all out of rum.'

'They had better be okay,' Shaun spat.

Bobby shrugged. 'I got sold this same as I sold it to you. I do my bit, convince you to do your bit and they do theirs.'

Shaun felt his anger flare. He was about to direct it towards Bobby when voices filled the radio again. The location was close to a police office. Two patrols had covered the distance and arrived at the scene at the same time. They described a dirt track entrance, no vehicles and an old farmhouse that appeared derelict in the distance. The controller confirmed that the female had said they were in a house.

The radio went silent.

Chapter 7

The thump from the other side of the building was loud and sudden. The door to their makeshift cell rattled in its housing and the woman swept her boy up in her arms, crushing him as she pulled him tight. She pushed her back firmly against the far wall while the boy stared wide-eyed and expectant at the door.

Another loud thud. Heavy footsteps and indiscernible shouts that filtered through the walls and the gap under the door. The boy took a sharp intake of breath and he pushed himself backwards into her chest. The door handle rattled suddenly. Then the door flexed from a solid blow with a cracking splintering sound. Another blow came a split second later and the door flew in on its hinges. The boy screamed.

A man strode in with a gun levelled in both hands. He wore a military-style helmet and his face was covered in a black material, but as she panned down his body, she saw the word POLICE stitched in white lettering onto his navy overall. All at once she felt her body slump as the fear and tension drained out of it to be replaced by a sudden swathe of relief. Tears blurred her vision of two more figures following behind.

'You're safe now, ma'am' The lead officer bent down and rested his hand on her shoulder. 'We've come to get you out of here.' The words were muffled through the material and were soft in her ear. She allowed herself to be helped to her feet, but she wouldn't let go of her boy — maybe not ever again. Her thighs burned as she found her feet, her muscles stiff from lack of movement, her whole body had been tight with tension.

The men led her through the house. She'd been blindfolded on the way in and this was the first time she had been able to see where they had been held prisoner. They had to walk up a flight of stairs from the basement and the front door was directly in front. It was a big house, old and run down. No one could have been living here. She was told to be careful on the stairs as some were missing. The floorboards on the ground floor were also gone and chunks of ceiling littered the hall. The front door already hung open, more officers were waiting for her. She narrowed her eyes at the sudden burst of natural light as she made her way through. A car was pulled across the entrance and a rear door was open. The hands that guided her in were gentle this time, the voices kind.

* * *

Shaun had dropped to a squat. One hand down, fingers splayed for support, his head bent forward as he listened to the updates over his radio. The team were in. They gave updates as they went through each room in turn. It was maddening. *'Ground floor CLEAR!'* he heard.

Shaun gripped his nose. He daren't breathe.

'Heading downstairs to the basement area. Locked door, standby, standby.'

The pause that followed seemed to go on forever. Shaun scrunched his eyes tightly shut. He didn't care about the instructions from Bobby anymore. He had plugged his earpiece back into his radio so he wouldn't miss a single word. He held it roughly in his ear.

'Contact, contact!'

They'd found someone — hostile or friendly? The longest pause yet.

'Two persons located, Control. An adult female and a juvenile male. It's gonna be our missing persons.'

Shaun spat out a sob. He had to bring one knee down as he threatened to topple forward. He opened his eyes and saw that Bobby had come off the edge and stepped towards him, just a pace or two. Shaun looked up. Bobby's steps were deliberate, as if in slow motion, but his expression had lost none of its intensity. He stopped five metres away from the ledge and bit his bottom lip.

Shaun spoke into his radio. 'Control, confirm the two persons are all in order?' His voice was still coarse. Bobby was still watching him intently.

'Yes, yes. They will be conveyed to a medical facility but both appear to be in order. Zulu Three, if you are still with the two persons can you confirm their details please.'

Shaun was still listening intently to his radio. Bobby was a little closer, he cast a shadow over him. Shaun rocked to his knees. The confirmation came through his earpiece of the two rescued persons. Their names and dates of birth. Shaun saw Bobby staring down at him, watching him intently. Bobby's hands suddenly rose to his cheeks and he expelled air. He must have seen at last the fresh panic that Shaun had done his best to conceal.

'It's not them, is it?' Bobby said. 'It's not your family!' He was already pacing backwards, a sudden beaming smile lifted to the sky.

Shaun found the strength to get back to his feet, his mind reeling. He started after Bobby. 'Bobby! Help me, Bobby!'

Bobby's backwards walk was halted as his hip met with the raised wall. He stepped back up onto the edge, his hands out towards Shaun. 'Not another step now, Sarge.

Stay there.' He cast a quick look over at the drop. The wind moved his hair round his face.

Shaun did as he was told. He stopped with a two-metre gap. Not quite close enough.

'I can't help you, Sarge.' A thick tear ran down Bobby's cheek. He did nothing to blink it away. He looked as if his eyes struggled to focus, the alcohol taking its effect. 'Just do as they say. You'll get yours back, too. I promise.'

'You can help me, Bobby. You're the only person who can. Do they have my family? Tell me where my family are, Bobby. Come down from there and tell me what you know.'

'I can't, Sarge. I can only help *my* family. My wife. My boy. Now you have them, you tell them I did this for them. That I died for something.'

'No one's dying here, Bobby.'

Bobby's eyes flicked to his watch. 'I hope you get yours too. Sorry, Sarge. Its 4 p.m. We're out of time.'

Bobby's right foot stepped backwards into nothing. Shaun had been edging forwards and he made a last-ditch dive. Though his footing was lost in the gravel, his right arm arched over the wall in a grab. He felt a wisp of hair.

But Bobby was gone.

Shaun's chest collided hard with the lip of the wall, his lungs were forced empty of air, his chin scraped on the brick. His feet scrabbled on the floor, his legs locked out, pushing him forwards so he could see over the edge and down. Bobby was already at the bottom, he was nothing more than a silhouette in the middle of the road, the red pool gathering around his body already visible, even from a hundred feet above. Shaun's legs buckled and he fell back onto the gravel, still fighting for breath.

Eventually, he managed to pull himself up to a sitting position, his back against the low wall. He twisted the radio from his belt loop and steadied his hands to work the buttons. He changed it back to the channel covering

Langthorne, to where patrols were now chattering excitedly about the mess on the pavement below. An ambulance had been positioned just around the corner as the negotiation had been ongoing. They were already with Bobby. Shaun knew it was hopeless; no one survived such a fall. Sure enough, the paramedic called *life extinct* after just a few moments. The patrol sergeant took over the air, he instructed officers to remain on their cordons, declared the area an incident scene and requested the detective sergeant on duty in the local CID to be made aware. All standard stuff. Some of the instructions were directed towards him too, he was told to remain at the jump site until he could be replaced by a patrol. They would carry out a search and then man a pointless cordon until the DS had been out for a pointless look. Shaun glanced back over at the bundle of Bobby's belongings and found his feet. The stuff was right against the rail line.

On closer inspection, the bundle was a long, black jacket and a small rucksack. He checked the jacket first. Bobby's wallet was in the inside pocket, it was busy with receipts, bus tickets and handwritten notes. Nothing that stuck out as significant. Shaun took out a provisional driving licence card: *Robert Leonard, 19 Sidney Street, Langthorne.* Shaun knew the road, it was a row of terraced houses at the top of the town. Most were council-owned two-up-two-downs. He took his notebook out of his pocket and calmed his shaking hands enough to note the details. The rest of the coat had some betting slips, more bus tickets and a bundle of vouchers for school computers from a local superstore. He threw it back on the floor and turned his attention to the rucksack. The front pocket had a packet of cigarette papers that had spilled out of a near-empty tobacco pouch, some remnants of cannabis, and a door key. He shifted his attention to the main compartment. He immediately saw a long white wire and pulled it free. He recognised a remote radio device similar to something he had used previously when doing covert work. It had a battery pack, a receiver unit with a switch to move up and down through radio channels and a microphone with a clip. The microphone was a specialised design that would transmit constantly when the unit was switched on, rather than only on the press of a button. He also found a small blue plastic box that snapped open to reveal a squashy headphone with a tiny aerial. The final part of the set, a fully concealable earpiece connected to the receiver unit. The only other item in the main part of the bag was a cheap-looking Nokia phone. Shaun nearly missed the final pocket on the back of the bag. It held a small white envelope, which he flipped over to read the front:

SHAUN CARTER

His pulse quickened again. In his eagerness to open the envelope, he ripped the single sheet of folded paper and had to hold it back together to read the message.

You'll know how to wear the wire I expect. We will require further assistance. Keep the phone on. This is how you get your family back. No one else is looking for them. This is just between us now, Shaun.

Shaun heard footfalls on the gravel behind him and he snapped his head around. Two uniformed officers approached, one offered a cheery wave. Shaun stuffed the note and the wire kit in his hoody front pocket. He pushed the phone into his jean pocket as he stood to greet them.

'Hey!'

'How's it going, Sergeant?' The cop had *PC LEVERITT, LANGTHORNE* in dirty lettering on a Velcro strip. 'I hope you're not in any sort of competition with the other negotiators?'

'What?'

'Competition? This would be a black mark, right?' PC Leveritt smiled.

'Oh. Yeah, I guess so.'

'No disrespect. I know you negotiators are well drilled but I always say if they're going to jump, they're going to jump. Not much anyone can do about it.'

'You might be right. One thing's for sure, though . . . I need to get on with the report.'

He brushed past the two officers without making eye contact.

Chapter 8

Shaun neared a place that was instantly familiar, despite never having been to this particular hospital before. Every hospital did morgues the same, and they were always found in the depths of the basement. As he approached, the heavy double doors swung open and he almost collided with a porter making his exit. He looked startled to find someone upright and talking. As the doors swung back to close, the thick plastic that hung from their bottoms swept the mottled concrete.

'You might not be expecting me!' Shaun blurted out, having been caught out himself.

The porter looked blank.

'Sorry, I'm Sergeant Shaun Carter, I'm part of an investigation following the death—'

'It don't matter to me. Who are you here to see?' The porter was curt, clearly having a bad day.

Shaun still clutched his warrant in his hand. He let it fall back to hanging round his neck on a lanyard. 'I'm here to see Leonard, Robert Leonard. He'll be your latest arrival I'd imagine.'

The porter spun silently on his heels and walked back through the doors. Shaun followed into a wide corridor with bare concrete walls busy with pipes and ducts feeding the living in the wards above. The left wall contained a number of whiteboards with handwritten names and admittance dates and times on them. The porter scanned these boards, moving along the wall as he did so. Shaun noticed the board labelled 'infants' and his discomfort increased. The porter continued to assess the boards and Shaun turned to face the opposite wall where a number of polished metal doors were arranged neatly over three levels. Each one represented the end of a human life.

'Be out in the overflow.'

'Oh, right. Busy then?'

'Not me. This ain't my job normally. I'm just the porter. I got to be down here covering. There ain't enough of us, see?'

'Seems a common theme,' Shaun replied. He flicked a glance at his watch, aware that he might not have much time.

The porter walked past him. 'Overflow fourteen.' He pushed back through the doors.

Overflow fourteen was near where he had first stepped out of the daylight into the underside of the building. The huge open space had been largely taken over by big squares of blue tarpaulin. Each could take eighteen of the freshly departed, stacked in feet-to-feet formation. They had zips down the middle of each side and a spinning fan. All the fans going at once combined to provide their own layer of white noise.

They stopped at number fourteen. 'He's in here. Middle left. I don't need to see it.' The porter walked behind one of the other overflow fridges before Shaun could assure him that, no, he didn't. By the time Shaun had pulled the long zip from top to bottom he could smell cigarette smoke.

The bodies were stacked three high and three along. The metal stretcher was on rungs, it slid out smoothly to yield up a black body bag. Zipping this open revealed a second layer: a white cloth bag stained a ruby red and tight enough for Shaun to make out facial features.

'Jesus!' He stepped back, just slightly. No matter how many times he saw the dead, no matter their state, he always half expected movement.

The cloth inner also had a zip. Shaun tugged this open and Bobby Leonard's dead eyes were revealed against his waxy skin. There was obvious trauma to the skull; it was severely misshapen and the hair matted with dried blood. The lower jaw was missing and it was obvious that the neck was broken — the head hung unnaturally low. Shaun pulled the tray out further, far enough to get two poles locked out from underneath that acted as a stand. The paramedics had cut Bobby's clothes in their futile efforts to keep him alive and Shaun took in his near-naked form. His leather hat lay on his chest. Shaun focused on what he was looking for. His attention moved to Bobby's head, which was turned sideways, left ear uppermost. Shaun checked it and it was clear. He had stuffed some blue gloves in his pocket from the boot of the car, he pulled them on and reached in, getting his palm under Bobby's right cheek. He lifted the head but couldn't turn it around, a likely combination of the muscles starting to stiffen and the damage to the neck. He had to make do, feeling until his fingers pushed into the right ear. Sure enough, he felt something solid. It took a couple of seconds for him to work it free. It was a clear, rubber earpiece. The same type as he had been left for his own use. His search moved down Bobby's body. Shaun searched the shredded shirt. He found a metal clip on the inside, just below a buttonhole, Shaun was sure it would have held the microphone. The rest of it could be anywhere. He continued down, patting each of Bobby's jean pockets. He stopped at the rear pocket, there was a lump and he pulled it clear — the remains of a small, white power pack. It was largely broken up but he could see it was switched to "ON." Shaun scooped up as much of the plastic pieces as he could and stuffed everything in the front of his hooded top, checking that the smoking porter had stayed out of sight.

'Is there a problem?'

Shaun was startled. A man stood in front of him. Shaun had missed his approach. He was tall, broad and in a shirt and tie. His top button was undone and the tie hung low in an untidy knot. His hands were pushed into the pockets of a brown jacket that hung open. He smacked of detective. Shaun recognised him from somewhere.

'No problem,' Shaun said. He patted Bobby's shins, the last part of his search.

'I wasn't expecting anyone else?' The detective was clearly unimpressed and did nothing to hide it.

'I didn't call up. I was called out as the negotiator. I was talking to Bobby, here, until he jumped.'

'I think he's done talking now.'

'I know. I had a good rapport with him too. This is something I do sometimes, you know? I like to come and see them when they are finally at peace. A little bit of closure.'

'And searching him. Does that help too?'

Shaun shrugged. 'It needs to be done, right? I thought I would. Two birds, one stone an' all that — seeing as I was here anyway. I thought it might be appreciated, it being a Sunday afternoon.'

'You're Shaun Carter then?'

'That's right.'

'Well, at least that's answered my question about where you'd got to. Seems talking to you became a priority during my journey over here. I've had some rather panicked senior officers wanting to know just why the hell they were being called out on a Sunday afternoon.'

'Called out? Why would they call people out?'

The man shrugged. 'I'm just the duty DS. The late weekend cover. I'd only just got my coat off and I get turned out to poke a body with a stick. I was on my way, stick in hand and then Major Crime call me and tell me they're making it their business. Seems they've been called at home and told to get their own poking sticks and to make their way out.'

'Major Crime?'

'That's right. Which means I've suddenly got a load of actions they want doing and ideally before they get here. Seems someone has come up with an alternative story to sad-man-jumps-from-height-to-end-it-all. One that involves murder.'

'Murder? He wasn't murdered. Unless you think I gave him a little shove — because there wasn't anyone else up there with him.'

'Unlawfully killed then. And no, I don't think you gave him a little shove. Not in front of that live audience.'

'Unlawfully killed? How did someone reach that conclusion?'

The DS cocked his head slightly to one side, his eyes held Shaun's for just a second longer than was comfortable. He shrugged again. 'Like I said, I'm just the bloke who's holding the fort. I need to get an account from you of what was said up there. I will warn you though mate . . . I know how they work. You'll be asked to give them the exact same account all over again when they get here.'

'Yeah, I've worked with Major Crime before, too.'

'Right then. I appreciate that the search is done but I'll have another quick look, if you don't mind — just so I can assure them it's been done and there's no knives or bullets stuck any place they shouldn't be. Then we can have a chat. There's a coffee place just in the entrance of the hospital upstairs. That sound okay?'

'Sounds fine, yeah.'

Shaun watched as the DS got to work, he pulled the bag open wider and gazed down at Bobby Leonard. 'We really are just a bag of bones, aren't we?' he said.

'We are,' Shaun replied.

'Largely broken ones in this poor fella's case. Well, he made his choice.'

'He did.'

The DS pulled a notebook from his pocket and readied his pen. 'For cause of death, what do you reckon? Gravity?'

* * *

The coffee shop was busy. It was indeed right by the entrance, and there was a steady stream of staff, inpatients and their visitors bustling through automatic doors that never rested. Shaun had always hated hospitals, but today his dislike of his surroundings was fuelled by his desperation to get away, to get on with finding his family. The DS sat down opposite him and fussed with his coffee. Shaun would need some information from the DS but he would have to be careful how he went about getting it. His next step had to be finding Bobby Leonard's family. Someone was controlling Bobby's every move at the last and it had all been for *him*. Every sentence he said must have been uttered into his ear, every move described in detail — including the final move: jumping from one hundred feet to certain death. And Shaun had to assume they'd heard every word he'd said to Bobby.

'So . . .' the DS began.

Shaun snapped out of his thoughts.

The DS smiled at him warmly. 'What's going on then?'

'Going on?'

'I mean, I don't really care to be honest. Major Crime are on their way, they're too full of their own self-importance to question why the sergeant of a town beat team lost a jumper and then followed him to the hospital to search his body. They probably won't even realise that's what you did. And if they did they'll definitely accept that you wanted closure and were trying to help. That's *almost* plausible. But I'm interested.'

'Who says that's not the truth?' Shaun bit back, it was a reaction to someone caught out with the sudden question and he knew it.

'I used to be a damned good detective, before they tied me to a desk and left me dealing with the irrelevant. A big part of being a good detective is following those first instincts and dismissing the *almost* plausible early. At least until it's the only explanation left.'

'I don't get your point.'

'You're a trained negotiator, deployed as and when you're needed. Your day job is running a town centre team. Nothing that has happened to you or that you have seen today should have lifted an eyebrow. How many ODs have you bagged up from the town's public toilets? Men and women you knew well, I'd bet. And yet here you are, chasing the ambulance so you could get here first to search poor old Bobby in there and then a bag of nerves under some light questioning.'

'I'm hardly a bag of—'

'What were you looking for?'

Shaun sat back. He shook his head. 'This is ridiculous.' He was stalling for time — floundering — and he was pretty sure that they both knew it.

The DS had sat back too. He was smiling again.

'I don't think you said your name.' Shaun huffed.

'I didn't. And, like I said, I'm just some desk sergeant. Someone else is on their way to take over. No one cares about my opinion and they sure as hell won't ask for it. I'm just interested. But you don't want to talk about it, and that's fine.'

'I came here to make my peace. Bobby really opened up to me. I've met him a couple of times. We got on well. He talked about his health, his family. I felt like I really got to know him, but I couldn't save him. I really thought I could help.'

'Maybe you did.'

'How so?'

'He's at peace now, is he not? I've dealt with my own fair share of suicidal people. Some of them genuinely want to die, right? We turn up and we can prevent it, we talk them down, tell them they've got everything to live for and everything's going to be okay. It's not always, though, is it Shaun? And then we just hand them over to some medical professional of some sort who might recommend a pot of pills to take the edge off their misery. Maybe today was the best outcome.'

'Not for his family.'

'Not in the short term, no. Today's a tough, tough day. But the rest of their life is easier, right?'

'You have a very unique outlook on life.'

'You might say it comes from a very unique life experience. You don't get this cynical standing in the sunshine.'

'I know you from somewhere.'

'I get that a lot. I'm George Elms.' He got to his feet and held out his hand.

'George Elms? *The* George Elms?' Shaun stayed seated and stared up.

'I get that a lot too. I'm done with you then, mate. I've seen the report from the last conversation you had with our Bobby on Shakespeare Cliff. Diagnosed with dementia, a bit of a drinking problem, murdered daughter — it's all on there. So today he talked about the same subjects — maybe forgot that he already had — and then jumped. You had no pre-warning and there was no opportunity to get him safely away from the edge. That sound okay?'

'That's about it, yeah.'

'Perfect. A standard suicide.'

'Standard . . . yeah.' George had stood but remained still. The pause was awkward. Shaun stumbled on. 'I err, I heard you resigned — you know, after all that happened.'

George pulled a small, bound notebook out of his pocket and scribbled on the top page. He tore it out and pushed it towards Shaun. 'My number if you think of anything more you want to add to my report. I suggest you do it quick, though . . . I've been told I can resign at any time.'

Chapter 9

George Elms had a small office in the training wing of Langthorne House police station. It was a large building, one of the biggest police stations in the county, and in his fifteen-year career George reckoned he had worked in just about every part of it. He'd spent time at other stations too, smaller ones with just a response team based there and he preferred them if he was honest. The bigger stations had any number of office type workers and senior ranks who worked a standard working week: Monday to Friday, eight 'til four. These were George's working hours now too, since his enforced move away from actual policing. It meant that he no longer benefitted either from days off in the week or the late or night shift hours where senior management would leave you alone. Every weekend shift, however, had to have cover from a detective sergeant and this was getting more and more difficult to secure with the government cuts increasingly strangling resources and options. So George had been called in. Though he was pretty sure he'd been the last resort, it was nice to be sat in his office on a Sunday afternoon where he could finish his report in peace and quiet.

‘George Elms!’ a voice boomed out. George hadn’t heard it for a long time. It was unmistakable.

‘Major John Whittaker!’ George stood up behind his desk. He referenced the man’s title from his army days.

‘I think it’s Chief Inspector Whittaker these days, George, old friend.’

George extended his hand, Whittaker took it up with vigour.

‘I thought you always preferred *Major*, sir. *Chief* Inspector?’

‘I know, I know. I was quite happy, George, bobbing along at inspector rank. It’s the wife, you know. We went along to some tosh soiree with the upper echelons mincing about in their dress uniforms and her indoors gets talking to the other wives. She hears about this business of moving up a rank or two in your twilight years to bang up the pension. Sure as eggs is eggs, she sees it fit for me to do the same. Pretty much had it sorted by the end of the evening — she’d even spoken to the right people.’

‘Well, I suppose that does make sense, right?’

‘It does not, George Elms, I can tell you. I had a lovely little number up there at HQ. I was in a lovely office, with a desk and one of those machines that makes coffee from a pod at the push of a button. One button! That was pretty much all I was responsible for. Nobody bothered me, nobody needed me. I mean, I had a role to fill. Just no one knew what it was and I sure as hell wasn’t going to tell them!’

‘Well, why would you?’

‘Quite. So this promotion idea comes up and bugger me if they don’t get me to start working for a living! Most unacceptable for a man of my stature and advanced years wouldn’t you say, old friend?’

‘Scandalous, sir. I wonder how you’ll cope.’

‘Eighteen months until retirement George. That’s how I will cope. We’re just back from Cyprus. I was posted out there in my fighting days, see. Beautiful part of the world. Looking for a nice villa or two out there. That's how I'll cope.'

'Two? You going into the rental market then, sir?'

'Rental! Pah! No chance friend, I can't be bothered with all that nonsense. I figured I should look at two, just in case the wife wants to move out there too!'

Both men shared laughter. CI Whittaker's laugh was from his very depths, the sort that could rattle windows.

'So, what on earth are you doing here then, sir? I mean, you're always very welcome of course.'

'I would like to think so. Although I notice you've done nothing to make the wets since I've been here.'

George held his smile. '*Wets*? You army boys have your own language. I only do tea. How do you take it?'

George turned to his own tea facilities on a low desk under the only window.

'Black these days, George. Can't touch the dairy anymore. Intolerance apparently. Who would have thought it? All these years dealing with foreign invaders and street shits and the only lasting intolerance I develop is to the tit of a cow.' Whittaker bellowed laughter again. George couldn't help but join in, it was infectious.

'So I'll ask again . . . why are you here?'

'Well, this is me now, see? I'm the chief inspector overseeing Major Crime. I'm going to need an inspector soon actually, maybe two. That sort of thing float your boat George?'

George shook his head, 'I don't think promotion is for me, sir. Although I would like to see the looks on some faces when you suggested it. I'm being very much kept out of the way.'

'Of course, I heard all about that business. It was all very nasty down here for a while, George. Terrible business. But this is an organisation with a perverse knack of promoting the trouble makers. You never know.'

'You might be right. I hear there's a vacant inspector's job looking after a coffee machine at HQ?'

Whittaker bellowed again. 'That's the George I remember! Imagine my surprise this afternoon when I get a call making me aware of a potential kidnap and murder and I get told the DS running the show is none other than my old friend George Elms! I had heard you had retired of course, but no one was really sure.'

'Very nearly. The chief constable offered it to me himself. He promised me the full pension and said I could walk into the sunset.'

'Why wouldn't you do that?'

'A good question! I had some time off before, sir. You might have heard about it. It wasn't so good for my health. My wife and daughter have gone off on their own for the time being and I was left in a situation where I could sit at home and potentially self-destruct, or I could stick to all I've ever really known until I get some sort of direction back. It's not a great plan, granted.'

'The wife? Gone? Christ, man, after all you've been through.'

'Yeah, I know, but that was the reason to be honest and I certainly don't hold it against her. It might even be the right decision — for now at least. I still hold out hope.'

'Charley — that's your kid right?'

'That's her. She's nearly nine.'

'Nine, is it? Do you still see her a lot?'

'No, actually. We talk on the phone. One thing I know about Sarah . . . when she does something, she does it properly. She's disappeared if I'm honest, I don't even know what part of the country they're in. You might even move next door to them in Cyprus!'

'Imagine that! You could find her, though, right? I don't know anyone better at all that lark, George.'

'I could, yeah. I did once. It didn't end so well. The problem with finding someone who doesn't want to be found is that they don't want to be found. It's not a great starting point for any sort of relationship. I was kinda hoping on an invite one day. I've spent the last few years fucking up, sir. I figured that the only thing I hadn't tried was doing nothing.'

'So that's your plan.'

George shrugged. 'For now.'

'Well, that's all the small talk I've got in me now, George, I didn't get called in on a Sunday to come and listen to your sorry state of affairs. What is going on with this whole thing today?'

George chuckled as he finished the drinks. 'I don't know too much really, sir. I'm the duty DS and I get a call to go out to a jumper before I even get my coat off. Standard procedure I know . . . a DS will always get sent to a suicide. While I'm on my way, I get an update that two people have been pulled out of a building after being snatched off the street in Canterbury at gunpoint and someone has made a link between the two. Seems the woman and boy are related to our jumper. Someone's put two and two together and come up with a bona fide conspiracy theory.'

'You're not having it then?'

'Oh, I didn't say that, sir. It's a hell of a coincidence, and you know what us detectives think about coincidences.'

'I imagine I do. It will all come out in the wash anyway. I have a couple of good detectives with the two victims of the kidnapping as we speak. I did get an early update that they weren't engaging. Worst case, we leave them alone for the night and revisit tomorrow. They've had quite a day.'

'And you get to go back to your Sunday afternoon!'

'Fair point! She'd done a lovely roast dinner too.'

'You left that?'

'Did I hell! I finished it before I came out. By the time I got a call we'd got our kidnap victims back and our jumper friend was well and truly jumped. Who was I going to rush around for? I'll be honest, I didn't have to come in at all. I only came out because I'm still trying to get my head around all this and I figured I could do with getting ahead before I get the third degree tomorrow morning. And then I saw your name all over the log and I knew I had to come in.'

'To check I wasn't fucking it up?'

'Well . . . that — and I just had to see for myself that it was really you. A slightly fatter, older you, but you all the same.'

The two of them laughed and raised their tea mugs to each other.

* * *

Shaun was so tautly wound that he flinched when the front door to 19 Sidney Street moved without warning. He was sat in his car further down the street on the opposite side, where the straight line of houses broke for a primary school set back off the road. Cars were bumper to bumper all the way down. The streetlights had just started to blink on as the afternoon gave way to evening. He slipped a little lower in the seat, but there was little chance of him being seen. From this angle he could see part of someone in dark clothing and still facing into the address. Then came the unmistakable forms of two police detectives, who stepped out and the door closed quickly behind them. Shaun watched as the male and female exchanged a glance and the female shook her head as they walked away. They got into a car, it was facing away from Shaun and he watched it out of sight as it drove off.

He gave it a few minutes then stepped out. Nineteen Sidney Street. Bobby Leonard's family home. He had read the log, he knew his wife and grandson had been unwilling to speak to police at any length after their ordeal and being told of Bobby's demise. He guessed by the reaction of his detective colleagues that they had tried again and got the same response. But Shaun needed to know if they could help him. Despite knowing that just knocking on their front door might put his own family at risk, he couldn't just sit and do nothing.

He hesitated again at the door. He took a second to look around. The world around him seemed to be going about its business. He knocked twice.

'Who is it?' A female voice. She sounded annoyed. It came from the other side of the door. There was a spy hole and he held his warrant card up to it.

'My name is Shaun Carter. I'm a police officer, but I'm also a negotiator.'

'I've spoken to you lot. I've told you that I'm done with it for today. I just want to be left alone.'

'I was with Bobby. When he jumped.'

There was no response.

'I was trying to talk him down. I couldn't do it, I'm sorry . . .'

Shaun paused for a reaction. He got nothing but silence.

'If you have any questions or anything you need to know, I'm here. I'm so sorry.'

Shaun left it a full minute. He couldn't be sure she had even heard what he had said. He considered his options and took in his surroundings again. He was starting to attract attention: the net curtain of the bay window next door twitched; a group of lads slowed as they walked past with a football. He made a decision. He pushed off the door and headed back to his car.

* * *

Shaun made straight for the police station. He booted up the Automatic Number Plate Recognition database and selected the cameras shown at the exit from the port. By selecting a short timescale he was able to identify the traffic leaving the port that was likely to have come from the *Spirit of Britain* ferry docking. The search on the ANPR system could be further narrowed as it filtered down to vehicle type and specifically for anything Spanish registered. He swigged at a cup of water as the system ran the search criteria. It took nearly a minute for a shortlist of six thumbnails to appear with the time next to each. Two lorries had left together at 15:58 hours. One had *Manesco* daubed on the front in small letters. Shaun noted the registration number and put it back into the search database. Another minute passed while he watched a maddening circle twirl on the screen. The hitlist was short again. One hour, twenty minutes after hitting the outbound ANPR camera at the port, it had hit again. This time inbound. They'd got back on a ferry. Fuck! They were gone!

Shaun stood up and backed away from his terminal as if it had suddenly burst into flames. His breathing shallowed as panic rose up through him. They'd made a drop somewhere within a thirty-minute range of the port and then they'd headed straight back to the continent. There was no quick way of tracing them now. And without that lorry he had run out of links.

He thrust his hands into his pockets and pulled out the handwritten note with George Elms's number on it. He couldn't sit on his hands until tomorrow and then hope he got his kid and ex-wife back safely. He had to be doing something. He needed a Plan B. He needed help.

Chapter 10

George was just back home when he got the call. Home was the top right flat in a large building built in the shape of a crescent on Langthorne's seafront, which he'd rented both for the proximity to work and for the views. He'd just made a coffee and was on a wooden seat fitted into the bay window, watching an orange moon reflected in the fidgeting water. It was 9 p.m.

'George Elms.'

'George, hey! It's Shaun Carter. We met earlier today.'

'Of course we did. How you going?'

'Fine yeah. I didn't know if you would still be at work.'

'I am technically. I knocked off a half-hour ago. I mean I'm still on the clock but the night cover DS came in and sent me home.'

'Oh. I'm sorry, is this a bad time? I didn't know you would have your work phone still switched on at home.'

'I don't. I haven't switched that thing on for months. That's why I gave you my personal. Everything okay, Shaun? Did you remember something about your conversation with Bobby Leonard?'

Shaun didn't reply immediately. George gave him time. 'Yeah, I guess I did. I remembered quite a bit actually.'

'Okay, so do you want to meet?'

'I could do with it, I think. Yeah. But I've got a bit of a problem . . . it's more urgent than you might realise.'

'Tonight then. By the time tomorrow comes this is all someone else's problem anyway.'

'You can do tonight?' George could hear the relief in Shaun's voice.

'Sure. Have you eaten? I haven't yet. There's a pizza place I know.'

'I haven't, but I think it will have to be the police station. I don't know if there's anyone watching me.'

This was disturbing. George took a second or two before responding. 'This sounds rather serious all of a sudden. Takeaway it is then.'

* * *

George parked in a side street and slipped into the rear entrance of Langthorne House police station. The oversized pizza box was cumbersome as he bundled into the service lift. When he got to his office the lights were already on. Shaun Carter was pacing the middle.

'Shaun.'

Shaun span to meet him, he immediately looked a man under stress. He was shorter and stockier than George. His arms were thick and well developed and he wore a wristband suggesting he was ex-military.

'Thanks for coming in,' Shaun said.

'You're welcome. What's this all about?'

'My conversation with Bobby Leonard was quite different to what you think. To what everyone thinks.'

'Okay.'

'I was picked out. You know I spoke to Bobby on a clifftop a few weeks ago. We spoke for a while and he got some information from me. He knew that I was covering all the weekends as negotiator, that I preferred to work alone, and he knew about my family. My ex-wife and my boy.'

'Do you normally go into that much detail?'

Shaun shook his head vigorously. 'No, I didn't tell him all that. I don't know how he got the information about my family. He said that he got picked too. He said that these people have my boy and my ex-wife. They grabbed them from the street in Canterbury. He said he had a message for me from these people and if I did what he asked I would get my family back unharmed. I called up, did the checks I could from the top of that viaduct and there *was* an abduction job running in Canterbury. It sounded bad. I panicked. I did what he asked and the update came out on air almost straight away that the two people from the abduction had been released.'

'It wasn't your family.' George was almost thinking out loud.

'It wasn't. Bobby knew it would be *his* boy and *his* wife getting out. He had obviously done what he needed to do. Then he jumped.'

'Shit! So your family are okay?'

'No. Far from it. I couldn't get in touch. It's not unusual for my ex to ignore my calls so I went round to her house. It's all in darkness. Then I got this through after I spoke to you on the phone.'

Shaun passed his phone over. George read a text message from the screen from *Carol*. It said, *Do as they say, don't know where I am Shaun. We are okay x*.

George handed it back. Shaun fiddled with the phone, then passed it over again. A second message on the screen from the same contact read: *CLEVER BITCH HIDING THE PHONE. FEEL FREE TO TRACK IT. SHE'LL BE LONG GONE.*

Have you had any further contact? Any more demands?'

'Nothing.'

'So they have your phone number. We can assume that's how they'll contact you?'

'I guess so, yeah. There was nothing else.'

'And Bobby was our link.'

'Yes, and it makes sense now. His whole demeanour wasn't right. I mean, I know people under that sort of stress. They don't come across like normal people, but he was all over the place. I couldn't put my finger on it. Then when you caught me searching his body I had found a wire on him.'

'A wire? What sort of wire?'

'Similar to what we use but a bit more up to date. A Bluetooth earpiece, the battery and device were all one, and I think it was the sort that uses a 4G network rather than a radio signal.'

'So they were in contact with him while he was up there talking to you?'

'The whole time I think. One of the rules was that I didn't go out of earshot. They must have heard everything that was said and were pumping information into his ear. He genuinely might not have known any of it and was just repeating what they told him to.'

'What did they have you do?'

'I've been seeing a girl who works down Dover port. It's nothing serious. I was holding out you know . . . with the wife. Look, she basically runs the team that assesses the vehicles coming off the ferries. They have a small in-house intel cell and they can stop and search what they like. I was told to contact her and to make sure that a vehicle got through. An HGV that was showing as transporting tomatoes.'

'Any idea what they were really transporting?'

'No. Bobby probably didn't either. But whatever it was, they went to a lot of effort to make sure it got through the border.'

'Do you remember the details?'

'I have them. I found it on the ANPR system. The same system that tells me that the lorry was back on a ferry an hour later. I've lost them, George. I've lost everything. I don't know what to do. I'm desperate here.'

'Desperate enough to call me.'

'I'm sorry. The last thing you want is to be dragged into something like this, George, but I don't know who to talk to. They made it clear that I shouldn't talk to anyone. Definitely not other coppers. They said just to wait for further instructions. I know you by reputation. This might be a complete fuck-up, but I figured that if anyone understands how to get things done away from alerting the rest of the world, it might just be you. You've been in my shoes before, right?'

George ran his hand through his hair. He scratched thoughtfully at his cheek. 'I suppose so, but the motivation is different.'

'Bobby Leonard played by the rules, I'm guessing he did what he needed to do by isolating me and getting my assistance. As soon as he did that his family were released. Totally unharmed. If I don't fuck up, if I play by their rules then maybe they'll just release my boy too?'

'If you believed that you wouldn't have called me. You're a copper. The second they involved you, they upped the ante.'

Shaun flopped in the chair on the opposite side of the desk. George remained standing, the delicious-smelling pizza was still untouched on the table.

'I don't know. I just don't know. That was my plan — to play by their rules I mean. To do what they say. But I wanted a Plan B. If it all went wrong, if they didn't give me back my boy I wanted to at least have a start on these people. If they hurt Tyler—'

'I know how you feel, Shaun. I've been there — my kid threatened, my family threatened. I know what it's like, that tense knot in your stomach. You did the right thing talking to someone else. I didn't. I kept it all to myself and

I made mistakes, the sort of mistakes that put everyone at risk.'

'These people seem to know so much about me. I figured you're a clean break. If I don't know you, they can't either.'

'I've been described as many things. That's a new one.'

'What do we do, George? Where do we go from here?'

George pondered his answer for a few seconds. 'If you're serious that these people might be watching you, then I suggest you do nothing. Let me do the legwork for now. I skimmed the details earlier. I need to review the whole thing, see if there's anything relevant.'

'I tried to talk to Bobby Leonard's family. They might be the only link left.'

'That would be the next obvious move. What happened?'

'I went to the home address. I watched a couple of detectives go in. They must have only been in there five minutes — maybe less. They got a pill to be honest. I knocked on the door a few minutes after they left and she wouldn't even open the door to me. I've checked the log and they're just not engaging with us at all.'

'She's back at her home address then?' George typed his password into the computer so he could access the police systems.

'Yeah. Refused to stay in protected accommodation. Major Crime had sorted a hotel.'

'That's good for us.'

'It is?'

'Yeah. She's not under guard and she's at her home. I'll go and speak to her there.'

'She won't speak to anyone, George.'

'Hold tight. We just need a different approach.'

Chapter 11

9:40 p.m. George Elms stepped out into an evening where the shadows were long. The cool air concealed the lightest of drizzle. He left his car parked some distance away from the address and walked Sidney Street, along the pavement opposite the target address. It was a tightly packed row of terraced houses, two front bay windows top and bottom, a front door tucked in one of the corners. Typical of much of the terraced housing stock in Langthorne. As best as he could tell from his position, there was a weak light coming from a room at the back of number 19 and on the ground floor. Probably the kitchen. He walked past, continued until he reached the other end of the street, then he crossed over and doubled back. He gripped half a house brick in his jacket pocket, sourced from a building site on the way. A front door opened a few doors down from 19 and a man strode out purposefully. He called back towards the house as he walked a few paces across the pavement to his car. It was an angry shout and he didn't look back as the front door was slammed shut from inside. The car revved hard as it pulled away. George had slowed his pace and dipped his head. He needn't have bothered. No one was taking any notice of the figure walking close to the building line. When George got to number 19, the curtains had been pulled across untidily, bunched up on the back of an armchair that was pushed into the bay window. They left a gap, enough that he could see the light better, a light bulb hanging bare, off-centre and towards the rear in the ceiling. No signs of movement. He took a step back and checked around for a final time. The street had fallen back to silence. He pulled the brick from his pocket and took aim. The lounge window folded inwards with little resistance. The curtains fell shut as the brick pushed through. The tinkling of glass lasted just a few seconds and the street fell back to silence. He slipped off the gloves as he paced calmly to his car.

He took his police radio out of the door pocket. By the time it had connected to the network the report was already being put out.

'Zulu Four, can I divert you to an immediate please?'

'Zulu Four, go ahead.'

'Zulu Four, thank you, we are receiving a call from 19 Sidney Street, Langthorne. This is the victim of a kidnapping earlier today. She states that someone has just put her front window in. She is home with her young son.'

'Received that, Control — show me en route.'

George cut in. 'Yankee One, Control.'

'Yankee One, go ahead.'

'I caught the last, Control. I'm just out for some refs. Confirm that was Sidney Street, Langthorne?'

'Yes. Yes, Yankee One.'

'Received that. I'm just around the corner. Keep that uniform patrol running but can you show me going to take a look.'

'Received that. Thank you, Yankee One.'

George pulled his car around and parked untidily into a space almost opposite. He was still clutching his radio as he got to the front door.

'Yankee One, show me TA, please.'

'Time of arrival noted.'

He knocked at the door. 'Police! Sharon, are you in there? It's the police.'

The door was pulled open almost immediately. He flapped his warrant card at the pale, stick-thin form of Sharon Leonard.

'Come in!' Her wide eyes gazed beyond him, out into the dark street. He pulled the door shut as he stepped into the lounge.

The house brick lay with glass all around it on the cushion of the single-seat sofa. The lounge was small and busy inside; wall units, sofas and a cluttered coffee table gave it a claustrophobic feel. A hanging coat prodded him in the shoulder.

'Bloody hell, Sharon!' George exclaimed. 'Are you okay? I was just around the corner. What happened?'

Sharon had her hands over her mouth. Her face scrunched into a silent sob. She wore a threadbare dressing gown that George could see through to a cotton nightie underneath.

'Are you and your boy okay?'

Sharon jerked a nod and took a sharp intake of breath. 'He was in bed. I was making a coffee. I just heard this smash all of a sudden, like. I didn't see nobody, I didn't go and have a look. I stayed in the kitchen back there and I called you lot.'

George heard a car pull up hurriedly outside. Two doors opening and closing, then a torchlight against the window.

'Looks like my uniformed colleagues are here, Sharon. I'm Detective Sergeant George Elms. I'll get them to do a good sweep so we know you're safe. Then we need a good chat about what's going on — about how we keep you safe from now on, yeah? I know you've had a hell of a day.'

She managed another nod. Her eyes flashed to the door as someone knocked on it. George showed the officers in. He led Sharon back through to the tight kitchen at the rear where she found a seat at a small table propped up against the wall. He noted a mug next to a kettle that still puffed steam from its spout. It jostled for position among the bottles of alcohol on the kitchen bench.

'I'll finish making your coffee.'

'And then you can go.' Her voice hardened.

George flicked the kettle back on and turned to face Sharon. A young boy appeared from the bottom of the stairs, he paced in without a word and stood next to his grandmother. She wrapped an arm around his waist.

'Of course. If that's what you want.'

'Of course it is!' Sharon snapped. 'That's all I've wanted all day. I just want to be left alone. I want to be safe in my own home and I want to be left alone. And I don't want to be asked any more questions. All day, all people have done is ask me questions. I don't know the answers. I don't know what you people want me to say.'

George took up the empty seat opposite where she held her head in her hands. She lifted her eyes to meet his.

'I'll tell you what, Sharon, call me different, but I don't want anything from you. I'm not here to ask any questions. I only came here to make sure you were all right. I'll just make you that coffee and then I'll be here if you want to ask *me* any questions. How about that?'

'I don't want to ask any questions. There's nothing I need to know. Nothing I want to know. Bobby's gone, I know that. What more is there?'

'Then I'll leave.' George stood back up to the kettle. 'Before I came here, I was debriefing the officer who was up with Bobby. He was the last person to talk to him. He feels awful, really bad about the whole thing. He told me what they were talking about. Bobby talked about you two, about his daughter. And about the people that made him do this. He said you wouldn't talk to us, Bobby did. Not straight away at least. He said we'd have to wait until you got angry. He said you're formidable when you're angry.' George moved the coffee in front of Sharon.

'Like I said, I'm not here to ask you any questions Sharon, but you have this opportunity now to ask me anything.'

'I've told you, I don't want to know anything.'

'Because you're scared?'

'Wouldn't you be?' Sharon suddenly became aware of herself. She spoke to the boy, 'Connor, love, why don't you go back up on your console for now. I'll come up and see you when the police have gone. There won't be any more noises. The policeman said it was an accident.'

'Was it an accident, nan?' The boy looked despairingly at Sharon. She met him with watery eyes and ran her fingers through his fringe.

George answered for her. 'A heavy lorry drove past. It ran over a stone and flicked it up through your window. We've checked it all out and we know that's what happened. It's a one in a million chance, little mate.' He smiled reassuringly. 'I don't reckon it could ever happen again.'

The boy met his gaze for just a second before he was back on his nan.

'Watcha playing? On the console I mean?' George asked.

'Fifa.' Connor replied.

'Good choice! I always play as Millwall. They're the best.'

'Millwall! No they ain't! I always play as Chelsea.'

'I thought you supported Millwall? There's a flag on the wall in there?'

The boy broke into a smile. 'It's my granddad's. But, yeah, I support them. But they're rubbish on Fifa.'

'I see. Maybe I can come over and play you sometime. I used to be good at the football games.'

The boy nodded at his nan. She managed a weak smile and he left back up the stairs.

'He's doing well.' George said.

'He has no idea. In a few days, when he starts realising that his granddad is never coming back, we'll see how well he is doing then.'

'I'm so sorry, Sharon. I can't imagine how difficult this has all been for you. You might have just had the worst day I have ever heard of.'

'You might be right.'

'I'm not here to make it worse either. If you want me to go I'll go. I get the feeling you're not the shy type, Sharon. If ever you wanted to swear at a police officer, to tell one to piss right off, now's your chance! I wouldn't blame you — I wouldn't even hold it against you. But I don't want to leave you while you're scared. That wouldn't be right.'

Sharon's smile was now more genuine. 'There's still some water in that kettle. You can make yourself a tea?'

'Very kind.'

'Sarge.' A male voice cut across. Sharon dipped her head again, her smile falling away.

'Yeah, you okay?'

'We're done, Sarge. We've done a good area search — there's no one about. I'll seize the brick and a glass sample for forensics. We got pictures of the damage. I've arranged for a marked car to be parked outside.' He addressed Sharon directly: 'It won't have anyone in it, ma'am, but it's a proven technique. It'll keep people away.'

Sharon looked questioningly at George who smiled broadly. 'Think of it as like a police scarecrow. This is how bad the cuts have got, see? We can also get a mannequin in a police hat, holding a truncheon if you think it will help? We can paint a very stern look on its face.' They both chuckled.

'Well, I feel a lot safer,' Sharon said to the uniformed officer. 'Thank you.'

'Well, good. I'll give boarding-up a call, Sarge, to secure that window. Do you need us to wait around for it or will you be staying? They're normally here within half an hour.'

'That's okay, I'll wait. I can't guarantee Sharon here won't kick me out sooner than that, but I can sit in my car.'

'You're all right,' Sharon said.

The uniformed officers left. Sharon waited for the front door to be pushed closed. George used the excuse of swigging at his tea to get Sharon talking first.

'Did he talk about me really?'

'Of course he did. He has nothing but admiration for you, Sharon. He was talking about how difficult things have been. This family has had its challenges, seems you've risen to every one of them.'

'I've had to. I just feel so exhausted. I've had enough.'

'There's nothing more tiring than having to keep getting back up, Sharon. That I know.'

'Got to, ain't I? For him.' She gestured at the stairs.

'Family's the only thing worth knackering yourself out for if you ask me.'

'I reckon you're right too. He was a good man you know, was Bobby. And he just wanted to see us happy. Me and the little man.'

'Connor seems like a good kid.'

'He's had a hell of a life. We lost his mum — terrible thing that was. She was killed by an animal of a man. He used to ply her with drugs so she would pretty much do what he wanted. She was just a plaything to him. But she was so much more than that, so much better. He wouldn't have Connor around. She accepted that, we wouldn't see her much at all then when I did see her she'd lost weight and all self-respect. She ended up your typical junkie. We did what we could but it got her bad.'

'I know how it can get them. I see it all the time.'

'I bet you do.'

'It's different when it's one of your own.'

'It is. I mean we all have our battles. Me and Bobby have always liked a drink most days. Never so it got in the way. We cut right down when Connor came to stay.'

'Kids change everything.'

'Do you have children, Sergeant?'

'I have a little girl. Similar age to Connor. And call me George.'

'I've never been so terrified, you know. When they grabbed us today, when they pointed that gun at Connor. They were pointing it at me too, but I didn't care. I was just terrified they were going to hurt Connor.'

'They didn't though, right?'

'They didn't no. Not Connor, not me either. Not physically. They pushed us around a bit — I got a kick so we went where they wanted. They hurt other people though — they hurt them bad. They drove that car right through the window . . .' Sharon tailed off, her voice breaking. She lifted her hand to cover her mouth. 'People were screaming out, it was panic at first but then it was pain. People were hurt. They got trapped under the car and knocked down. They killed people, George, and why? To get to us!' Sharon lost her composure completely. Her head fell forward and George laid his palm flat over her hand on the table. He leant in close so he could talk softly into her ear. She smelt sickly sweet up close, like day-old alcohol and cigarettes.

'It's okay, Sharon. It's okay. You're away from them now. You're safe.'

'He said that if Bobby did as they said we'd be fine. They said he was a good man and we had nothing to fear. I was praying, George. I was praying that he just did what they wanted him to do. I know he can be a stubborn old bastard — he doesn't like being told what to do. All I wanted was for him to listen and to do it. I didn't realise they were going to make him do himself in! I didn't know.'

'You couldn't have known, Sharon. I know you would never want him to do that.'

Sharon sat back up and dabbed at her eyes. 'There was two of them. One stayed with us most of the time but he kept going into another room where the other one was. Every time he came back from there he would say that Bobby was doing well. They must have been talking to him on the phone in there. They got us food. they asked what we wanted and Connor said that he liked McDonalds. They got us some and we'd only just finished it. And then — just like that — the other man came in and he threw me a mobile phone. He told me where we was. He said I had to count to a thousand. Then he said I could call the police. He said he would be counting too, and if I called the police or left the house before he had got to one thousand he would shoot us both. He had a big rifle thing — said he had trained as a sniper. We counted to one thousand together, taking it real slow. Then I called the police and we just waited. I didn't want to leave that house, I thought he would be waiting for us out the front, like it was some sort of game. A sport.'

'You did well, Sharon. I don't think anyone could have done better. In those situations you just have to do what you can to stay alive. You and Connor walked away.'

'I was so happy when I saw your lot. But the man with the big rifle said not to tell you anything about them. He told me we had to go home. He said we would be offered somewhere safe to go, but I had to insist on going home. Do you think it was so they would know where we are?'

'They want you frightened, Sharon. Their hold over you depends on it. They want you frightened so you don't speak to the police. Personally, I think they're done with you now, but you have to do what you think is best to keep you both safe.'

'I can't move. I came back like they told me too. I thought that Connor could have some sort of normality too. They offered us a hotel a good distance from here but I didn't want to take him away from all his mates. This is a funny old place to live, you know. That brick through the window could just as well be one of the locals getting the hump with all the police attention. They must think I'm talking to you. I ain't no *grass*, but I've had nothing but coppers coming to and fro here.'

'Could be, Sharon. But this isn't like squealing up some local for dealing a bit of green, though, is it? I can still make a few calls and get you both into a hotel. I'll make sure it's more local than you were offered, maybe just the next town but somewhere they won't know?'

'I appreciate the offer. But we're staying here. We've been here nearly twenty years and I ain't ever run away from nothing. I'm not about to start now.'

George grinned. '*You* don't strike me as the running sort. You're sure though, Sharon? Connor will be okay. He can take Fifa with him. It would be a bit of an adventure.'

'I think we've had enough of them for one day, George.'

'Fair point.' George scribbled his telephone number on a piece of paper. 'I'll leave this here. For anything you need.'

* * *

'Late finish?'

Shaun jumped at the sound of the voice. Jess stepped out from the shadows of the front entrance to his building. He had ignored a couple of her calls earlier in the evening. He had intended on calling her back. It was 11 p.m. She was dressed in her navy-blue work trousers and a black fleece. She must have finished her late shift and come straight over.

'You could say that,' Shaun said. 'Sorry I didn't get back to you, it's been a manic one.'

'Don't worry.'

'Everything okay?'

'Yeah. I was just worried about you.'

'That's not like you!'

They both chuckled but it was strained. Shaun used his key to open the door. A sensor detected his movement and light flooded the hall. 'I'll put the kettle on, then.'

Shaun's cat immediately provided a trip hazard as he pushed through his front door. It was on the top floor, views overlooking a park in Canterbury's city centre. It was a small flat in a good area. — the best option after the breakdown of his marriage.

'How did it go then?' Jess folded her arms and leant on the units in his kitchen.

'How did what go?'

'Did he jump?'

'Yeah.'

'Shit! I'm sorry Shaun. Did you see it?'

'Yeah, I saw it.'

'These people. It's so selfish. They don't care about the people that have to clear up after them — or the people they leave behind.'

'They don't. They're not in the right state of mind to think like that, I guess. I hope I never understand how that feels.'

'You okay?'

'I'm fine. I think he was always going to go, I don't take these things personally.'

'But you must have been talking to him for hours? Was he up there all this time and then he just decided to jump?'

'No. He jumped bang on 4 p.m. I don't know why, but that seemed like an important time to him.'

'You can't have been doing paperwork all this time?'

'No. There were some bits to do as you can imagine. Then I went round Carol's house. I haven't heard from her or Tyler all day. I'm starting to get worried about it.'

'That's not unusual, is it? Was she in?' Jess's tone now carried an edge. It always did when Shaun talked about his ex-wife.

'No. No sign of life. House in darkness. Phone rings out.'

'She's probably playing her games again.'

'Probably.'

'Did you go back to work after?'

'Yes. There was a kidnap job here in Canterbury. I was hanging around to see if they were going to call a negotiator. I didn't want to book off just to get called back in again.'

'A kidnap! I thought Sunday was the day of rest.'

'It appears the criminal element were not aware. I wasn't needed in the end anyway.'

'Did it get resolved okay?'

Shaun hesitated. He considered telling her everything he knew. He was desperate to share it with someone else and he knew the pressure of keeping it to himself was affecting his behaviour.

'It got resolved. There's more work to do, but not for me. The investigation team took over and I did what I could to help.'

'Anything come of this intelligence you had around that lorry?'

'The lorry? Oh, I didn't really do much with it. That's someone else's problem.'

'Are your lot doing some sort of enforcement on them?'

'I don't know what the plan is, but I checked the ANPR system before I knocked off and it left already.'

'What did?'

'The lorry. It spent half an hour, tops, in the UK before it was back at the port, waiting for the next boat out.'

'Oh really? So they dropped whatever they had and then went straight back. I assume you didn't want the drivers then?'

'I didn't personally, Jess. Like I told you, I don't know what the interest was in that lorry or anyone connected to it. It may well be a small part in a bigger puzzle. They might have let them run this time in anticipation of them coming back for the enforcement phase.'

'And you don't know when that might be or what they were dropping off?'

'I told you I didn't'

'You did. But, like I said to you on the phone, I've had those sorts of calls before from the police. Holding information back like we don't matter down there.'

'Jess . . . Jesus! I told you everything I knew. I wasn't calling so you missed out on a good job. I was calling so you didn't get hurt.'

'So you said.'

'Is that not enough?'

'I don't like being part of someone else's game is all.'

'Your wellbeing isn't a game to me, Jess. I've had a long, shit day. If you only came over here to lecture me about inter-agency intelligence then perhaps you could save it for another day. I need to get some sleep — I have to be back in early tomorrow.'

'What do you mean? You're off tomorrow. We were doing breakfast before I go on lates.'

Shaun had forgotten they had plans. 'I can't make it. I have got to go in now. I'm sorry. I'll make it up to you, though, yeah?'

'Don't bother, Shaun.' Jess pushed away from the unit and made for the door. 'I'll see you around. You just let me know when it suits you, yeah?'

Shaun remained still. He heard Jess scuffling to get her shoes back on and the front door slam. He didn't have the energy to chase her and argue. He would make it up to her, but it could wait.

His phone vibrated on the kitchen bench. *George Elms* appeared on the screen. Shaun was suddenly aware of how drained he felt.

'George.'

'Hey. I've just come away from Sharon's'

'Who?'

'Bobby Leonard's other half.'

'Yes? Is she still not talking?'

'She talked to me. She just needed some assurance. She doesn't feel safe at home so I was able to tap into that.'

'Is there still a threat there?'

'I don't think so, no. I think she's done her bit for these people and they couldn't care less about her anymore.'

'And? Did you get anything relevant?'

'Not much we can use. Sharon said there were two of them for most of the time. They had automatic rifles, access to at least three vehicles and they were highly organised. It sounds like they were communicating with Bobby from the same house they were holding his family. I don't think she helps us much.'

'So we need to go to where they were found. See if there's anything left that might give an idea where they went. Or who they are?'

'I don't think so. They told Sharon where she was and to call the police. Then they left. If you know the police are coming to a location you clean it real good. There won't be anything there other than whatever they want us to find. Besides, it's still a scene — there's a search team due in there at first light.'

'So what now? I can't just sit here and do nothing.'

'There isn't much else you can do. I suggest you try and get some sleep. It's going to be a long day tomorrow. I'll go back in and see what's been updated on the log. There might be something useable.'

'You can't tell anyone about this, George. I trusted you. I don't really know why. I just thought if anyone would understand how important it is to play by their rules for now, it might be you.'

'Don't worry. I know we have to be clever about this. Or subtle at least. I'll talk to you in the morning.'

The conversation ended and Shaun stared at his phone. He knew George Elms by reputation only. And that reputation was not of one for subtlety.

Chapter 12

'Tee' was even bigger than Jake Jones had expected. Not just tall, but thick set, with electric-blue eyes that stood out from tanned skin and darker stubble. He was older too, late forties Jake guessed. His age helped with his presence, even his walk exuded confidence. Tee was his street name. No one seemed to know much about him. Jake certainly didn't. Jake had been doing some work on the outskirts of the 'Tee Line', as it was known, but had recently stepped up to become a bigger fish. But he was well aware that it was Tee's pond.

He had been told to meet with Tee tonight. The location was phoned through to him at the last minute. The message he had received was that tonight was all about loyalty. He had no idea what this meant and as Tee approached him, emerging from the darkness into the headlights of two parked cars, he had a sudden sense of dread — like this might not prove such a good career choice after all.

Jake was a drug dealer. Small time. He had been a labourer until recently. He was getting regular work on sites around the county, mainly prepping land for new housing. He worked with large crews, mainly groundwork. It was tough graft and the men and a few women worked hard and played harder. Drugs played a big part: the crews had a demand for cocaine, amphetamine and cannabis that Jake had been able to fulfil almost accidentally. He had kept in touch with an old school friend who he had known to be involved in something the wrong side of the law and somehow it had escalated and brought him to this place. It had once been a road that linked Dover with Ramsgate, but was now a dead end with grass growing up its middle and sliced in half by the building of a new bypass.

Jake held his hand out to shake with Tee. It was ignored.

'You're the new boy I understand? You want to work with me?'

'That's right. It's good to meet you, man.'

'I'm not your man. I'm your boss. You should call me boss.'

Jake took his hand back. 'Boss it is.'

Tee's face broke suddenly into a wide smile that reflected the headlights pointed at Jake's back.

'I wanted you to see something tonight, new boy. This is a lesson. I don't care who you are. I don't care how connected, big or fucking clever you are. I just want you to be loyal. Can you manage that, new boy?'

'Yeah, I can do that.'

'People tell me you've got a good market. People tell me I should work with you. We can grow this thing together. But before I work with anyone I always have this same conversation. I think it's better if we both understand each other from the start.'

Tee turned and walked away. Shadows either side of him moved and he was flanked by two men in dark clothing. Jake hadn't even noticed them. He could see the red taillights of a car further down the road. Tee walked towards them and called out, 'Let's take a walk!'

Jake started after him, taking time to peer right and left as he walked. Dark woodland leered back at him, green leaves and brown branches soon gave way to thick trunks of mature trees; beyond this was just a solid blackness. Ahead, and some way in the distance, he could hear the dull roar of the new bypass. He felt for the phone in his pocket for a crumb of comfort. It didn't have the desired effect; there was no one he could call that could help him now.

Jake made it to the rear of the parked car. It was a Ford, an old black Mondeo. The paintwork blended with the night; the round red lamps stood out like evil eyes, watching his approach. The boot lid was up. Some carrier bags and dried mud littered the inside. Tee stopped level with the driver's door and called back, 'I want you to meet two other people that I had a similar conversation with! They were new boys, too.'

Jake peered in through the windows. The interior light was on and he saw the man in the driver's seat first: a white male, mid-twenties, around his age. He had a tattoo on his neck and behind his ear. His skin was a shocking white, no doubt worsened by the harshness of the interior light. His eyes bulged wide with terror, his head pointed forward like it was held by some invisible force, and sweat ran freely from his temple. Jake stooped to take in a better view. He could see a second man in the front passenger seat. He was similar looking and had the same tense stare forwards. Both took hurried, shallow breaths.

'We can talk.' The driver spoke with effort in a heavy, Eastern or Central European accent. He didn't deviate from staring forwards. Jake looked ahead to where the headlights of the Ford arrowed up the road. 'We can still talk,' The driver said again.

Jake stepped back. Tee pulled gloves from his pocket and slipped them on. He reached through the open window. The engine of the Mondeo fired.

Tee leant on the door. 'Put it in drive.'

'We can still talk!'

'Now you want to talk? Now you want to talk to me? Do you have any idea the problems you've caused me? The humiliation? You think I went to all the trouble of bringing you back from your hidey-hole in Paris so you could talk? I brought you back so you could die.'

Tee stood away from the car and turned to Jake. 'You get good at this sort of thing you see.' He stepped around Jake and beckoned to him from the rear of the car. Jake walked dubiously over.

'Cable. Strong cable,' Tee said, and he leant down and pushed down on thin, grey cable that ran up into the car from the darkness. Jake had missed it as he had approached the car, but he could see it now. He could see that it rose up through the boot and creased the top of the driver's headrest. And there was another one too, running over the passenger's headrest. Jake walked back up the side of the car. He leant into the front window. He could see now that the wires were looped tightly around the necks of the two men. The man in the driver's seat thrust his eyes right, straining to see.

'Please. Please help us,' he whispered to Jake.

Jake was suddenly aware of Tee close behind him.

'Help you?' Tee called out, 'but then he'd be sat in the back seat. I don't think that's going to happen, now is it? Nobody's here to help you. I think it's time.'

'I got children. Two children.' The man spluttered. The sweat had pooled on the end of his chin. The man in the passenger seat stayed silent. He'd scrunched his eyes shut and seemed to be battling with his breathing.

'Yes you have. And you remember what happens to them if you don't do what you're told right? You're lucky I didn't bring them back, too. This is merciful.'

Jake stepped back, it was like it wasn't real. Like he was watching a recorded nightmare.

'You've got twenty metres or so. Make the most of it.' Tee's voice carried sudden authority. This was an instruction. 'That's more than enough to get up enough speed for it to be quick.'

'I can't do this.' The stricken driver raised his voice. 'I CAN'T do it!'

Tee's hands made a slapping sound as they came down hard on the roof.

'This is what you get. You think you can betray me? There's nowhere you can hide from me. This is where it ends. Now you have a choice and I will only offer it once more. It ends like this, with you at the controls, quick and easy. Or we move onto much slower methods. I know you've seen that. LAST CHANCE!'

'LET IT GO!' Tee shouted to the rear of the car. Jake could her a rustling in the wooded area, some twigs snapping. The cable that had been taut fell slack instantly. A man appeared from the woods and threw two coils of the wire on the floor under the boot. Two ends still trailed into the woods. Suddenly the Mondeo revved, though it stayed where it was, shaking on its chassis as it fell back to idle. It revved again, but this time the front wheels spun as the gear was engaged. Jake heard a terrible shout from inside the car. It surged forward. The coils of cable quickly unravelled in front of him as he watched the car surge away. His attention turned back to the quickly unravelling cables. Both tightened within a split second of each other. Then they dropped to the ground. The Mondeo still moved away but the revs dropped. It veered to the left, the rear taillights bucked into the air and stayed at an angle. The car came to a sudden stop with a terrific noise.

Jake felt physically sick. Tee looked very satisfied.

'We just need to be sure the matter's finished and then I think our meeting is concluded. I think you understand what it means to be working for me, right? It's Jake, right?' Tee's hand was now extended. Jake was on autopilot as he reached out. Tee's crushing grip shouldn't have been such a surprise and he locked Jake in an intense gaze.

'Are we walking?'

Jake had to swallow hard to form words. 'Yeah, boss.'

They walked side by side towards the car. The engine had stalled but Jake could still pick out the lights in the darkness. It was thirty metres ahead. The night sky was clearing and the moon peeked out to provide sufficient light for Jake to follow the road and to pick out some details. He could see the two cables trailing up the middle of the road. He stepped over one of the wire loops where the cable had pulled tight. It was still whole, it's surface slick with something, enough to reflect the moon. His stomach churned like he might be sick, his mouth filled with saliva and he had to swallow a couple of times for it to pass.

'In every walk of life you get tested,' Tee said. 'You take any job for any company they're going to come test you somehow. You go work for a bank they're going to test your mental agility, you work for a newspaper, they're going to test your ability to structure arguments in your written work. I run a business, just like them, but loyalty's what matters to me. That's all that matters. These two men you see tonight, they failed my test and they put my whole business at risk. I don't accept that, I can't accept that. You understand?'

'Never clearer.'

'Good. Then you'll never be driving hard into the darkness.'

Tee produced a torch and shone it on the back of the Mondeo. They were just a few paces short now, the car had ridden left until it had come to a sudden stop against a tree. Jake braced himself as he walked up the offside of the car. Already he could see the rear window had a red hue. Tee shone the light into the front and beckoned for Jake to peer in first. It was unreal, like a scene mocked up by a special effects team. A torso, a red fleshy lump on top of it that had once been a neck, eyes gazing up from the severed head that had gathered in the footwell. Blood still dripped in clumps from the roof lining. Jake could fight it no more, he spun away from the car and wretched. Tee thrust him a bag.

'In here. We leave nothing.'

Jake took the bag. Bent double, he dry retched. He got control of his breathing and he could hear laughing. The bastard was *laughing*! It stopped suddenly, sudden enough for Jake to turn around where Tee was leaning into the car.

'What the FUCK?'

'What's the matter?' Jake said.

Tee straightened up quickly and swung the beam of his torch into the woods beyond.

'Where'd he go? Where'd he fucking GO?' Tee moved to the front of the car. His torchlight picked out some trampled grass leading away. He plunged into the woods to follow. Jake peered back into the car. The interior light was still on. It was dulled by a slick layer of blood but it was bright enough to see that there was nobody in the passenger seat.

Chapter 13

George Elms had come to hold a deep dislike for night and the silence it brought. For a man suffering a constant whooshing and whistling in his ears, silence could be a form of torture. Since tinnitus had become a part of his life, he'd learnt to function with very little sleep, most of the time dozing through the night on his sofa with the television on low or in bed with the radio on. He was dozing when his phone rang. The sound of the television remote control falling onto his wooden floor was what shook him awake.

'George Elms.' He sat up, opened his eyes as wide as he could then squinted against the flickering light of some shopping channel. It was 2 a.m.

'George, sorry to wake you. It's Shaun.'

'Don't worry about it. I can only assume it's important.'

'It might be, yeah. I couldn't sleep. I took my police radio home and I've been listening in tonight. I know no one's out looking for my family but they might have got away . . . I don't know what I was hoping . . .'

'You don't need to explain to me, Shaun. I've been there, I've got a good idea of how you're feeling. What's happened?'

'A traffic patrol came over to the local channel. They found someone walking along the motorway, back towards Langthorne. This bloke was covered in blood and when they picked him up he said it wasn't his. He said that someone had killed his brother.'

'Okay.'

'The update didn't have much detail on it, it was just a summary over the radio. But this bloke asked for police protection. He said that the people that killed his brother meant to kill him too. He knows they'll be out looking for him. He said he was smuggled back into the country with his brother earlier today. He was smuggled through the port. On a lorry.'

'And you think this might have been the same lorry that you made sure got through?'

'I do.'

'People get smuggled through the port all the time, Shaun. Don't pin your hopes. But I agree, this is worth a look.'

'I think I'll go into the nick near me. Have a look at the log and see if there's any more detail on there.'

'Don't do that. You can't walk into a police station in the middle of the night without prompting questions — and you can't give a good reason. Where is this bloke?'

'They arrested him. I assume he's at Langthorne House custody.'

'Makes sense, I suppose. Best way of making sure he's safe while they do some more enquiries. He'll probably be there most of tomorrow too. We have a small window to get to him.'

'We can't just walk down there and talk to him though. Major Crime will be all over him. Neither of us will have a good reason.'

George stood up from his sofa in a stretch and walked towards the kettle. 'That's true. It might need a little creative thinking. I'll think of something. Is that all we know from the radio updates?'

'So far. They're still looking for where he's come from. He's a foreign national. He was lost when they found him and he doesn't know how to get back there.'

'Nationality?'

'Polish. He's known though. I heard them run him through PNC. He has an intel marker.'

'Any details on that?'

'It was an urgent interest marker. Any stops were to be reported to the Op Vapour intel team. Do you know it?'

'Yeah. It's the county team combatting the movement of class-A drugs around the county and from outside.'

'The marker said that if the stop was in office hours they had to call direct through to a DC Ryker from the Vapour intel team The log has been tagged for him, so I guess he'll pick it up in a few hours.'

'Her.'

'Her?'

'DC Ryker. She's a *her*. Emily Ryker.'

'You know her?'

'I know her, yeah. I know her very well.'

Great. So she'll help us?'

'She might help you.'

'Why would she help me? She doesn't know me.'

'She doesn't *like* me.'

'You'll try though, right?'

'Yeah, of course. First thing in the morning.'

'The marker has her hours as eight 'til four. I think we need to speak to her straight away.'

'I'll call her earlier than that. We need to get to her before anyone else does.'

'Won't that piss her off even more? We need to be careful about it all, George. About what we say. How are you going to explain your interest?'

'We'll need Ryker on board, Shaun. She's the best intelligence officer this force has. The only way to get someone like that on board is to tell them something they don't already know. We need to tell her everything.'

'We can't do that! I've taken a punt telling *you*. The circle of knowledge needs to stay at just us two.'

'I trust her, Shaun. There are very few people I would say that about. We're up against it with just the two of us. The rest of Lennokshire Police are running investigations into the same people we are, but they don't know your family are still part of it. Ryker could be very useful in keeping us up to speed with what's going on.'

'I don't know . . . I just don't know what to do.'

'We'll meet her. You can judge her for yourself. I'll set something up for around 7 a.m. We'll meet at the nick first. I'll drive you out so no one follows. Keep your phone on for details.'

'And you think she'll just agree to a breakfast meeting with someone she don't even like? What happened for you to fall out?'

'It's a long story, Shaun, but it won't be an issue. She might not admit it, but she definitely still likes me. And I owe her a breakfast.'

* * *

Emily Ryker was already seated in the corner when they arrived. George made a 'drink?' signal with his hand as he stood at the counter. She shook her head and lifted a mug. George noticed her attention shift immediately to Shaun, who stood behind him at the till. Shaun was eyeing the occupants of the café nervously; he looked decidedly uncomfortable. George led Shaun over to Ryker's corner and put two teas down on the table.

'Thanks for coming out,' he said.

‘What can I say? I’ve never been a fan of the lie-in anyway, George.’

‘I’ll make it worth your while.’

‘Fucking right you will. I’ve had a look at the menu and they do some house challenge heap for, like, fifteen quid.’

‘I saw the poster. You’ll never eat all that.’

‘Not even close.’

‘But you’ll order it anyway.’

Ryker smiled. And those big brown eyes came alive as they always had when she smiled. She wore her short brown hair pushed over to one side and was dressed in dowdy jeans and a fleece top with a zip collar that was pulled right up so she could dig her chin into it. George always liked the way she was unquestionably attractive but did nothing to accentuate it.

‘You’re lucky,’ she said. ‘I can’t do food this early in the morning. Who’s your mate?’

Shaun fiddled with a sugar sachet. ‘Shaun Carter.’ He smiled weakly. ‘I’m a skipper from one of the town beat teams.’

‘Carter, yeah. I think you might have done some warrants on mutual targets over the last few months. You’re new in, right?’

‘To you guys, yeah. I’m a transferee. I was Sussex for nine years.’

A young girl appeared at the end of the table. She chewed gum, had a blue pinny and looked expectant.

‘I think we’re just doing drinks for now thanks, love.’ George said. The girl slunk away.

Ryker put down her tea mug. ‘What’s this all about then?’

George shared some eye contact with Shaun and then took the lead. He brought Ryker up to date with everything he knew. Shaun stayed quiet throughout, offering a few timely sighs and shakes of his head.

'Fuck, Shaun! You must be doing your nut!' George recognised this as Ryker's best attempt at support.

'I don't know what to do to be honest. Bobby Leonard did what he was told and he got his family back. I'm praying they have the same intention with mine. I don't know if it was right to involve anyone else, not George and not you. George said you could be trusted.'

'Jesus! Well, okay, that's quite a start. I mean I don't think I could just sit and wait either. I take it there's no one looking for your family officially? The cops rescued Bobby's family and they're thinking it's job done, right?'

'Yeah. It seems that was the plan all along and you have to say they did it well.'

'They run the risk of them being reported missing by someone else though. They'll be missed surely?'

'Carol works part-time. She's not due in until Tuesday. My boy starts half term. Carol speaks to her mum most days, but it will be a few days until she thinks there's something wrong.'

'And that's the strength of it,' George said. 'Anybody who gets concerned about either of them would get in contact with Shaun here. He can keep any concerns at bay for a day or two without any problems. That's obviously enough time for these people to achieve whatever it is they want to achieve.'

'Do we have timescales?' Ryker leant in.

'I'm expecting something today. No idea when.'

'Bobby told you that?'

'Yeah.'

'How will they communicate with you?'

Shaun took a second then shrugged, 'I don't know. They used Carol's phone to send me a message so they would be able to get my number easy.'

'And what do they still need from you?'

'I don't know. I could guess that it would be the same as before. Maybe they've got another couple of lorries coming through.'

'Fair guess. They obviously chose you for your link to the port. And your girlfriend, she doesn't know what's going on?'

'No one else does. I considered it, but she's a bit of a hothead. She wouldn't be able to sit on her hands. If I have to involve her again I might have to reassess.'

'How long have you been together?' Ryker asked.

'Nine months. It's nothing serious, you know. We're just messing about really. I was married a long time . . .' George remembered that Shaun had said he still had feelings for his wife but, even if he hadn't, it was plain to see.

'And this Polish man is the only link you might have to whoever has your family?'

George produced a crumpled piece of paper from his pocket. 'Aleksander Nowak. I had twenty minutes reading the log before I came out. He's at Langthorne House in a cell. They've nicked him for murder and the two main actions for the morning are to question him and to find the body. From the log, it looks like he made some initial significant comments about drug dealers killing his brother and demanding police protection, but he clammed up when he got arrested.'

'That might work in our favour,' Ryker observed.

'How so?' George said.

'If he doesn't talk to the detectives on record, he might talk to intel *off* record. I can really push that angle — use it as an excuse to get in the room with him.'

George felt encouraged. 'That's a very good point. DCI Whittaker's running the show as well. He's one of the few senior officers who isn't hell bent on keeping me at arms' length from police work. Major Crime are going to be stretched. They've got a bloke covered in a missing person's blood. It's their worst nightmare. I reckon they might jump at the chance of palming off the kidnap and suicide to other teams. Whittaker might have got a call and be in early this morning. I'll get onto him.'

‘Did this Polish lad say anything? About what happened to his brother?’

George’s enthusiasm drained away. He tried to avoid close eye contact with Shaun as he considered his reply.

‘He just made a few comments before he clammed up. The officers wrote on the log that he was in shock. He was complaining of pain in his shoulder and he had a slim cut to his neck. He was found with some pliers on his person and the running theory is that he cut something from around his neck and escaped.’

‘So his brother was hanged? That wouldn’t explain the blood.’

‘No, it wouldn’t. The log reads that he might have cut something from his neck before it took his head off. I don’t know—‘

‘I need some air.’ Shaun’s chair scraped and he left hurriedly, his hand covering his mouth.

‘Just come right out with it, George!’ Ryker said, once Shaun had gone.

‘We’re all coppers, Ryker. And if these people might have his family, it’s all the more reason to know what it is we’re up against.’

‘How’s he holding up in general?’

‘Who knows. He’s under a lot of pressure. He hasn’t really had the opportunity to do anything stupid yet. He’s difficult to read, actually. At least I know what he’s going through.’

Ryker swigged at her tea but her gaze remained on George the whole time.

‘What?’

‘You know what. We never talked after you were a dick the last time. Why didn’t you tell me what was going on? You let me go and I could have helped. Then you tried to get yourself killed and when that didn’t happen I heard you got offered retirement. Pension, payoff — the whole shebang. The last time we met, you couldn’t wait to get out of this. Why aren’t you retired?’

'Maybe I learnt my lesson, Ryker. You're the only person I'm telling this time. And it wasn't retiring that I wanted. It was my family.

'I thought that went hand in hand?'

'So did I. And then it didn't matter whether I was a copper or not, she still left.'

'But surely staying in this job gives you less of a chance of her changing her mind?'

'It gives me more of a chance of having something to give up for her. When she realises that, maybe everything can be all right, I'm going to need a life worth giving up. So she knows I'm serious.'

'That's some twisted logic there.'

'There's nothing logical left. I've tried logic.'

'Maybe it isn't meant to be with you two. Maybe she won't come back for you at all.' Ryker tilted her head as if in sympathy.

George felt a flash of anger. He took a moment before he replied. 'Maybe you're right. This job has made me do some pretty terrible things, Ryker, and for a long time I had a real battle with myself. I felt I had become this terrible person. But I've made peace with myself — as best I can, at least. I worked out the difference between good and bad, between the criminal and the hero. Do you know what it is?'

'I have a feeling you're about to fill me in.'

'Motivation. That's it. That's the only difference between us and them, good and bad. Shoot a man in the face for his wallet and you're a criminal, a bad man. Shoot a man in the face because you truly believe it is the only way to stop him doing the same thing to your family, or to the innocent — you're a hero. I've never done anything for personal gain. I'm not a greedy man, I don't want anything but a healthy, happy family life. I can't be a bad person. And another thing I worked out is that we need more coppers like that.'

'So you're a hero now?' The look on Ryker's face was playful.

'I've ordered a cape.'

Their chuckling had died down by the time Shaun made it back to the table. He held three new mugs. Some of the colour had returned to his face.

'Sorry about that,' he said. He sat down untidily. 'Listen, thanks for your help, both of you. What do you need me to do?'

'I ain't done nothing yet, Shaun.' Ryker's smile was warm. 'You need to stay available. Are you due to work today?'

'No. I'm on a rest day.'

'Then I suggest stay by your phone and try and do what you would normally do.'

'Okay.'

'Ryker, your name was all over the file when they ran this Polish guy through,' George said. 'Do you know anything about him that may help?'

'Not off the top of my head. I'm involved in intelligence gathering around the movement of class-A drugs. We're currently monitoring nineteen supply lines, most originate outside of the county. If someone is stopped anywhere in the county and gives cause for the officer to suspect them to be involved in the supply of drugs, their intel report is marked up for Op Vapour. If they get stopped again after that they will automatically have the marker on PNC to contact me in office hours. It's all part of the chief's vision around drugs now. He has this mantra . . . *make the most of every opportunity*. Unless someone is a main player, though, I won't know much about them. This bloke isn't a main player — certainly that's known. I need to get back into the intelligence database. I'll see what we know about him and in what context. There might be something for you to do from that, Shaun, I'll keep in touch.'

'Whatever you need from me, just let me know.'

'Let's see what we can get done before they call again.'

'Under the radar,' George said, draining the last of his tea.

'Well, if there's one thing you're good at . . .'

George returned Ryker's smile, but noticed how, as they left the café, Shaun was still stony faced.

Chapter 14

'Aleksander Nowak.' Emily Ryker strode into his cell two hours after her meeting with George and Shaun Carter in the café. Detective Sergeant Holly Saunders stepped in after her. Aleksander looked up at Emily. His eyes were glassy, the skin surrounding them red. He looked exhausted. 'Shit night?' Emily said.

'Very shit.' His accent was thick, but he understood her clearly enough.

'I'm sorry to hear about your brother. I can't imagine what it was like — to be there when it happened.' Aleksander's head dropped. A CSI officer in a white paper suit was scraping at the underside of his nails. His hand lay flat on what looked like a large white napkin, it was designed to ensure nothing that dropped off him was lost. Emily was aware that upstairs Nowak was being referred to as 'Scene One'; in reality, he was currently the only scene they had.

'I do not know anything for you.'

'Anything you know, Aleksander, is not for me. It's for you. You're in a lot of danger.'

'Not here. Here I am safe.'

'You can't stay here forever.'

'I did not kill my brother.'

'Then you definitely can't stay.'

DS Saunders stepped in. 'Aleksander, I'm going to interview you shortly about what happened, but it takes time. We need to get you processed here first, then we need to wait for your solicitor and your interpreter. You've said you need both right?'

'I said this. I do not know what I need. I have not been arrested for murder before in England.'

'No, I'm sure you haven't. I'll make sure we have these people here for you and then we'll make a start. But before that, is there anyone in danger? Anyone that might need our immediate help?'

'No. He's dead. My brother is dead.'

'I'm sorry Aleksander. I know you've told us that but can you be sure? Maybe if you tell us what you know now about where this happened we can send medical assist—'

'No! He is dead! Very dead.'

'We haven't found him, Aleksander. Can you help us with that?'

'Without my solicitor? Is this right?'

'This isn't an interview. I just thought you might want to help us. You say you didn't kill your brother. The sooner we find him, the sooner we find out who did.'

'Not without my solicitor.'

DS Saunders checked with the CSI officer, he needed twenty minutes more. She led Emily out of the cell. 'I'll make sure we are ready to go as soon as he's processed. I don't expect him to talk in interview but we will need to give him that opportunity before you speak to him.'

Emily nodded. 'Understood.' She pulled her phone from her pocket as she mounted the steps leading away from custody. George Elms sounded hassled.

'You okay, George?'

'Yeah, I'm okay. I spoke to Whittaker. Offered him assistance on the kidnap and suicide case. He turned me down flat.'

'Turned you down?'

'Yeah. Seems he's passed this over to the local CID. He said that he just needs it to be *ticking over* for now, until they get a handle on our Polish friend downstairs. Maybe I'm reading between the lines, but he certainly seemed less enthusiastic about working with me today. I'm guessing he dropped my name somewhere and he's been given a pill.'

'Okay. We can still keep up to speed on that investigation between us, I'm sure.'

'Yeah, it just means I don't quite get the access to Bobby's family I could have done with. I've got a feeling our blood-soaked man is our best bet anyway. How did you get on with him?'

'Well, he's not blood-soaked anymore. CSI are just about done with the washing, seizing his clothes and scraping. His interview's imminent, but no one's holding their breath that he's going to talk. Are you in the building?'

'Yeah. My office.'

'Sounds grand.'

It isn't. Third floor. I'll put the kettle on.'

* * *

George's office was small and the furnishings were a mishmash of whatever the property team could find. He'd stopped apologising about the broken chair on the visitor side almost immediately.

'So, what about the intel approach?' George asked. Do you think he'll talk to you?' He tipped milk into two cups from a flask. Emily perched gingerly on the chair opposite.

'I'm not convinced. I've had a look at him on our systems. He first came to our attention ten years ago. He's twenty-eight now and he's been arrested twelve times in those ten years. Eight of those arrests were in London. That means they will have intelligence on him too — I've already requested it. As long as they don't demand a guv'nor to sign off the request it won't be a problem.'

'Are you expecting that?'

'No. A month ago and it would have been a different story. Now I've been on Op Vapour a while, I've got a contact or two in the Met. They shouldn't even blink. I've also put in requests with the European Liaison Unit. You can bet he's got form in Poland too but that might be much slower in coming.'

'You mean you don't have an ELU contact? Is that a first, Ryker?'

'*Yet.* I bet they've heard of me though,' she joked. 'I would certainly bet they've heard of you!'

'Yeah, my name is the last one you should drop, though, Ryker. Seems everything I do is destined to be questioned forever.'

'Means you need me, George. So you have to be nice.' George felt her lingering gaze as he turned to finish the drinks.

'So what sort of thing is Nowak known for?'

Emily cleared her throat. 'Robbery and theft from person to start with. Drugs more recently — only ever possession. He's on the watch list for Vapour because he has links to the T Line, him and his brother.'

'What's the link?'

'A combination. First he was found at warrant on a house full of Eastern European workers employed by a salad factory. They were thought to be dealing Pico to other Polish and Slovakian workers from the premises. Nowak wasn't named personally, he was just noted as living there with his brother.'

'Did they find anything?'

'Some evidence of Pico preparation. But nothing that would stick — they didn't get lucky with the timing.'

'Pico? That's like crystal meth, right?'

'Yeah. Just a cruder version. Nasty. It's the same stuff they gave Nazi soldiers to keep them awake. It had a wonderful side effect too — it meant they could kill indiscriminately. It's still big in Eastern Europe. Since that raid there's been more specific intelligence around Nowak personally — he's supposed to be involved in the supply of crack cocaine. Source information names him and his brother as using a local supplier to be the go-between to the Eastern European community. His brother is believed to be the primary.'

'Was.'

'Well, yeah, assuming we believe him.'

'Do you?'

'Yeah, actually. The basic outline of events he has supplied are plausible, right?'

'They are. And you think that explains how he could have upset someone?'

'It could, yeah. Let's be honest, supplying to our European friends is a growing market. Maybe they betrayed that trust?'

'What do we know about this Tee Line?'

'Not so much. It's well established. Originates from London but first sprung up down here a few years back. Margate now seems to be where the line is run from. We're getting this more and more . . . drug lines initially look to branch out from London but they reach an untapped market and realise that there's more profit to be had from basing themselves there, rather than staying in the capital. Most of the drugs in the coastal towns are controlled this way now. The local supply was all a bit amateurish, I think the established lines couldn't believe their luck. Our methods were amateurish, too, George — these lines are well run and they have incredible business models. We're not even close to understanding them. The MET are better. We need what they know. The Tee Line have one consistency it seems . . . they like to use extreme violence.'

'Enforcement?'

'Debt enforcement, yeah. You wouldn't want to owe these people money. But claiming and defending territory as well. I'm sure these people wouldn't take too kindly to a dealer letting them down.'

'He's definitely not one of ours, Ryker? We're not running Nowak, are we?'

'I've checked as far as I can without upsetting anyone. I don't think he's the source for any of the information we have on the Tee Line. To be honest it isn't really good enough for me to think we've got anyone in among them.'

'That is a shame. It would all be rather convenient if he was already a source. We wouldn't even need to lean on him.'

'The problem we have now is that I don't think there's any desire to lean on him straight off. They're already talking about treating him as a witness. His story about his brother is plausible. He can't tell us where the site is but he's willing to show us. Major Crime are already planning a drive-out.'

'Makes sense.'

'Either way, George, I can't see us getting much from this today. He might show us the site, but he's made it clear that he won't talk about who was behind his brother's murder. Not until he knows he's safe. It'll take a couple of days to get him into the witness protection scheme. He might talk then, but I don't think we have a couple of days.'

'I agree. We're all out of lines of enquiry here. Help me out, Ryker. How do I get to speak to him?'

'I don't think you do. Unless you can convince Whittaker that you have some sort of special power that might make him talk, you've got no chance. And even if you did, you'd have a Major Crime chaperone.'

'And I certainly don't want one of them.'

'Are you in touch with Shaun?'

'I will be. I'll give him a call and we'll talk about where we are.'

'It might be that we have to wait. They're going to pop their heads up to speak to Shaun soon, right? That has to give us something. It might even give us the man's family back. Then we can all back away and let Shaun reveal all.'

George was unconvinced. 'It bothers me, Ryker, sitting on our hands and waiting for them to get in contact. You know me, I'm never comfortable to let the criminal have control of the timetable. You have to disrupt them, even if it just pisses them off or keeps them on their toes. You can't let them think they are getting it all their own way. Kidnap is all about absolute control.'

'I'm all ears if you can think of something.'

'I'll go back through the material we have. Will you get an update after the interview?'

'I will make sure of it.'

'You never know your luck. Something might come out of that.'

'Something might.'

'You don't sound convinced.'

'Nor did you.'

* * *

Shaun Carter looked a little brighter than he had at 6 a.m. Maybe it was because he was in the surroundings of his own flat, Ian Brown playing softly over a Bose speaker system. He had changed into shorts and flip-flops, a tight-fitting t-shirt with a zip-up top hanging open. His flat was impeccable: everything perfectly in place, the carpet swept in fan-shaped patterns.

'You didn't need to tidy up for me, Shaun!' George joked but he watched closely for reactions. Ever the suspicious detective, someone reacting to his ex-wife being kidnapped by cleaning his home was always something to be considered.

'I've been pretty restless. I couldn't sit down, so I hoovered.'

'You look a little better. Did you get some rest?' It was just before 11 a.m. He was pretty sure Shaun wouldn't have had time to sleep.

'No, it's a lot of coffee and a lot of nerves. Did you want a drink?'

'No thanks. But feel free if you're making yourself one.'

'What's the update then? Take a seat, George.'

Shaun led through to a large living room at the front of the flat. He had the middle floor of what would once have been a large manor house. It looked out over council maintained parkland. From the living room George could make out a kids' play area that was busy with excited movement and the River Stour beyond. The house was central in the city of Canterbury. George guessed that it would be an expensive place to live.

'We aren't much further, Shaun. I've given that update many times in my career, but it's hard to say today. I know how desperate you must be feeling about the whole thing but we still have options.'

Shaun had remained standing but now slumped into the chair opposite. 'I can't see any options, George. I can't see anything clearly right now.'

'Nowak is being interviewed as we speak, I would imagine — or very soon. They were fussing over an interpreter and it was holding things up. Ryker is poised to get the update from that the second it's available. He might tell us something in that we can use.'

'Is that likely?'

'They killed his brother. That's normally the sort of thing that could prompt a man to tell all that he knows. Ryker's pretty sure that he has no choice but to help us now. Not only for his brother's sake — he's in a lot of danger. If we were to release him he wouldn't last the day.

He'll know that. The problem is that he knows the system and he'll use it to his advantage.'

'He knows that we won't just kick him out to fend for himself all the while he says he is in trouble?'

'Exactly. And I don't see him talking to us until he knows he's safe. Or at least feels like he is.'

'Witness protection?'

'It'll have to be.'

'That'll take days.'

'It will. I've had some experience with them. They're a funny bunch. They do things a set way, but there's method to their madness. Nowak's safe in custody, so they'll be able to take a few days to get everything sorted out before he's released. They won't move him until that's all done.'

'And he won't talk until he's moved.'

George shrugged. 'We'll get an update from Ryker soon.'

'You said we had options. Is that it? Wait and see if the impossible happens?'

'No. The other option comes when they make contact with you. The longer they keep your wife and boy, the more the risk of someone else missing them. They won't want anyone looking for them. I think they'll be in touch soon.'

'But then we're at their mercy. It's all on their terms. You said right from the start that you wanted to avoid that.'

'I did. I do. It's not my first choice, but it'll give us an opportunity. It'll give us *something* at least.'

'They're not just going to give my family back, George, are they?'

'When they call, we'll see what they want.'

'I won't do anything to risk their lives.'

'This is why you were right not to involve the police as a whole. Nobody will do anything without you saying so. When it comes down to getting your family back, it will be you calling the shots. I'm not here to put them at risk.'

'Or to be at fault when it all goes wrong and they end up hurt. Or worse.'

George stood to leave. 'Stay positive, Shaun and stay available. And stay in touch.'

George was shown out without another word.

Chapter 15

'Jesus, Becks! What the fuck has he done to you now? We've got to do something about this!' Alice's pulse had quickened from the moment she had received the text from her sister. It had just said *I need to see you. I'm at the back of Subway.* Alice knew where she meant, the Subway restaurant just off the A256 between Sandwich and Thanet. It had been a regular meeting point for them previously. This was the first time Alice had seen her sister for almost two months.

'I'm taking you to the police!'

'No Alice.' Becky even sounded different where her face was so swollen. Her bottom lip was split, too, and she kept rubbing spittle away as if it was numb. Her nose was red, shadows had already started under each eye and she had dried blood above her top lip.

'I can't go to the police.'

'It was Jake, right? Jeez, Becks, what the fuck did he do this for?'

'He was different, Alice. He's not normally like this.'

'You expect me to believe that?' Alice scanned the interior of the Vauxhall Corsa. Becky had owned it for a couple of years and every time Alice had been in it, the little car had been a clutter of makeup items, wet-wipes, CD cases and food wrappers. Today it was spotless.

'Do you have anything I can clean you up with?'

Becks shook her head. 'No, I checked. I was going to go into the garage but I didn't want to get out of the car looking like this.'

'What about Subway's toilets?'

'It's shut.'

'Okay, hang on.' Alice pushed open the passenger door.

'Alice! Don't call the police! Where are you going?'

Alice leant back into the car. 'Calm down Becks, I'm just getting my bag.'

Alice walked just a few paces to where she had parked her Renault Clio and retrieved her bag. By the time she climbed back into the Vauxhall, her sister was crying. It was a silent cry and she was attempting to conceal it behind her hand. Alice grabbed her sister firmly in a hug. 'Christ, Becks! Look what he did to you! I've never seen you cry. We got to go to the police.'

'No, Alice. I said no. I can't do that.'

'You're not going back, though, right? You can't go back. Not now he's done this.' Alice had backed away, she gestured at Becks's bruising. Her sister grimaced a little as she turned to face forwards.

'Are you hurt anywhere else?'

'No.'

'Becks! Are you hurt anywhere else?'

'Jesus, Alice, I called you so I wouldn't get the third degree.'

Alice snatched at her t-shirt and jerked it up over her black bra. Becks was just as quick to pull it back down, but Alice had already seen a flash of angry red on her ribs. She gave Becks a look that said resisting was futile and she reached out, pulling the t-shirt up again, slower this time. Becks just cried in response.

Alice resisted the urge to shout, fought back her emotions. She waited for her sister to start talking.

'He was so angry. I promise I have never seen him like that before. He's aggressive, but it's always just intimidating. He doesn't threaten me straight out, he just says things in a way so I know I have to do what he says.'

'What was he angry about?'

'I don't know. He got in late. The second I saw him I could tell he was stressed out. He was pale and sweaty, he looked like he'd seen a ghost! He woke me up coming in and I lay awake for ages. He didn't come up, so I started to get curious — then worried. He didn't turn on the telly, didn't make a drink and he didn't even turn a light on. So I went downstairs after a while. I turned on the light and straight away I could see he was in a state. I was worried about him, Alice. I asked him if he was all right and he just dismissed me. He said he needed to wash his clothes — he felt dirty. He told me to go away.'

'Was he drunk?'

'No, he doesn't even drink. I think he uses sometimes. A white powder. He says it's called spice and that it's legal, but it makes him *different*. Angrier. He was terrified of something, though, Alice. I've never seen him so scared. You know Jake . . . he's always full of himself. But all that was missing.'

'Spice? That ain't legal, Becks. Just Google it for a second. When did you become so naïve?' Alice was furious, but she took a moment to collect herself. 'Sorry, Becks, this isn't your fault. I'm just angry you got hurt.'

'It's okay. I have been naïve, Alice. Fucking stupid more like.'

'Stop it, Becks. So he was dirty then? What had he been doing?'

'I don't ever ask — I know it makes him angry. But I had to ask last night and that's what made him flip out. I think he thought I'd left the room. He took his jacket off and his t-shirt underneath had blood on it — loads of it. I thought it was his, Alice!'

'It wasn't his?'

'No. I asked him if he was all right and he said that one of his mates got into a fight and he helped clean him up. There was a lot of blood. I asked what he had been doing and how his mate got so badly hurt. He just hit me. I didn't see it coming, I didn't even know what hit me. I took one to my face and the next thing I knew I was on my back looking up. Jake stood over me and he hit me a few times again. Then he kicked me — that's when my ribs got hurt, I think.'

'Fuck, Becks! He can't get away with this, babe! You're the one with all the brains — he can't get away with this, can he?'

'No, you're right. He can't. This is it for us — I'm not going back.'

'And you need to call the police. You need to report it.'

'No, Alice. Please stop saying that. I told you I don't want to. I just want all this over. I'm not going back. I called you because I need somewhere to stay. I can't go to mum and dad's while I look like this. I'll just stay with you until it's all gone down. Is that okay? I promise I won't be a bother, I'll stay out of—'

Alice cut her sister off with a fierce hug. 'Of course, Becks, you don't even need to ask.' She pulled back to assess her sister's face again. She couldn't stop looking at the angry bruising, the swelling and the streams on her face where tears had fallen. Becks was her older sister. It was Becks who had always looked out for her. She'd never needed her help for anything before.

'Thanks. I won't be a pain, I promise. If you need to go to work or whatever, just do what you need to do.'

'I'm due on a late shift this afternoon, Becks. I'll call in sick.'

'You don't need to do that.'

'I want to look after you. I don't think you should be on your own at the moment. Just in case he comes looking.'

'He's not going to come looking for me. And if he did it would only be if he's realised what he's done and he'll be all dopey. He always gets angry then gets really dopey and sorry straight after. He'll be really suffering right now. It was my fault, really. I know what pisses him off and I still asked those questions.'

'Don't even start, Becks! Don't you dare make excuses for that animal.' Alice twisted the rear-view mirror so her sister could see her own reflection. 'Look what he did to you! Don't *ever* forget what he did to you. No one deserves that. And what did you do? Ask him if he was alright because he had blood on him! You're too good for him, Becks. You were too good right from the start.'

'I did try telling him that.' Becks started to smile. She flinched and her hand rose to her swollen cheek.

Alice's anger flared suddenly again. 'Listen, my mate at work, she's dating this copper. He sounds alright, you know. We could speak to him off the record, like. Just see what—'

'NO! Please, Alice. Please don't do anything. We'll think this out.'

'Fine. Let's get you home. Take what you need and get in my car. You can leave this one here.'

* * *

George Elms lifted the phone hastily to his ear. 'Ryker? Give me just a sec!' He dropped the phone back to his waist then spoke to the youth stood at the till in front of him.

'I'll just take that one. With the receipt, he can bring it back right?'

'Yeah, I guess so.'

'You guess so? What do I need to do to get a definite answer? Speak to someone who works here?' Despite his frustration at the service it was George who felt out of place. He was in a videogame store, surrounded by a generation that might as well be another species. The boy shrugged his shoulders. It wasn't confusion, it wasn't that he didn't get the sarcasm and it certainly wasn't anger. Apathy, George guessed — the one word that summed up the youth of today. George slapped a twenty-pound note on the desk and scooped up the bag. He lifted the phone and scurried towards daylight.

'Sorry, Ryker. I was just trying to communicate with someone below the age of twenty-five.'

'I can see why you might find that a challenge.'

'What, because I'm so intelligent and on a higher academic plane?'

'No. There isn't anyone under the age of twenty-five left with less qualifications than the likes of us now, George. I just meant that you're so out of touch.'

'Suits me, Ryker. What the fuck do you want anyway? I assume there's an update from the interview?'

'He didn't say much more. Nothing more that's useable for us. He confirmed that he and his brother were brought over on the ferry, in a lorry carrying tomatoes, by a gang involved in dealing drugs. He confirmed that he had dealt drugs in the past and he owed these people a debt. He didn't say how much.'

'Must be a hell of a debt for them to go to all that trouble.'

'I agree. Then he said that he and his brother were driven to a location and his brother was killed. Decapitated. He wouldn't say exactly how, just that they tried to do the same to him and he was able to escape. He showed off a red mark round his neck.'

'So I was right! How on earth do you escape a decapitation with a red mark round your neck? It's either off or it isn't, right?'

'He did mention a car on a road. We've had gang members killed in cars before, where they had something tied around their neck and then tied off round something fixed. The car then accelerated until the rope tightens. It's pretty effective.'

'Fuck yeah! I think I heard of it once a long time ago. That was a suicide though?'

'That's the point, force them to drive and it looks like suicide. We talked about this before, remember? The best way to get away with murder?'

'Make it look like a suicide,' George said.

'Exactly. Or at least make sure the death is never investigated as a murder. These gang members had suicide notes for their family — the whole hog. They may have been genuine of course.'

'Wouldn't work so well with two in the car though. That's always going to be investigated as a suspicious death.'

'True. I'm not saying that they've tried to make *this* look like a suicide, there's no body for a start.'

'No. I guess there might have been. They may well have had to change their plans when our Polish friend managed to wriggle out of it.'

'Pliers, I think. He found a pair of pliers in the boot of the car. Reading between the lines I think they got him to set it all up himself. It's like digging your own grave. That's pretty evil.' Emily sort of chuckled.

'And sensible. That way the only prints and DNA belong to the victims. The poor bastard would have tied his own noose.'

'And his brother's. He must have cut the wire round his neck when the car started.'

'Yeah. Can you imagine the panic, he can't have been the driver. He didn't manage to cut it completely, just weakened it enough that it snapped.' George exhaled loudly. 'Think of that, Ryker!'

'He wasn't quick enough to save his brother.'

'Horrible bastards.'

'Exactly, so he's suitably terrified of these people and he's doing exactly as expected, promising to talk to us when he knows he's safe. There's a lot of work going on in the background to get him moved over to Witness Protection in the next twenty-four hours. The one thing they were able to convince him to do was a drive-out.'

'To ID the scene?'

'Exactly. The DS is going to take him back to where he was picked up and then around the area to see if he remembers anything. Without that scene there's nowhere to start. The DS has asked me to ride out with them.'

'She asked you?'

'Yeah, she thinks I might be of use from an intelligence point of view. She seems to think I have a photographic knowledge of all criminals and their vehicles under Op Vapour and I'd be able to effectively spot a tail.'

'No pressure, then!'

'None at all. I think they're arranging a marked car to chaperone — just to put off any efforts by the gangs to continue their conversation with Mr Nowak. But I don't expect that's high on their list. They'd be far better slipping quietly into the background for now.'

'I agree. That's if they somehow expected us to do it. Let me know how you get on.'

'Will do. What are you up to? I guess we're running out of lines of enquiry until they make contact with Shaun. We're not going to have a Plan B after all.'

'You're right. There is something I wanted to revisit. I think it's a case of wait and see for now.'

'That won't go down well with Shaun.'

'No, I saw him earlier and wait and see is obviously the last thing he wants to do. I totally understand it, you just want to be out standing on the throat of whoever it is that's got your kid.'

'We are getting closer, George.'

'We are. It's not a giant leap for a gang forcing men to take their own heads off in a speeding car to convincing other men to jump from a viaduct. We're very close. But close means nothing right now.'

'I'll be in touch when our tour of the county is over.'

'Speak soon.'

George had made it back to his car by the time the call had ended. He had crossed the pedestrianised area of Langthorne's town centre and walked through the main bus station. His car was in a one-hour bay, pointing away from the town centre. He pulled back out into the flow of traffic. Radio 2 came on with the ignition: The Beatles — *Here Comes the Sun.*

* * *

The door was opened with some trepidation. The sort of open where it was clear it was ready to be slammed closed at any point. Through the slim crack George could just make out the gaunt face of Sharon Leonard peering through her own door. She fidgeted and looked down like someone was tugging at her leggings. George smiled and tried to look reassuring. The sun had indeed come out, it was high enough in the sky to arrow through the slit in the door over his shoulder. Sharon was squinting.

'You can tell me to go away, Sharon, I don't need to talk to you. I just came to see how you were getting on. And to drop this off.' George pulled a slim object from a carrier bag and pushed it into the gap. Sharon's eyes moved to it, she stepped back and it was pulled through. The door pushed shut and George waited. A few seconds passed, some muffled words and then the door opened wider.

'What's that for?' George could see all of Sharon now, but she still stood blocking his entrance.

'I honestly have no idea. I think it's a computer game, Sharon, but my goodness have they changed since I last played them. You ever play Pac Man? I was good at that.'

Sharon's expression warmed a little. 'I did actually. They had one in the Working Men's Club down the road.

My dad would be drunk in there — too drunk to take care of me. I used to steal change off him when he fell asleep. Nothing else to do.'

'Dammit. There was me thinking I had picked something I was best at. You could probably give me a run for my money.'

'What do you want?'

'Someone bought me a voucher I won't ever use. I figured Connor might appreciate a new game. Unless you like first person shoot-ups? I don't even know what that is, but it sounds horrific.'

'Well, thanks.'

'Yeah *thanks*!' Connor's excited chatter came from behind his nan. 'It's the new one, nan!' Sharon smiled again as he disappeared.

'I just wanted to see you were okay is all. I didn't come to ask any questions.'

'Makes a change from you lot. They do keep coming, you're persistent if nothing else.'

'We get called a lot worse.'

'You want a cup of tea? I was making one.'

'That would be lovely. As long as you don't have Pac Man. Now I think I might get shown up.' George walked into the living room behind Sharon. It was not a home that looked better in the daylight. It was still cluttered and untidy and George could now make out a thin layer of dust wherever there was a surface. The curtains were still roughly drawn so the natural light was limited, the light from bare bulbs added to the bleakness.

'Sorry I ain't done nothing with me face, or tidied up or nothing. I'm normally good with the housework. Just not been in the mood you know.'

'I can imagine. Housework might just be the last thing you want to do.' George's mind flashed back to his conversation with Shaun an hour or so earlier where he had taken out his nervous tension on his vacuum cleaner.

'I didn't sleep much.'

'It'll take you a long time to get over these last couple of days, Sharon. I know that better than anyone. Don't think you need to be making excuses either. Everyone will understand that you've been through a hell of a time.'

'You've had it then? Days like I had?'

'I've had my fair share of trauma, Sharon. Sign of getting older, isn't it?'

'Who knows. I see some of my friends, they ain't never known nothing like it. Charmed lives they've got. Me and Bobby always used to say the same. These people don't know they're born.'

'I know what you mean. It never seems to be spread out evenly does it.'

'No. I musta got all of theirs. You people any closer to finding them what did this?'

'No. We don't have much to go on, Sharon. Whoever these people are, they seem to have a real influence over their victims. No one's telling us much. It's what these sorts of people do. They're bullies, and any bully knows that the seat of their power is fear.'

'Too right it is. I ain't no coward, but I got my boy to think about. And it's just me now, Bobby may not have looked much but he was handy, you know. He could look after himself and he would certainly look after me if he needed to.'

'I bet he could.'

Sharon led through to the kitchen. George stopped short of going in, leaning on the surround while Sharon made the tea. A round dining table was tucked against the wall, it was busy with paperwork. He peered back into the kitchen. A calendar hung from a kitchen unit — March was a perfectly manicured cat with long white hair and a red bow — and George noted that today's date was filled out with the words *Anniversary! Don't get that long for murder!* George allowed a smile. The jokes were the same, no matter the couple. He turned back towards the table. On top of the paperwork was a manila envelope. It had been ripped open and a white card embossed with raised lettering was visible — a gift card. George checked Sharon was still busy making his tea, he reached over and tugged out the card. He spun it round. *Happy Anniversary to a wonderful wife.* He flipped it open. The whole card was handwritten text, a long love letter signed *Bobby xxx.* George scanned it as quick as he could. Sharon finished the tea and he was out of time.

'Have many people been round? I assume you have friends and family in the area?'

'Pfft! Nosey fuckers, more like it. They all just want to know what's going on. They see the cops coming round. They see Facebook about someone jumping and it gets out it's my Bobby. They come round saying how sorry they are, they should just come right out with it and say how nosey they are.'

'I didn't realise the timing.' George took a mug from Sharon. He gestured with his eyes towards the calendar as he took a sip.

Sharon sighed long and hard. 'thirty-two years today. Every one of them a slog. But I would give you anything and everything right now for that man to walk back in through that door.'

'I understand. Marriage isn't easy, but it's an awful lot harder to live without.'

'Are you married, Sergeant?'

'For now.'

Sharon afforded a smile. 'Planning an upgrade?'

'Goodness no! I'm already batting well above my average. I'm just trying to cling on, we've had a difficult couple of years ourselves.'

'You cling on all you can then, George. A good one is worth fighting for.'

'He knew he was going, yesterday, didn't he?' George watched closely for a reaction.

'What do you mean?'

'He didn't make the decision yesterday. He must have had contact with these people before they took you off the street. Did you know about it?'

'I don't know what you mean? I thought you weren't here to ask me no questions.'

'I'm not. Nothing that you have to answer. The card he sent you, did it arrive today?'

'The card?' Sharon bustled past and snatched it up. She walked it back into the kitchen and scowled. You been going through my stuff? That ain't even legal! I let you in here because you've been nice. Because I thought you was here to be nice.'

'Sharon, I only came round to see you, to see the boy. But this card, the note inside . . .' George reached for the card but Sharon snatched it closer to her chest. 'It reads like there was money in there. A fair bit. If he had contact with these people, if money changed hands, there might be a trail. I want to find the bastards that did this to you, Sharon, that did this to your family.'

'The card arrived today. He sent it me, he wouldn't be the first bloke to plan his own death. He's been threatening to do it for months.'

'He just needed that final push didn't he Sharon. No pun intended. Maybe Bobby would still be here if these people hadn't got in touch.'

'And maybe he wouldn't.'

'Maybe this worked out better for you? How much did you earn out of this?'

'Get OUT!' Sharon lunged towards George. She raised both her hands and punched George in the chest. George got hold of her flailing hands, wrapped them up and got hold of her by her elbows. She was sobbing hard, she couldn't talk and she stepped into George.

'Sharon, it's okay. I know you didn't want this. Just tell me what happened.'

Sharon fought to get herself back under control. She pushed George away and turned back into the kitchen.

George noticed movement at the foot of the stairs. Sharon must have seen it too. 'Go back to your bedroom, Connor!' she snapped. Connor was gone.

George stayed still. Sharon busied herself on the kitchen surface. A hot drink was no longer on the agenda, she reached up to a cupboard and pulled out a white bottle of liquor. She turned a tumbler up the right way from beside the sink and poured a good measure. She had thrown the card onto the side and it had spilled open, Bobby's handwritten words right in front of her eyes. She took a swig of the liquid, her lips curled back over her teeth as she took it neat. Her eyes seemed to scan the words.

'I didn't want no cash. And nor did Bobby. I just wanted Bobby to get better — or to at least *try*.' She scooped the glass for a second tilt and the liquid was all gone. 'Bobby got approached a few days after he first tried it. He took a load of pills sat here with a load of drink. In this fucking house!' She forced a laugh through her tears. 'It was never going to be enough. I thought it was a cry for help and we could get through it, you know. He'd only just had the news and he hadn't taken it well. The street got to know about it. I told you what it's like around here.'

'All streets are the same.'

Sharon shook her head and she lifted watery eyes fleetingly towards George. 'Nah. It's worse round here. No one works see, no one's got much going on so the only thing to hold their interest is what everyone else is doing. Someone gets so desperate they try and take their own life, that's big news round here. Keep them all chewing the fat for a good few days.' Sharon sighed, she poured another good measure. 'I suppose I was the same once. Did you want a proper drink, George?'

'Definitely not one of those.'

Sharon smiled. It was weak, but it cut through the gloom a little. She clicked the kettle back on and prepped a mug with a teabag. 'Very sensible.'

'So what changed?'

'Changed?'

'Neither of you wanted any cash. You wanted Bobby to get better. And here we are, you got a payment and Bobby's gone.'

'Twelve grand.' Another weak smile. 'Thirty-two years married, they offered us twelve grand to bring it all to an end.'

'And you took it?'

'No! I know what it looks like to you. You have to understand that Bobby was suddenly in a different place. I ain't never seen him like that. He was a strong man. He lived through some terrible things and he took it all in his stride. Lizzy's murder hit him hard, knocked him for six for a good few days but just like that he was back on it. He focused on Connor. He wanted some sort of normality for that boy and he just switched back on. He missed Lizzy every day of his life, but he never let it beat him down. But this diagnosis, it got to him. You can see from the moment the doc told him, you could see that he knew it was going to get him and he knew how. He had an uncle that went the same way, you know. Bobby watched it happen, I think. He saw what it does to you. He never fought it, not for one day.'

'He didn't think he could beat it?'

'He *knew* he couldn't. And he didn't want to fail in front of Connor. He loved that boy more than I've ever known him to love anyone. And he has this vision of himself — he's the strong, masculine fighter. This disease would have taken that away from him. He wanted to die, George, but on his terms.'

'What terms were they?'

'We got a knock on the door. Some lad we've known for a long time, I looked after him when he was a baby, changed the fucker's dirty nappy. He'll be well known to you people, he's been in and out of trouble. Done some time behind the door recently.'

'A name?'

Sharon bit her lip. She fidgeted again — this time in a drawer, from where she produced a cigarette. She pushed the window open over the sink. 'You don't mind, do you?'

'Your house.'

'I gave up. I was off 'em for six months up until a few days ago.'

'You can quit again.'

Sharon chuckled. 'Yeah. Until the next disaster. I don't know about names, George, I ain't talking to you on record. None of this.'

'It's best you do talk to me, though, Sharon. Here with a fag on the go. Better that than down the nick with you under arrest for conspiracy to murder.'

Sharon's face hardened, 'What are you talking about? I didn't murder no one!'

'Perverting the course of justice at best, Sharon. If you knew Bobby was planning on killing himself, if you knew he was being manipulated to do it and there was a cash payment involved to you, there's questions to be answered. I should have nicked you already. I don't want to. I'd rather you talked to me now. Tell me what happened and who was involved. I don't think for one moment that this is the outcome you wanted, but imagine the gossip around here when you get taken out in handcuffs the day after Bobby dies. Connor in emergency care.'

'You wouldn't.'

'I would. I don't want to, Sharon, but I would. I'd much rather have a cup of tea with you here and we can talk about how we find the people that did this. Even if you don't want to, there's a bigger picture, other families are being affected by these people and I don't have much time.'

'Other families? What are you talking about?'

'You first.'

'Christ, George!' Sharon finished the tea, she slopped it down on the side close to George. 'This lad knocked and spoke to Bobby. He wouldn't speak in front of me but I managed to get a gist of it from being stood in here. He wanted Bobby to meet with someone, he said it was mutually beneficial. He said that a lot. I know it wasn't him saying those words — this kid don't know words like *mutually beneficial*. Someone sent him here with his head full of something.'

'And Bobby did meet?'

'Yeah. He went down the pub and some fella bought him a beer. I know what you're going to ask me, I don't know okay, I don't know who this fella was. I just know that he's not someone Bobby knew, which means he ain't from Langthorne. And he was all dressed up like — a suit and shit.'

'What was his business?'

'Drugs. They're all about drugs ain't they? You see kids out there, ten, eleven years old on their push bikes with drugs in their backpacks. I only got to walk to the shops and I see them all out and about. Sickens me.'

'You're not wrong.'

'Bobby wouldn't tell me what it was all about, but he suddenly seemed brighter, you know? Like this meeting had given him something to be cheery about. I couldn't put my finger on it. Bobby ain't ever been one to sell drugs. He was always dead against it, even when he was younger. When Lizzy got stuck into them he turned even more against them. He got into a few fist fights with local dealers after she died. He'd see a deal go down in a beer garden or a car park and he'd just flip out. I had to drag him away.'

'So it's strange that he'd meet with someone involved in drugs.'

'He got his head turned. I couldn't get no truth out of him — nothing about what had happened. Then we had a few beers. Connor was round his mate's house and he was staying out. He's mates with a good family on the other side of the tracks. Nice people, decent people — I could tell they was decent 'cause they wouldn't let their boy come round here.' Sharon allowed another smile. She poured another measure, a little smaller this time. 'We had a few of these and I got him talking — I've always known how to get him talking. They offered him a deal. Enough cash to set his family up and all he had to do was get some information from the police. The police got called when he took the pills so he was on record for having mental health issues for trying to do himself in. Seems they needed someone like that.'

'What information?'

'He had to go stand on a cliff. I remember it was a Sunday a few weeks back. It was a specific time and he had to pretend like he was going to jump. They send out negotiators, your lot — you know that already though, right?'

'I know how it works, Sharon, sure. But you tell me what you know.'

'He was up there for ages. He had something in his ear, someone was talking to him the whole time, telling him what to say, what to ask. Then, after a while, he got talked down and the cops walked him down to where I was stood with the ambulance. They took him to A&E, he got some pills and we was home by midnight.' Sharon stubbed out the cigarette forcefully.

George swigged his tea. 'So they must have approached him again then?'

'They must have. Bobby told me that he had to do it again — the same deal — and then he would get a little bit of money. He told me he didn't know what the information was for, and I believed him. You live with someone for forty odd years, you know when they are lying to you.'

'I guess you do. Did you know the timing of the next one?'

'No. Bobby said he didn't either, but now I know he did. He was upset last week — more and more upset the closer it got to the weekend. Then on Sunday, he said he wanted to go out and watch the game down the pub. Millwall were on at two in the afternoon and then there was some other game straight after. He was going to be out all afternoon, so he gave me a couple of hundred quid and said I should take Connor into Canterbury for some shopping. I can't remember the last time I went out shopping with money on the hip, George. I jumped at it.'

'You didn't think it was odd?'

'Only that he had the money. Since Connor came to stay, he always felt guilty if he went out. It wasn't out of character, but he was odd. He told me he loved me Saturday and he hugged Connor so long on Sunday morning that we all felt uncomfortable. I thought he'd started on the beer early.'

'You think he knew you were going to get kidnapped?'

'No! Definitely not. He would never have put Connor through that. I think those bastards upped the stakes at the last minute. I don't think he was ever supposed to jump, George. I think they took us and they told him what he had to do for us to be safe. And he did it.' Sharon broke down again and wiped away thick tears with hands that shook. She steadied them enough to light another cigarette.

'And you don't know who these people are?'

'No.'

'Who's this lad that made first contact, Sharon?'

'I can't, George. You don't talk about people round here to the cops.'

'I need to know, Sharon.'

'Bobby's gone, George. Ain't nothing bringing him back. We got played and we lost. I'm talking to the council about getting a move. I want out of here, out of this area and maybe we can have a life.'

'There's more to it. Bobby was part of a much bigger picture, Sharon. You need to understand that this isn't just about you and him. When they snatched you from the street they did it as loud as possible so the police would throw every resource they could at it and they wouldn't see that you weren't the only people snatched from that town.'

'What do you mean?'

'Another family was taken. Plucked from the streets. We don't know how or when, Sharon, but you and Connor were a diversion. And we fell for it.'

'They got someone else? Why?'

'I don't know yet. But they weren't released like you, Sharon. And I don't know how this ends unless you can help me find them. I need the name of your mate, the lad that came knocking on your door and started all this off. Do that, and I promise I won't come after you for your part.'

'I told you, I didn't play no part!'

'Knowing is playing, Sharon. And you aren't the only person that stands to lose. Help me with the name.'

'I've spent all the money. You can't have that back.'

'I don't want your money. I just want a name.'

'Damon — Jesus, Damon.'

'Damon? Damon who?'

'You know him. You all know him round here.'

'Damon who Sharon? They might already be dead. Help me. Give them a chance.'

'Alcott. Fucking hell, Damon Alcott.'

George showed himself out.

Chapter 16

Emily Ryker was designated driver. Aleksander Nowak was led to the rear passenger seat by two uniformed officers. He had to stoop his wiry frame to fit in to the family hatchback. Detective Constable Nicola Anstis filled the front passenger seat with her day book ready and open; she had been briefed to act as scribe. Detective Sergeant Holly Saunders was already in the seat behind Anstis. Emily watched in her mirror as she smiled reassuringly at Aleksander. One of the officers passed her his seatbelt and she clipped it in.

'Really? With these?' Nowak held up his hands. They were still handcuffed in a 'front stack', one hand lying flat over the other with rigid metal keeping them apart.

'Sorry, Aleksander, you're still under arrest.' The DS still held her reassuring smile. Emily didn't know Saunders very well, but she had a reputation for being very thorough. A good investigator by all accounts, but who was only recently promoted to sergeant. 'I can't even imagine the paperwork if we managed to lose you.'

'I do not want to be lost.' Aleksander peered out of the window.

'They're not too bad, just try not to move too much in them.'

The two uniformed officers moved to their marked vehicle. They rolled up to the speed gates to exit the station and Emily pulled the unmarked Vauxhall Astra up behind them.

'We'll wait for you just up the road.' The transmission from the car in front came over the radio far too loud and Emily hurried to turn it down. They were working on their own talk-through channel so they could speak to each other easily.

Emily pushed a dash-mounted button to reply. 'Understood.' She pulled through the gates and then came to a stop, watching the gate slide shut in her rear-view mirror. It was a new directive: in the modern world of terrorists targeting police officers, you had to watch the gates shut. It took just a few seconds and they were on their way.

From Langthorne, the convoy of two headed for the A20, coast bound, where they would pass the port and come out the other side of the town of Dover. From there they took the A256 towards Thanet and the area where Nowak had been found walking down the hard shoulder, covered in his brother's blood. No one knew quite what to say and conversation was stilted to the point where Emily turned the radio on to cut the atmosphere. The A256 got a lot slower as they passed a building site that was soon to be thousands of new-build houses. The road works were severe: a new roundabout was being installed to link directly to the new estate. They got clear of the road works, still in convoy. They'd had a brief conversation before leaving the station and one of the uniformed lads had suggested he might know the road Nowak had described. Emily followed the marked car as it took the slip road off where Richborough Power Station had once dominated the skyline. Now it was two piles of rubble and a husk of a building. The roads became more rural, with fields either side and woodland straight ahead. The marked car slowed for a road flagged by a dead-end sign. It curved gently into the woodland and Nowak suddenly became agitated. Even from her position watching him in the rear-view mirror, Emily knew they were at the right place.

'We'll drive it through first — make sure it's clear of vehicles.' The marked car ahead rolled into the road and was quickly out of sight. Their update came in less than a minute.

'All clear.' The marked car reappeared, facing them this time. Emily pulled past it into the road.

'We'll hold here and make sure nothing comes down.'

Emily drove slowly. After just twenty metres, the marked car behind was hidden by the bend in the road.

* * *

In the marked police car, PC Dave Laughton laid back a little.

'By the time the suits have done their dicking around down there and we hold their hands all the way back to the nick, it'll be time to go off duty.' He rested his knee against the centre console. 'Yup. Another day closer to retirement.'

PC Debbie Nicol grinned across from the driver's seat. Dave noticed her narrowed eyes.

'What?' he said.

'I reckon you'll be disappointed to get this one done.'

'Why on earth would I be disappointed?'

'Well, without at least getting to know that doe-eyed intel officer a little more. What's her name? Emma?'

'Emily.' Dave sat back up straight. He felt his cheeks warm a little.

'Ah, Emily is it? Why don't you ask her out? I don't think she's got anyone on the go at the moment.'

'I'm not sure it's the right time — you know, over the radio and her with a car full and all that.'

'I don't mean right now, you dick!'

Dave saw a flash of movement first — behind Debbie — then he felt the impact behind him, enough to shove him hard in the back, his head forced so far forward it bounced off the handbrake. Dave managed to look up, his neck shot with pain, the whole side window was instantly filled with blue. Despite the pain, he was groggy, his vision hazy. Debbie's scream cut through the haze. Dave was aware that his car was still shaking, the roof of the car banged. He turned to look through the windscreen just as it shattered inwards and something heavy bounced off the dash and crushed his hand. He yelped in pain. Boots appeared on the bonnet. A figure dropped to a kneel.

'Alright, pigs!' a man's voice muffled by the black material pulled tight over his face. Debbie screamed again.

'The FUCK?' It was all Dave could manage.

'You see that?' The figure on the bonnet leant in and pointed to Debbie's window. Dave followed the gesture. A large digital clock with an old-style font was counting down from fifteen minutes. It looked like it was suckered to the glass. 'Move out of this vehicle before that gets to zero and you're fucked. You understand? It's rigged to something highly sensitive. You don't want to be moving now, you hear me?'

The man made exaggerated tip-toe movements down the bonnet of the marked car. He jumped backwards off the end like a showman enjoying his own performance. He raised his finger to his covered face like he was *shooshing* them. And then he was gone.

* * *

'Is there anything you recognise?' DS Saunders asked Nowak. DC Anstis scribbled in her day book.

'This is for sure where they brought us. It was darker, but the street light I saw at the start . . . this is for sure the right road.'

'Okay. Do you remember how far in you were?'

'The bend finishes and you can see far. We were a little way along.'

Emily slowed further as the bend did indeed straighten out. In the distance she could now see a hedgerow that marked the end of the road, beyond that the tall street lights and gantries of a main 'A' road were visible.

Nowak was animated suddenly. 'Can we stop?'

Emily let the car roll to a stop with the engine ticking over.

'We hit hard. There will be a tree with marks at least. This side.' Nowak pointed to the woodland on the near side. Ryker rolled forward a little until they came to an area around two thirds along the straight where the bank was a little churned up. The ground looked disturbed — not as much to suggest that a car had left the road and ploughed into the woodland, but the foliage just looked out of place. A mature tree stood a few metres from the road, its lower trunk shrouded by a dense bush. Emily stepped out and walked over to the tree. As she got closer, she could see that it didn't look right, the bush had been cut; this wasn't the spot where it had spent its life. Somebody had cut it and moved it here. She pulled away to reveal a fresh, ugly scar gouged deep into the tree.

She stepped back to the car where the DS looked questioningly out through the rear window. She wouldn't be able to open the door from the inside — standard on police cars. Emily pulled it open.

'This is it. Someone's made a token effort to hide it, but—'

'Stay where you are! Don't you fucking move!' Emily turned to the sound of the gruff voice and was immediately struck hard in the face. The force pushed her back against the car and she lost her footing. In her confusion she was aware of the rear door being slammed back shut and movement from the other side of the vehicle. Someone stood over her.

'Don't you fucking move, bitch!' Her vision cleared enough to see the outline of a man dressed all in black, his face covered.

'Stay here for fifteen minutes. If you are seen to move in the next fifteen minutes we will be back and we'll make sure you don't move again. You understand?'

Emily jerked a nod.

'Fifteen minutes! And count yourself fucking lucky.'

The man was gone. Emily managed to push herself to a sitting position, her back against the front passenger door. She could feel the car rock as someone inside moved, a door creaked from the other side of the car. She struggled to her knees, looked down the road towards the dead end where what looked like two males dressed in black walked either side of Nowak. A few more seconds and all three plunged left into the woodland. And they were gone.

'The radio! The fucking radio's not working!' DC Anstis threw her handheld radio back onto the driver's seat and pulled out her phone. 'Nothing's working!'

Emily managed to stand. She tried her own phone — *no service.*

'What do we do?' DC Anstis looked from Emily to her sergeant, her eyes wide and her breathing shallow. Emily looked at her watch. It was ten past two in the afternoon. She felt a calmness that belied their situation.

'Wait fourteen minutes. Then walk to find help.'

* * *

It was ten minutes later that help came to them. Emily saw the officer who had introduced himself as Dave limp into sight. DS Saunders jogged to meet him.

'You okay?' He looked directly at Emily who was holding a piece of gauze against her eyebrow. It had been bleeding intermittently. She took the pressure away and checked. It came away clean.

'Yeah, we're okay. We lost Nowak.'

'Jesus. We never stood a chance up there. Two 4x4s just rammed us, blocked us in both sides. They put some countdown timer up. None of our radios are working.

'Countdown timer?'

'Yeah, they said it was rigged. It isn't. They just wanted to slow us down. They must have a car nearby. Their trucks are still up there. I got a phone signal half way to you and called out the cavalry. Everyone's on their way.'

'I bet. They'll be long gone by now.'

'We've got a lot of explaining to do.' Dave shook his head. He was clearly suffering the effects of shock.

'You just explained it perfectly to me,' Emily said. 'We've all got families to go home to. There's nothing we could have done differently.'

'I'm not sure the bosses will have the same idea.'

DS Saunders was in her own state of shock, she was mumbling, repeating herself. 'How could they have known? There was no way anyone could have even known we were coming here . . .'

'We don't need to worry about that right now. We're all okay, that's all that matters. Dave said the cavalry was on the way. We wait and then we can start working out what the fuck just happened.'

Chapter 17

When the cavalry did arrive, George Elms was part of it. He had heard the breathless shout over the radio and he knew Ryker was part of the away party. By the time a second update stated that she had been injured, he was already on his way.

He had been in the station at the time of the shout, finding out as much as he could about Damon Alcott. He had tried getting hold of Shaun — he reckoned that he could be very useful in finding Alcott and helping to convince him to talk — but his phone was going straight to voicemail. Whatever. That could wait until later.

George had taken one of Major Crime's unmarked vehicles: a black Skoda VRS with concealed lights in the grill. He drove like a madman on lights and sirens, and he was the first from Langthorne House to make it to the scene. A police dog van that had been in the area was there already, along with a patrol that had turned out from Sandwich. He was aware of the whine of a helicopter overhead as he stepped out of the car.

The uniformed officers present would be expecting detectives to be deployed, and they would expect them to take over the investigation as soon as they arrived. George took advantage of this, barking questions and getting quick-fire replies to the point where he was up to date by the time he made it to where Ryker was sitting on the ground, leaning against the bonnet of the dog van.

'Hell's teeth, Ryker, they said on air that you were injured but I couldn't get in to ask for an update.'

'Somebody hit me, George.'

The point of impact was obvious. There was clear swelling above Ryker's right eye and an angry red split that would probably scar. She was padding the swelling gingerly.

'So I see.'

'*Me* though, George! You hear of officers getting assaulted all the time. It's terrible it is. A right liberty. But I don't get hit, George. I made that quite clear when I started out on this career — I'm too fucking good looking to get hit.'

'You won't find me arguing.'

'I should hope not.'

'Not because I agree, but because you're angry, Ryker. And I don't like you when you're angry.'

'I am angry George. I got hit.'

'I wouldn't take it to heart. At least you got hit by professionals.'

'What do you mean?' Ryker's expression was more serious.

'Looks like it was a simultaneous hit on both vehicles. They threw jammers under both the cars to stop your radios working. They blocked uniform in with two cars that were nicked in the early hours of this morning and they left on foot. At least until they got to another vehicle. They didn't give us much to go on, Ryker.'

'How did they know what we were doing though? The ride out was deliberately low key.'

'Knowing that is the key to finding who hit you, Ryker. There won't be anything here.'

Ryker narrowed her eyes. 'Is there something you're not telling me, George.'

'There's always something I'm not telling you. You want me to drive you back?'

'Fuck yeah. The longer I stand here, the more chance I have of being swabbed.'

Once in the car, George paused before starting the car. 'You're okay though? I mean, it can't have been nice. That might need a staple in it too?'

'Are you being caring, George Elms?'

'You know I care about you, Ryker.'

Ryker shrugged. 'Shit day, George. They'll get theirs. We've got other people to find first. I take it Shaun hasn't had any contact?'

'Not that he's made me aware of.'

George pulled back onto the A256. Twenty minutes later they still hadn't made it past the roadworks. George turned on the aircon as the sun burst through the cloud cover to beat at them through the windscreen. They were monitoring the police channel on the radio where the hunt for the people that had taken Nowak was continuing. Two detectives gave an update regarding the vehicles used to block in the police car. Both were stolen from a garage that had a stock of around forty cars; it was on the border where Langthorne met with Sussex. It had been a 'car-key burglary', the thieves forcing entry to the sales office to get the car keys. The update finished with a dreary line about the garage's CCTV system being 'hit and miss' and out of action at the material time. Ryker was staring out of the window.

'Fancy a diversion?' George said.

'Huh?'

'A diversion. You fancy a quick chat about those stolen vehicles?' George gestured at the radio.

'Sorry, George, I was only half listening. They were nicked from a garage, right?'

'Yeah. We should go and talk to the poor victim.'

'Major Crime just did that right? I told you I'm fine. This can wait another day. We need to get back looking for Shaun's wife and kid. They could get in touch any time.'

'You're right. So we don't have any time to waste.' George flicked on the lights and siren for a second time that day. 'Do me a favour would you, Ryker? Give your intel office a call and see what we know about the owner of this garage.'

Ryker shook her head but did nothing to argue.

* * *

'Roland Merrington Auto's.' George read the livery clinging to what had once probably been the canopy for a petrol station forecourt. It had that look, a large square structure on struts with a glass-fronted office at the back. The pumps were gone, replaced by lines of shiny cars parked in rows and at jaunty angles. It was off a busy road that ran all the way through to Hastings and onwards and was prime for passing trade. George parked in one of the visitor bays. A stocky man in a suit and day-old stubble was on him and smiling before he'd shut the door. He looked the Skoda up and down and then did the same to George.

'Good afternoon, sir. How are you today?'

'Very well, thank you.'

'What can we help you with, sir?'

'I was hoping to speak to Roland.'

The man's smile dropped a little, but he recovered it quickly. 'He's not always on site. He lets me deal with matters most of the time. Are you sure there's nothing I can help you with?'

'Is he on site now?' George flipped over his warrant card. The man's eyes flicked from George to Ryker who was also holding her warrant up.

'He's in the office.' The man turned sharply and walked away.

Roland Merrington was a big man. He wore his trousers pulled high over his rotund waist and held in place by a set of braces. His tie hung loose, his shirt undone to facilitate his chin. He stood up to greet George as he walked in, but his smile dropped away as George introduced himself as a detective sergeant.

'I've spoken to you lot already.' Merrington fell back into his plush swivel chair and rocked back, steepling his fingers.

'I know that, Mr Merrington.'

'So why come back?'

George gestured at two seats that were tucked under his side of the desk. 'Do you mind?'

'Go ahead, if you're staying. Call me Roland.'

George and Ryker each pulled out a chair and sat down.

'So what more do you need? Your colleagues felt that there wasn't much more I could offer. I got my crime reference number, too. I just got off the phone to the insurance company.'

'What was taken?'

'You don't know?' Merrington suddenly appeared flustered. 'Your colleagues knew the makes, reg numbers, the lot. All the stuff I gave over the phone. Why are you here now if you don't even know what this is all about?'

George studied Merrington closely. 'My colleagues knew about the vehicles and about the incident earlier this afternoon, but they didn't know about you . . . Roland. I've been doing this job a long time and I like to look at the victims first. I like to try and understand the motivation. Sometimes victims are *chosen.* If I can understand the reason why, I'm a lot closer to finding the culprit.'

'What are you talking about?' Merrington's cheeks flushed a deeper red. 'In the early hours of the morning, some chancers nicked two of my trucks. They broke in here and they took the keys and then the trucks. Your colleagues tell me they were used in some sort of ram raid or something. I'm a victim because I had two trucks. They were probably out looking for them and there they were, sat at the front of my place.'

George turned to take in the forecourt. 'They were out the front?'

'Yeah. On the grass by the road. They were my prime draws, the first cars you'd see.'

'At the end of March? I saw an Audi TT out there, two of those little Mazda sports cars and a BMW Z4. All convertibles. Surely they're a better bet for your passing trade starting to think about the summer. Am I right?'

'I rotate them — move them around a little. People might be looking for a bargain on a 4x4 because it's spring.'

'And your CCTV wasn't working?'

'No. I mean it does — it's intermittent.'

'But it wasn't working last night?'

'It's been down the last seven days.'

'Exactly?'

'What do you mean?'

'Seven days exactly?'

'I don't know if it's exactly, I—'

'Can we check?' George pointed at a monitor stood on top of a black box marked *Lenovo*. 'That's the system, right?'

Merrington had to shift around to see it behind him. 'Yeah, that's it, I don't really know how to work it so good—'

'I do. Doing this job, I use these systems all the time. You've probably set it to run constant during the day and then it's just motion activated at night, right? So it doesn't fill up the hard drive.'

'Yeah, I think I d—'

'And if it does get full up it starts overwriting itself. You'll probably get about a month back. But you can free up space. Do you know how you do that?'

'I don't think I've ever—'

'You just select to delete a seven-day block. It's easy. It only deletes in seven-day blocks, see? Most people would get rid of the oldest week, but you could wipe the last seven days, almost at the touch of a button.'

Merrington took a second to reply. 'Are you suggesting I deleted my own— '

'How do you know Shaun Carter?'

'Shaun? I don't. I—'

'You'll note the way I worded the question, Roland. I know you do. I also know how you do. So this is the bit where I determine for certain if you are lying to me or not.'

Roland reached for a tissue and dabbed at a run of sweat. He rocked forward in his seat and straightened a pen on his desk.

'I know his dad. Or I *knew* him, I should say, a long time ago.'

'We're getting somewhere now, Roland. Now I do know something my colleagues that were here earlier don't. Now, still assuming that I already know the answer, tell me what happened this morning.' George met Ryker's stare briefly. Neither spoke.

Merrington sat back and expelled a long breath. 'He's a good kid, you know — just like his dad. The last person I ever expected to turn up and tell me that he was in trouble — that he needed my help. He was here before eight o'clock. I was here early — I always am. He had cash. Said he wanted to use the trucks. He didn't have enough to buy them but he said I had to report them nicked anyway and I could do the insurance money. He begged me, Sergeant. I mean *begged*. I know a desperate man when I see one, and whatever trouble Shaun's in, it's deep. I locked the office up and he got in with a wrecking bar from the garage and broke the safe to get the keys so it would look like a burglary.'

'And he didn't tell you why?'

'Nothing. He just said that I had to give him twenty minutes and then make the call to your lot. We stuck some different plates on them — just stuck them over the existing ones. I didn't ask too many questions. I know what he does for a living. I know he's one of your lot, so I guess I kinda thought whatever it was he was up to, it might be for the good, you know? I didn't know what to think. A kid turns up like that, someone I used to know and begs for my help. I just did what he asked.'

'Was he on his own?'

'Yeah.'

'And he left on his own, did he?'

'He must have.'

'In three cars? Come on, Roland. You need to do better.'

'Fuck, I don't know. I'm not on the block here, I just helped out a mate!'

'For cash, Roland. Your mate out there with the cheap suit didn't give him a hand then? Maybe for his own share?'

'He don't know nothing about it.'

'Where's he gone?'

'I don't know . . .' Merrington dabbed at his face again. 'Has he gone? He does have some errands to run this morning.'

'I'm sure he does. He doesn't like police, does he? You can give me his details and maybe I'll find out why.'

'Your mates spoke to him already. If he told them, he told them. I don't know much about him.'

'They did speak to him, and to two other employees. One who said he was your mechanic and the other called himself a valet. Neither of them were too friendly, Roland. They don't like the police much either? Why might that be?'

'I don't know. I don't know much about them outside of here — none of them.'

'I'm sure you don't. They just work for you. If that's the case I'll have someone I know go through your books and tax returns. Literally brushes his hair with a fine-tooth comb. Wears glasses and everything.'

'Fucking hell! I'm not the criminal here! I was just minding my own—'

'And the other car Shaun took. I'll need the details of that.'

'There weren't no other car.'

'You're doing well, Roland. Don't lie to me now. I have the ability to ruin your day.'

'I don't know nothing about no other car!'

George sighed and stood. 'Roland Merrington, you are under arrest for fraud by false representation. You do not have to say anything—'

'An old Vectra. Silver! Fuck, it was just about the shittiest thing I had — he didn't have no money left.'

'Where are the documents?'

'He took them in the car. That was legit, I didn't report that one.'

'Of course not. That was his getaway car, Roland. What sort of person does something for the good and needs a getaway car? You think about that. I really should take you in, you know. The registration number?'

'God dammit.' Roland tugged a hardback A4 book from a drawer. 'Every car I ever had,' he mumbled. He scanned the pages, scrawled something on a post-it and handed it to George.

'And this is the number plate it left with? You didn't mess with this one?'

'No. There wasn't the need. Look, I ain't bothered about no insurance money, I'll call them back and tell them.'

George stood. Ryker did the same. 'Do what you think is right, Roland. We weren't here for you. Or your employees.' George said.

Ryker stared straight ahead as they made it back into the Skoda.

'So Shaun hit me?'

'Probably not. He wouldn't want to risk being recognised. He probably just drove the getaway car.'

'How did you know the link with Shaun in there? What's going on?'

'I didn't, Ryker. Not for sure. It just didn't feel right to me. I couldn't get hold of Shaun and that assault on you all was too perfect. All our cars are tracked. If you had access to that system, knowledge of jamming radios and could listen in to communication between the two cars you could carry off that snatch with perfection. Without any one of those things it wasn't even doable.'

'So it had to be a copper.'

'And one with a motivation to get hold of Nowak. Shaun lived in Sussex for a while, too, before he transferred to Langthorne. Then we got lucky in that fat boy in there doesn't perform well under a bit of pressure.'

'So what does Shaun do now?'

'I don't know for sure. But I think he's got himself his own Plan B.'

'We need to find him.'

'Because he hit you?'

'Because he's going to get himself killed.'

'Do me a favour . . . Call the PNC bureau and get the Vectra's details uploaded to the ANPR hotlist. But I don't want it broadcast if it pings, I want us to know and nobody else. I can't run the risk of it being stopped. And try and get an idea where's it been pinging in the last 24 hours.'

'I'll use my intel excuses. We can put a silent marker on it. I can review the ANPR hits back at the office.'

'You can, but I plan another diversion. You fancy going to see a drug dealer?'

'Hell, yeah! You really know how to treat a lady . . .'

Chapter 18

Midday. Shaun had turned on the earpiece ten minutes before, as instructed. He wasn't sure what the battery life was like for the equipment he had been given. It looked much slicker than the set he had used for covert operations. The earpiece was Bluetooth, the battery pack and the radio itself all one slim piece of plastic. The channel was a digital display: a black four against a green background.

Right on time, a small light flashed on the top of the radio unit. His earpiece whooshed then a voice came as clear as a smartphone call.

'It's midday, Shaun. It's been quite a time, right?' A male voice, a little older than him perhaps. Well-spoken — a slight cockney accent maybe? But then so many people were imitating Londoners these days that he couldn't be sure.

'What do you want from me?'

'Straight to business! I guess I should appreciate that.'

'Just tell me what you want and give me my family back. I don't care about anything else.'

'Ideal. You're doing very well. You will need some tools for the next part. Go to the front desk of the Grand Mersin Hotel in Langthorne. Do you know it?'

'I know it.' Shaun knew it by reputation only: shit hole.

'Good. There is a package there for you. You are booked into Room 224. Take the package to the room. We will talk again then.'

'Wait! I need to—' The sound in his earpiece changed back to the constant whoosh. The man was gone.

Shaun walked back to the silver Vauxhall and got into the driver's seat.

'What now?'

Shaun met eyes with Nowak in the rear-view mirror. He was sat awkwardly, his hands cuffed to the door handle.

'We move.'

'You don't kill me yet?'

'I'm not here to kill you.'

'Who you talk to? They will kill me then.'

Shaun spun in his seat, 'Right now you're alive. You should be thankful for that.'

* * *

The hotel car park was mainly at the rear, but there was some overflow parking underground. The slope down to it was so sharp that the front of the Vectra grounded out where it levelled. Shaun found a space as far in as he could. He was one of only four other vehicles. When he tugged the rear door open, he forgot that Nowak was attached to it.

'Now what?' Nowak said.

'We check in.'

'I don't.' Nowak smiled. 'Why would I do as you say?'

Shaun unlocked the cuff attached to the door handle and wrapped it round his other wrist. He slid off his jacket and folded it over the cuffs to conceal them.

'I'll shout for help.' Nowak said.

'Do it.' Shaun pulled his warrant card from his pocket. 'I'm a police officer. Anyone challenges me and I'm simply on an operation down here and you are under arrest. We are conducting a search and then I'll be conveying you to custody.'

''You're not a cop!'

'I am. And I'm trying to keep you alive. I work for Witness Protection. We have information that the gang you used to work for have people inside the police, but I couldn't find out who. There was a credible threat to your life today and I pulled you out before anything could happen. We don't do this sort of thing lightly, Mr Nowak. I'm sorry I couldn't tell you earlier.'

'You're lying. You hit me!'

'I can understand you being cautious. I'm sorry I hit you, but I didn't exactly have time to explain. I just needed you to do what you were told. If you don't believe me, feel free to try your luck when we get into the hotel. If you shout and scream loud enough someone will call the police. I cannot be compromised, Mr Nowak, so I will leave and let my police colleagues pick you up. It might all turn out just fine for you — our intelligence might be wrong. But the only way I can guarantee you reach Witness Protection is that you remain with me. Your choice.'

'Those other men . . . they police too?'

'They were. They're trying to get a hold on this threat as we speak. I get left to do the babysitting.'

'Babysitting?'

'English term. Don't worry about it.'

Shaun stepped back from the car. He walked to the boot and took out a bag. He pulled out his police issue radio and switched it on. It immediately projected excited voices.

'Looks like we got away clean.' For Nowak's benefit, Shaun hesitated with the radio in his hand — he knew it was an effective prop if Nowak was to believe him.

'So why handcuffs?'

'I don't know you. I don't trust people I don't know.'

Nowak pushed the door closed with his elbow. 'Lead the way.'

The Grand Merson lived up to its reputation immediately. It was a huge, imposing building with sharp edges that were slowly crumbling into disrepair. The revolving doors to the entrance wheezed and jerked to a start as Shaun and Nowak approached. The woman behind the desk wore an ill-fitting uniform that reminded Shaun of flight attendants a couple of decades before.

'Can I help you, sir?' The woman smiled. Shaun had been concerned that she would react to Nowak's bloody mouth, his sprawling tattoo running up the side of his neck and the dried blood on his neck wound. But she smiled like it was any other day.

'I have a room booked. 224.'

'She looked down and clicked a mouse. 'Mr Carter?'

'That's right.'

'For two nights.'

'Err, yes, that's right. Thank you.'

The woman turned to rows of pegs jutting out of a wooden board behind. The key came with an oversized pendant.

'And did you have a package for me?'

'Ah.' The smile still held. She moved through to an office at the rear, she reappeared in seconds. She put a box on the desk, it was shoebox size, wrapped in brown paper.

'Enjoy your stay!'

'Thanks.' Shaun eyed the parcel. He lifted it off the counter, it was heavier than he had expected.

'Second floor, out of the lift and it is on the left!' The woman called out. Shaun heard her but did nothing to acknowledge.

Chapter 19

The approach to the grey, pebble-dashed council house was through any number of bikes, bits of bikes and upturned bins. The grass was long and unkempt, the front of the house was flat and featureless. There were greying net curtains in each of the windows and George couldn't see in. He knocked on the door. A dog barked immediately. It sounded small but the immediate thud against the door suggested otherwise. He waited for a minute or so. Besides a lot more thuds there was no other sign of movement.

'You reckon this is the best address?' George turned to Ryker who had backed away to get a view of any twitching curtains on the first floor. She had made some furtive calls during the drive to get the most recent intel on their target.

'It's where we've had the best success before. But he's got around thirty addresses linked to him. None of them show as his home address.

'But this is the missus, right?'

'Yeah. Sometimes.'

George knocked again. He took some of his frustration out on the door. The dog went banzai in response.

'Hang on!' A gruff voice from the other side. 'I'll just put the dog away, yeah?'

George smiled at Ryker. 'I just wasn't knocking right.'

The dog barking didn't relent, but it did get a little quieter. The door was pulled tentatively open, a slim woman in tight-fitting jeans and a vest top stood in the gap. She was probably late thirties, but the bad skin and shading under her eyes made it difficult to age her. Her hair was tied back firmly.

'Sorry to disturb you. I was hoping to speak to Damon.'

'Damon ain't here.' The gruffness in her voice now suited her. 'I ain't seen Damon for ages.'

'I thought he lived here?'

'He don't live nowhere. What do you lot want with him?'

George smiled. He hadn't shown his warrant or mentioned he was police, but she had known instantly. 'Just to talk to him. He might be able to help us with something that's rather urgent.'

'He getting nicked?'

'No, not at all. The last time he got nicked from here we sent out a whole tactical team, right? I wouldn't turn up here in me best tie, now would I?'

'Yeah. He don't like you lot. I'm sure it ain't personal.'

'I'm sure it is.'

'Well, I ain't seen him.'

'Any idea where he might be?'

The woman shrugged. 'Got fuck all to do with me what he does, know what I mean?' Her forced laugh revealed browned teeth.

'Thanks for your help.'

Back in the car, George paused. 'So where did you say he would be?'

'I told you he wouldn't be there, George, didn't I. It's my job to know where people are, all the recent intel shows him out serving up heroin during the day. He'll be in or around the park on Canterbury Road.'

'I heard you. And I knew you were right.'

Ryker made a face. 'So why did you just waste my time knocking on her door?'

'Because that's his missus, right? She'll have called him already, told him the filth are looking for him. So when we find him there's a good chance he won't run away. For once, we really do just want to speak to him. I'm not interested in the forty deals he's got stuffed in his underwear.'

Ryker smiled. 'You've done this before, haven't you?'

'Once or twice.'

Damon Alcott didn't run. He was sat on a bench on Canterbury Road, the alleyway to the park directly behind him. His legs were splayed wide apart as he eyed the Skoda and its occupants as it pulled up beside him. With hands firmly in his pockets, Damon was doing his best to look disinterested as they approached, but George knew his interest had been spiked.

'You the copper what wants to speak to me?' He had to raise his voice over the din of the traffic.

George had known the name from somewhere. He remembered him now. He had dealt drugs all his life. George had contended with him and his brother when they'd been quite the formidable team in town and run the scene for a while. George recalled that the brother had died from an overdose a few years back and that Damon couldn't hold onto the scene on his own — not since he got addicted himself. There was always someone bigger and more ambitious ready to take over a patch. Every bit of Damon looked small time now: his worn tracksuit bottoms tucked into tatty Nike trainers, an oversized hoody covering his wiry frame and a DIY haircut, his brown tufts jutting out at differing lengths.

'Long time no see.' George said by way of introduction. He didn't bother offering his hand — no telling where Damon's had been.

'I know you?'

'Long time ago. I certainly know you. You and your brother were working together then.'

'All your lot know me.' Damon was clearly proud. 'My brother been gone five year.'

'Like I said, long time.'

'So what do you need?'

'Your help.'

'Why would I help you?'

'Someone's in danger. A woman and a young kid. I think you can help us find where they are before they get hurt.'

'I don't know nothing about no woman and kid.'

'You know about a gang, though. There's a new setup in town, sends out messages by the name of "T".'

'So you say.'

'I guess that's who you're working for these days.'

'Self-employed me. Always have been.'

'Tell me about Bobby Leonard.'

'He's dead, mate. Suicide. Not much more I can tell you.'

'I think there's a lot more. That's not being investigated as a suicide, Damon. We know he was manipulated to jump, to take his own life. He left behind a little lad who really needed him. I know you don't care about that, Damon. I won't even try appealing to your good nature. But I know you're interested in protecting yourself.'

'What you mean?'

'You went to see Bobby. He got paid to go up on top of that bridge where he died. There are serious offences there, Damon, and yours is the only name I have that I can link to them.'

Damon suddenly got to his feet, he freed his hands from his pockets. 'I thought you weren't nicking me? It'll take more than you and your bitch there.'

'I'm not. I could, Damon, but I'm not.'

'You think you could?' Damon stepped in closer. George ignored his snarl, kept his eyes locked and stood his ground. He was close enough to Damon to feel his stinking breath.

'Not a single fucking doubt in my mind. But I don't think it would do me any good. I don't think you're the man who put up the money. The man who put up the money is running the show in this town right now. He ain't out here, plucking deals from his arse for a tenner a go.' George locked eyes. Damon broke off first. He stepped back. He picked up a carrier bag from beside the bench.

'We're done, yeah? You trying to rile me up so you can take me in for a bit of sport? I'm older now — I don't go for that shit no more. And even if I did, you wouldn't get nothing from searching me.'

'Of course I wouldn't. You've had enough time to sort that out. I just want to know the name of the main man in the town. And how to find him. I don't care about small time dealers, Damon.'

'Why the fuck would I talk to you?'

'Tell me what I need to know. Or my next stop is a crackhouse I know half a mile from here with a search team parked round the corner. They go through the door and everyone's arse gets searched.' George raised his voice. 'Ryker? Where's that new setup?'

'Green Lane. Bottom flat of the new-build on the left.'

George watched every detail of Damon's face and knew that Ryker's intelligence was bang on the nail.

'What do I care if you go knocking on some other fucker's door?'

'You care, Damon, because I'm careless. Horrible fuckers in there — London boys if I'm right. Maybe sent here by the very man I need to find. I'm going to search their arses, then I'm going to ask them about their man. And I'm going to make sure they know I got the information from you. All of it.'

'You didn't get nothing from me man!'

'You're right. But then, as we both know from our respective career paths, the truth isn't really what matters, is it?'

'You won't do that. Coppers don't go round talking like that. You lot can't go and put people in strife — they'd fucking kill me!'

'And they know all that, same as you do. So when I slip up and drop your name, they'll absolutely know it's true.'

'You fucking wouldn't.'

'I'm a desperate man, Damon. We don't have much time. Ask yourself, do I value the life of an innocent woman and her little boy over yours? Because that's the decision for me. It's a simple one, right?'

'You lot have a pop at us, but you're the scum.'

'That might be right, Damon. But I suggest we continue this conversation in the car. How many people do you think have seen you talking to us while we've been stood here? All you're doing is making me more believable.'

Damon swore. Then swaggered into the back seat of the Skoda. George drove them all somewhere a little quieter.

* * *

The hotel room was basic. An off-white wardrobe fixed to the wall on the left that made opening the door difficult. There was a bathroom immediately to the right. It was clean but tired, a theme that continued into the room itself, where two single beds were separated by the width of a bedside unit. The beds both pointed at a small tube television that sat on a slim desk against the wall. Shaun locked the door. He took the key with him as he walked the length of the room to the window. They were a long way up. He peered down at the activity below. Cars moved, people walked, the boats in Langthorne harbour opposite fidgeted as the tide nudged them while sweeping in over the exposed mudflats. Nothing looked out of place, but then Shaun had no idea what he should be looking for. He put his bag on the bed closest to the window.

'So why all the effort for me?' Nowak stood by the entrance to the bathroom.

Shaun shrugged. 'Who said it was for you? There's a much bigger picture than just keeping you alive.'

'You need information from me?'

'Yes. Urgently. And the more information you give me the easier it is to keep you safe. We need to know what we're up against.'

'Animals. These people, they are like animals.'

'How so?'

'They killed my brother. I saw him dead. His . . .' Nowak's face flickered with emotion. He got it back under control by biting down hard. 'They do not give a good death.'

'Is there such a thing?'

'For me? It is old and in Poland.'

'Tell me what you know and I'll see if I can't make that happen.'

'I am alive because you need to know what I know. When I tell you, I am not needed. I told police back at the police station, I will tell you everything you need to know when I am safe.' Nowak gestured at the tired décor. 'This is not safe.'

'It's the best I can do right now. Who wants you dead, Aleksander? You must understand how it is important for me to know that?'

'A very bad man.'

'I might need a bit more information than that. And why so much effort just to get you back into the country? Do you owe him money?'

Nowak chuckled. 'You think this is about me owing money? I owe money but he does not want my money. You really know nothing.'

'Then tell me.'

'These people, they work in drugs, right?'

'We know that much.'

'Two markets. He is big in cocaine and some amphetamine. He likes this. They are weekend drugs, yes? Cocaine users are smart — smarter than the dirty people for heroin. He does the best cocaine — eighty percent pure — eighty pounds a gram sometimes. His customers can boast they have the best cocaine. If you want good cocaine in south England it is likely you buy from him.'

'That's a big demand. He must have a big supply.'

'From Europe. Amsterdam some. Barcelona and other places I think. I do not know this. But they come through on lorries that deliver other things. Food, beer, plastic—'

'Tomatoes?'

'Yes of course! I was surrounded. Maybe ten million euros of cocaine. Very pure, one of his biggest. But this was not the biggest on there.'

'Not the biggest?'

'I said two markets. He is heroin now too. He does not like so much. But cocaine at the weekend is one thing, heroin is every day — *all* day. The demand is constant, the money is constant.'

'Was he not making enough money from cocaine?'

'Millions of euros! Every week, more and more and more. But this is not a man who has enough money.'

'So there was heroin on there too?'

'Yes. But he is known in cocaine. He is Mr Cocaine! The very finest. He wants to be the same for heroin. It is a good business plan. When you are the best you charge most. And people will pay.'

'So his is purer?'

'No. There was no heroin on that lorry, there was just cutting. Fentanyl.' Nowak had a wide grin. 'This is something special.'

'Fentanyl? As a cutting agent?'

'This is right.'

'That's pain medication, right?'

'One hundred times stronger than morphine. This is not for the amateur. You dying of cancer, this is the last thing for the pain. Regular users will pay for this and they will pay good.'

'So it's just a stronger hit?'

'This is like no other hit. It is known, the first heroin hit is like nothing else. The best, the most amazing. They spend their whole life trying to get that again. They won't, this is not possible, the body has resistance. Fentanyl takes them back to their first hit and it will do it time and time again. People pay good for this. This is what they want.'

'Those that don't die.'

'This is very bad. Lots of people die. Some taking this for the first time die. This is very bad. Many overdosing. Many die in making it too.'

'Making?'

'It is a powder mainly. A white powder. Very dangerous. This powder on your skin soaks through and you can overdose. I have seen this.'

'So how much fentanyl did you have with you in that lorry?'

'As much as they could! This can wipe out England yes! And the man, he buys this for a lot less than heroin. He can cut it, little heroin, a little fentanyl — best hit of your life. A very rich man.'

'So that was the reason for getting the lorry through.'

'Yes. He has tried before. He has many lorries being stopped recently, this has not happened before. He knows he has a problem — somebody talking maybe. He is very paranoid. He loses money like this.'

'Is that what he thinks you did?'

'No. I was doing similar business in Poland. I came to England to sell to Polish people — there is a lot more money here for buying. He asked me to work for him so he could sell to Polish people. I stole his money and some of the cocaine to take home. Enough so I could be big there. I also took some spice. This is big here, not so much in Poland.

'Spice?'

'Man made. This is plant food! It is very bad. Sometimes it is very good, but it can give you a very bad time. He does not do this now. He cannot make the best of this.'

'How much money did you take from him?'

'Five hundred thousand euros maybe. As much as he makes in a week. I saw the amounts of money. I thought he would write me off as bad debt but he is not someone to cross. He is proud. He came for me hard. He knows that he needs to make an example.'

'Two birds with one stone. You and the drugs.'

Nowak nodded. 'Two birds.'

'Jeez.'

'I need go shit.' Nowak pressed a light switch for the bathroom. A noisy fan accompanied it.

Shaun stepped quickly past Nowak and into the bathroom. There was a small bath with an electric shower on one side, a white toilet with a worn seat on the other that backed into a raised bench under a mirror. On the bench was just a plastic beaker with what looked like serviettes — not even a complimentary soap. Nothing that could cause him any problems.

'Go ahead,' Shaun said, stepping back out. Nowak closed the bathroom door behind him.

Shaun pulled the rig out from his bag. He switched it to *on* and slid the all-in-one power pack and transmitter deftly into his back pocket. He had wrapped the microphone tightly; he couldn't be sure it wasn't transmitting permanently and this limited the chance of being constantly overheard. He unwrapped it and clipped it back into place. The earpiece was already whooshing. He sent a text to the only saved number that said simply: *ON.*

He turned his attention to the box. The paper cover ripped off easily. It was indeed a shoebox underneath, green with *Clarks* written in black lettering. He lifted the lid and took a sharp breath. His eyes fell first on the black handgun. An ugly thing, extended in length by what he recognised from movies as a silencer. Shaun had never liked firearms. Never understood those that did. He always said that nothing good had ever come from firing a weapon. The box also contained a black mobile phone. It was an identical Nokia, the type known as a 'burn phone' among the kids out selling drugs. He tipped out the other contents of the box. There was a flat piece of plastic he recognised as a replacement battery for his wire and a vacuum-sealed see-through bag containing what looked like three pairs of blue nylon gloves — the sort used at crime scenes, a soft bag, a cloth like you'd clean glass with and a roll of Gorilla tape. His earpiece crackled suddenly into life.

'You made it, Shaun.'

'I did.' Shaun's voice broke. Every time he heard this voice in his ear he wanted to break down, to beg for it all to stop.

'And you have our friend.'

'Yeah.'

'I appreciate that. It was a little unexpected that we would ask that of you, Shaun, but you did very well to adapt.'

'So I get my family back?'

'This was not meant to be my use for you, Shaun. This task still needs to be completed. Unfortunately, Mr Nowak decided to inconvenience us all. Mr Nowak will not be a problem for much longer, then there is a small task for you to complete and you have my

word that your family will then be returned. I really do appreciate your efforts, Shaun. You are proving to be both resourceful and reliable.'

'What other task?'

'First you need to finish the Nowak issue.'

'Finish? I got him here, I can walk out now and lock him in. He's yours. You told me to get him here.'

'I don't want him, Shaun. Not alive.'

Shaun's eyes flicked back to the pistol. He knew what it was for.

'What you do with him is down to you. I brought him here — that was my task.'

'The weapon in the box is loaded. Be careful with it, Shaun. Nowak needs to die and then you need to leave. Do it now, Shaun.'

'Don't be ridiculous! I can't kill a man.'

'Do it now, Shaun. You don't want to say no to me again.'

'I can't.'

'Are you saying no?'

'I can't kill a man! Jesus! This wasn't the deal . . .' Shaun picked up the weapon. He held it in a loose grip then threw it back on the bed in disgust.

'Do you have your police radio on you, Shaun?'

'Yes, why?'

'Turn it on. We are just crossing the motorway, a flyover near Dover. We were bringing your family closer, Shaun. They are with me here. Turn on the channel that covers that area.'

'Why? Can I speak to them? Please!'

'Last chance, Shaun. Nowak needs to die. Yes or no?'

Shaun stared at the ugly weapon. 'Can I speak to my family? To my boy?'

'Are you dealing with Nowak? Yes or no?'

'I can't kill a man.' Shaun pleaded.

His earpiece changed tone to the one he had come to recognise when communication had been cut.

Shaun heard a flushing sound. He quickly flicked the duvet over to cover the box and its contents. He retrieved the radio from his bag and turned the volume up. It was already monitoring the local area.

'You okay? You look worried?'

Shaun stared intently at his radio, he made no reply to Nowak who paced to the free bed. He lay down and kicked his legs up.

An update by an officer was interrupted suddenly, an excited call handler.

'Any Zulu patrol able to attend the M20 near the flyover to Hougham on the outskirts of Dover for an immediate call please? We have reports of someone going off the bridge into live traffic there.'

Voices replied immediately to confirm that they were attending. Nowak looked over, his interest spiked by the reports. Shaun turned to the window to hide his own reaction, his chest so tight he felt like he would never breathe again.

'Sounds bad.' Nowak offered.

Shaun didn't reply, couldn't reply. He heard bedsprings and half turned. Nowak was scooping up the remote and Shaun faced back to the window. The television clicked on.

The buzz in his earpiece changed. The voice returned, *'Listen to your radio, Shaun. Remember who's in control here and why.'*

Shaun's eyes clamped shut at the sound of the voice. As impossible as it seemed, he still had some hope that the report on the radio wasn't linked — that it was all just a coincidence. The voice coming back confirmed that this was all for him.

'Mr Nowak?' Shaun managed, 'can you turn that television down a little. I'm just listening to the radio.'

'Sure.'

The volume dropped.

'So he's there with you,' the voice through the earpiece was suddenly gleeful. *'You can just listen, then, Shaun. Your ex-wife suffered for your refusal. Your boy does not need to do the same. I think you understand what I mean?'*

Shaun opened his eyes. Suddenly they felt sensitive to the white light of the window. He heard confirmation on the radio of the first patrol arriving at the scene. They confirmed that a female had fallen into the live carriageway and been struck by a lorry. In a shocked voice the officer asked for more patrols. He sounded breathless and distraught. *'It's a mess, Control.'*

Shaun leant on the windowsill for support. He fought back a sob, He could feel his heart thumping, it beat behind his temple. This had all got out of hand.

'You need to deal with Nowak and you need to deal with him now.' The voice was back, keeping on the pressure. *'Yes or no, Shaun? I only ask once.'*

'Yes,' Shaun muttered.

'You speak?' Nowak called out.

'Yes,' Shaun said stronger. He spun quickly. He tugged the duvet so that it fell back to reveal the pistol. He scooped it up. Nowak was just a blur to him as he lifted the weapon and pointed. Shaun pulled the trigger three times in rapid succession. He was screaming out his frustration and his fury as he did it.

Shaun's eyes focused. Nowak was bleeding heavily from his chest. He was still on the bed, his eyes wide, his mouth opening and closing, fighting for a breath that wouldn't come.

'Sounds like you made the right choice, Shaun. There is a camera on the phone. Take a picture of Nowak and send it. Do it now. Then you need to move. Leave the old phone there. Turn your radio and your own phone off for now. You can be tracked on that. If they find you, this is all over. I will have someone clean your room. You don't need to be told what will happen if we do not find a dead Nowak.'

Shaun dropped the weapon and his hands lifted to cover his mouth.

The hiss in the earpiece changed to its flat tone. Shaun was on his own.

Chapter 20

A McDonald's drive-thru. Not a good place, too public. Shaun knew it the second the automatic doors parted and he nearly collided with a heavily tattooed man in work trousers and tool belt who was coming out. Shaun started and this shook him out of his daze. He kept his head down, mumbled an apology and slalomed through the bustling interior to the toilets. He'd left the hotel in a panic, got back to the car and driven blindly. He just needed to get away from that room and what he had left there. He had seen the McDonald's sign at an industrial estate at the top end of the town where he had intended to join the motorway. The urge to get away was suddenly replaced with the urge to scrub his hands. He scrubbed them hard, the water as hot as he could bear. The eyes that stared back at him in the mirror were exhausted and terrified at the same time — *what had he done?*

A phone vibrated in his pocket and he flinched as if from an electric shock. He had turned his own phone and his police radio off. This only left the phone he had found in the shoebox. Still switched on. He plunged a soaking wet hand into his pocket. It was a text message.

CALL THIS NUMBER AT 1430.

Shaun checked his watch. He had twenty minutes. He didn't want to be here to make the call, he knew what they could do with phone work — making a call was as good as putting a digital pin on a map. Finally, he was starting to think straight again.

He left the toilets, his face still dripped where he had splashed some cold water. His stomach now ached for food, set off by the smells. He couldn't remember the last time he had eaten, but it was probably more than twenty-four hours. He hurried back to his car with a burger meal and a well-sugared coffee to try and boost his energy levels. He discarded the food on the passenger seat and pulled out into the traffic.

The village of Hougham was a ten-minute drive, its elevated position made it the perfect choice for phone companies looking to put up a transmitter to service the area. Shaun pulled up as close as he could, just a few metres from where one of the steel cables reached up from a huge concrete slab, one of four anchoring the giant phone mast against the elements. He demolished his burger meal before making the call. He had recently been involved in looking for a missing person on a cliff top. The police had pinged the phone to try and get an idea of his position and it had come back as pinging from the base of this very mast. The officer leading the search had immediately dismissed the result. 'Happens every now and then,' he had said. 'It's an anomaly. That phone could be anywhere in five square miles of that mast — maybe even further. If it doesn't get a result it just shows the source of the signal as being the mast.' Shaun didn't think there would be a manhunt for him just yet, or that this number would be known, but he couldn't take the risk.

'Right on time, Shaun.'

'I've done everything you've asked, when you've asked. You've no reason to hold my family any longer.'

'Steady on there, Shaun. Our Polish friend was a bit of a bonus — a little unforeseen. But he was not the reason you were chosen. I still have a task for you. It's very simple. Then you get your family back — just like Bobby Leonard did.'

'I might not be able to do anything soon. Now there's a body in a hotel room it won't take them long to work out I walked in with him. Then I'm no use to you at all.'

'I told you I would sort that. But you do need to move fast. You've managed to carry out the perfect kill, Shaun. You're actually quite good at this!'

'Fuck you! A man died, I took his life and you're making jokes.'

'That's police mentality coming through, Shaun. Don't start losing sleep over removing that man from existence. I can assure you it won't be much of a loss to humanity.'

'And what about you? Jesus Christ, you murdered Carol! Threw her off a bridge like she was a piece of rubbish. And kidnapping a ten-year-old boy? These are innocent people. They did nothing to deserve this.'

'I stopped worrying a long time ago about my soul, Shaun. I know where I'm going when this is all over. You get to the point where it's too late, where you need to focus on getting what you want and putting off eternity for as long as possible. All that matters to you is that I am a man of my word. Do as you are asked and you get your boy back.'

'What more could you need?'

'A swap. A simple swap.'

'What are you talking about?'

'Someone works with your girlfriend that is causing me a lot of problems, Shaun. I need to know who that is and I need them to be delivered to me.'

'Delivered to you? What are you talking about? I can't just go picking people up and dropping them off for a damned madman. What person?'

'That's another part of the puzzle you see. You assisted me with getting a lorry through the port of Dover yesterday, but this is the first I have been able to get through for nearly three months. I have made numerous attempts in that time, but everyone has been stopped and searched and the cargo found. I accept the risk that there will be stops, that you can't always be sure of getting through, but for all of them to be stopped? I have a leak, Shaun — someone who has knowledge of my operation who is happy to share this knowledge with various aspects of law enforcement. Your girlfriend was the obvious choice. We built a lot of information around her, spent a lot of time watching her, planning our moment. All that did was confirm that she wasn't the source. All was not lost, however, it became pretty obvious that you were the better candidate. You could assist with getting what I needed through and with the added bonus of ensuring the lorry could move freely on the mainland. Now we need you to use your link with the port to find out who is the cause of stopping my cargo.'

'You mean your drugs.'

'Who cares. You certainly shouldn't. Just understand the lengths I have gone to for this information. Don't think for one second I wouldn't go further, Shaun.'

'I don't know what happens down there. I don't know who's stopping your damned lorries.'

'Jessica Norris does. You will need to get the information from her. And once you do, you will need to isolate this individual and deliver them to me. In exchange for your son, Shaun — just in case you were forgetting what is at stake here.'

'Then what? What do you do to this person?'

'What do you care? But if you don't deliver it will be your boy instead. I suggest you do as you are told. Call me on this number when you have what I need. And not before.'

* * *

George had seen a number of incident rooms before. They were an ever-evolving animal: chaotic, tense and exciting at the 'golden hour' stage, then staid, tense and often tedious in the many months that could follow. This incident room was still very much in chaos. He and Ryker swerved past the numerous bodies and through the excited chatter to get to the door marked *Chief Inspector J. Whittaker*. George knocked and entered.

John Whittaker was sat at a cluttered desk, papers strewn over his keyboard. The wall behind him had a whiteboard with hurried notes in black marker, some crossed through, some half rubbed out. Whittaker gave a tired looking smile over a ringing phone. He reached out and turned the ringer down.

'George, old friend, if this is work related I genuinely don't give a damn. I'm sure you don't mind me saying.'

'I don't mind at all. I'm sure you won't mind me ignoring you?'

'Everyone else has.' Whittaker gestured at a vacant seat for George. 'I'm very sorry, Emily, you'll have to drag a chair in from outside.'

'I'll stand.' Ryker said.

'You two know each other then?' George said. 'That saves the formal introductions.'

'Yes of course. Emily put some intel packages together for me in a past life.'

'Excellent. So, it's been a busy weekend, sir. Not the sort of weekend I'd want to be running Major Crime.'

'Feast or famine this lark, George, just like I remember from the front line. Of course, I was a much younger man the last time I was stood on it. Suddenly I'm the SIO for a murder with no body, a kidnap with returned victims who are suddenly mute, a dead man quite probably linked and we've just had a high-risk witness snatched from police custody. As far as shit storms go, this is a particularly stinky one. Are you okay, Emily? I know you were caught up in all that business?'

'Fine, sir. I'm just sorry it happened.'

Whittaker waved away her apology. 'As long as you're okay. We'll sort it out. We'll sort everything out.'

'You'll get a handle on it, sir,' George said. 'And from the amount of people just outside your door you've got enough to delegate some of the smelly stuff out to.'

'The buck will stop in this office, though, friend. And the more people you have working for you, the more stupid questions you get asked and the more people you need to think for. I can't say I remember trained detectives being quite so *needy,* George.'

'I think it's a culture thing, sir. This job is all about audit trails and arse covering these days. If they only do what they're told to do, it's not their fault if it's wrong.'

Whittaker rubbed at his tired looking eyes. 'I think you might have hit the nail there, George.'

'I can help, sir. I know you weren't keen on me taking bits on for you but the offer's still there. I can even think for myself.'

Whittaker shook his head vigorously. 'I know you've offered. From up high, though, George . . . I didn't realise just how much you'd pissed those people off, my friend. You know I would have you front line, stood beside me while this thing plays out, but I've been given a very severe word at the mere mention of your name. I can't have you involved. I have to say I'm a little envious to be honest. I was hoping someone would say they didn't want me involved either so that I could go home!' Whittaker's nervous laughter lacked its usual enthusiasm. George could tell that he felt awkward about the situation. He let him off the hook.

'I understand. It's better that I stay away then, sir. The last thing you need is to be spending any time or energy on me. You have a lot on, we'll leave you to it.' George stood back up. 'Unless you needed anything from Ryker here?'

'Not at this moment, but I know where you both are. Thanks, George. We'll catch up though, when this all calms down and my coffee machine finally arrives from headquarters. Come and talk to me. I'm serious about supporting you for the next rank up.'

George pursed his lips. 'Sounds like you've just experienced first-hand how likely I am to be considered for promotion.'

'It would definitely piss some people off, George. Some very senior people. But if you're supported and you meet the criteria no one can block you. The fact that it pisses people off is all the more reason to get it done, right?'

'We'll see, sir. Well, the offer stands if you need us for anything.'

George left the office quickly, his pace fuelled by his frustration. He heard Ryker calling out when they got clear of the incident room. He waited until they were in the lift before acknowledging her.

'We're not telling him what we know, then?' Ryker breathed a little with the exertion.

'No.'

'Because you're pissed off that he doesn't want you involved?'

'No.'

'It seems like it to me. I know you've got this male pride thing going on, but there's a bigger picture here, George. The information we have would progress their investigation massively. Maybe even to the point where an incident room of that size will find Shaun's little boy alive and well.'

'You heard what he said in there. He has a room full of detectives who are terrified of making their own decisions, of using their own initiative. If I tell Whittaker what we know he will be pissed that I didn't listen to him, that I didn't step away — and that I kept the information from him in the first place. Then he will make damned sure that I don't do it again and my day is over. The task of finding Shaun and his family then falls to a room full of people too scared to do what it takes to get the job done.'

'This again!' Ryker's exasperation was clear.

'Yes, this again.'

'This belief that you are the only person who can get things done, that everyone is else incapable of—'

'Not incapable, Ryker. There are a lot of good coppers in there. But they're all choked. They're all on a leash. They're all terrified of losing their jobs, of being prosecuted by their own employer.'

'I wonder if we are ever going to be able to get you back, George. I know what you've been through. I know it's changed your outlook. You're a different bloke. It's like you've lost all faith in everyone. But maybe you're wrong, George.'

'An incident like this, where you're against the clock isn't about being wrong or right. It's about getting things done. Major Crime got sent to speak to Bobby Leonard's family and they walked away with nothing. We don't have time to play by the rules.'

'Major Crime don't even know they're against a clock until we tell them. And get over yourself! You were first on scene when she gets a brick through her window, George. Of course she was going to be a little more receptive to talking to the police once she realised there might still be a threat to her and . . .'

The lift *bonged* impatiently, the doors opened and George stepped out, waiting for Ryker to continue. Her voice was hushed suddenly.

'You threw that brick, didn't you?'

'I needed her to talk to me. We don't have time to play games.'

'So you put a brick through her window?'

'What would you prefer? I play by the rules and knock on her door? Get told to fuck off like everyone else did?'

'I don't know. We don't know what we're up against. Shit, George! You throw a rock and marked police cars turned up to that house. We don't know what that might mean.'

'Well, all the more reason to do what we need to do to find out.'

'You're going to get yourself in the sort of trouble you can't get out of one day, George. You know that, right?'

'You're probably right, Ryker. Lord knows I've given it a good go.'

Ryker sighed and he felt that she was stepping down from her offensive.

'You can't go round doing stuff like that. Even you, George. You're a good detective, you don't have to step over the line to get results.'

'Yes I do. We all do. I am a good detective, and when you get a good detective to a point where he doesn't give a shit anymore, that's when you can become a great detective. I just want to find Shaun's family. Not for him, for *them*, because they don't deserve any of this. Protecting the innocent, that's what we do, right?'

'From bricks through the window, from being terrified in their own home.'

'You think Bobby Leonard is innocent in all this? And his wife? Do you think they play by a set of rules? The Leonards took money to get to Shaun. Whether they knew it would go the way it did or not, they took part. And Damon Alcott? He's a piece of shit and I'll lie to him every day about having a search team ready to do a bust if it means he tells me what I need to know. To protect the innocent. That's all I'm here for now. One day I will step over the line and Lennokshire Police will gladly get rid of me. It's all fucked, Ryker. Nothing has more rules and regulations than policing, and yet our very function is to pursue those who play by none, and for their own gain. Fuck 'em. Sometimes we have to even it up a little or we will never win.'

Ryker smiled. 'You feel better now?'

'No. I'll feel better when we win.'

Ryker shrugged. 'So how do we do that? We're at a bit of a dead end all of a sudden.'

'Yeah. We need to be out of here so we can work out what we know and where the gaps are. Then we can start filling them.'

Ryker smiled. 'Fine. But I'm choosing the place and you're not allowed to throw anything at it.'

He grinned back. 'No promises.'

Chapter 21

Follies was a French themed café, which meant the coffee was strong and the atmosphere hushed and personal. George and Ryker occupied a table upstairs in front of a large window overlooking a busy road at the top of town. George tried Shaun's mobile number for the umpteenth time, despite knowing it was useless. He slid his phone over the table top in response to the standard engaged tone.

'So, what do we know?' Ryker said.

He watched the cars bustle past through the window for a few seconds. Then he summarised as best he could. He tried to keep it chronological while Ryker made some scribbled notes. There was a silence when he finished that Ryker was the first to puncture.

'So the address that Damon gave us. That's the next obvious move, right?'

He shook his head. 'It's a viable address and it'll be a drug den no doubt, but I'm not sure it will get us any closer to our missing people. Damon might even have given us something that would slow us down. I don't think he would be offering anything that would help, assuming he even could. Without resources, we can't go knocking on the door anyway.'

'So we wait for Shaun to reappear? We have to assume he's back in touch with these people by now.'

'He must be, yeah. But Shaun's wife stands out for me. When I think about what we know and the vast amount we don't, that's what I would focus on. These people have got to know as much as they could about Shaun. It's fair to assume they would have spent as much time on his ex-wife and her movements too.'

'There's not too much we can do, though, is there? What can you get from looking at the outside of an empty house?'

'We don't know it's empty. I assume she lives alone now but we don't know that. For all we know she's a prisoner in her own home. But stuff like if there's a car on the drive, what her neighbours know. Basic investigation stuff, Ryker, you never know your luck.'

'Well, thanks for patronising me at least.'

'Sorry, I forget you're one of the good ones!'

'Well, at least you accept that they exist. That's the sort of thing that could be done for us by someone in that incident room, though. Maybe we should have told them what we know. I'm not sure if looking up the movements of the victim's car is going to get us much further. We need to find Shaun. Is it not better to make him our priority?'

'Shaun isn't behaving rationally. We don't stand much chance of finding someone like that, but we can find where this Carol lives. Then a little more about her maybe and who knows where that leads. Shaun will turn up.'

'What about Shaun's girlfriend down at the port? Is it not worth talking to her?'

'She has to be on the list. But she doesn't know what's going on and we don't know if Shaun's going to need her to help him again. I don't want to do anything to put his family at risk unless we really have to. I didn't get the impression from Shaun that he trusted her to do the right thing with this information. And if he doesn't, we sure as hell can't.'

'What about warning her? These people are snatching those that are close to Shaun. Surely she's at risk?'

'It's a valid point. Okay, maybe we could talk to her and see if there's anything we can get without letting on why.'

'That won't be easy.'

'I agree. We'll need to be a little creative.'

Ryker twitched, her right hand moved to her jeans pocket and she pulled out her phone to inspect the screen. She looked puzzled. George sipped at his drink while Ryker took the call. It was short and she said very little.

'That was the control room. My silent marker on Shaun's car? It's just pinged at the port — inbound.'

'The Vectra?'

'Yeah. Seems we might need to go see the girlfriend rather more urgently.'

'Seems that way. I'll head down there and see if I can find him.' George stood and led the way to the stairs.

'You don't want me to come with you?'

'No. I'm going to have to get a move on to get there, Ryker, I don't like driving like that with someone else in the car. And I think one of us needs to do the enquiries around his wife sooner rather than later. Can you find out where she lives do you think?'

'I work in intelligence, George. I reckon I can handle it.' She followed him as he walked to the door. 'Are you sure you're going to be okay on your own? Shaun's suddenly a lot less predictable and he might have Nowak with him.'

'Yeah. I think it makes sense to be on my own actually. He might not panic if he sees it's just me. If I want him to engage with me again I'm going to need him still to trust me.'

He slapped a ten-pound note on the counter, prompting a curt look from the woman stood behind it. He continued out through the door. 'You okay to walk from here?' he called out, already at the driver's door.

'Yeah. I've decided that cars are dangerous anyway. The last time I got in one someone hit me.'

'Oh really? You didn't mention it.'

Chapter 22

'Christ, Shaun! What's the matter?'

Shaun had checked himself in the car mirror before stepping out. He knew that he didn't look himself, his skin had a washed-out pallor and he could feel the sweat that had layered his top lip and held his t-shirt against his back.

'Nothing's the matter, Jess.'

'You look unwell, Shaun.' She looked beyond him, Shaun thought that she might be concerned he was making a scene, embarrassing her. Sure enough she moved him to a side office.

'What are you doing here, Shaun?'

'I'm sorry, Jess, I know you've just started your shift. There's been conversations at my place about this lorry that came through — about what we can do the next time. Now . . . I'm not making a panicked call through to someone I just happen to know down here. I know you weren't too impressed and rightly so . . .' Shaun knew he was floundering. 'But we need to be sure there's a system in place.'

'That's why you're here?'

'Yeah. I mean not officially. I was in the area and I wanted to talk to you. I wanted to say I was sorry too, you know? It wasn't ideal, calling you out of the blue like that — and then I was a bit of an arse about it after. I've been under a lot of pressure at work recently. I know I shouldn't take it out on you.'

'I've never seen you like this, Shaun. Has something happened?'

He could feel Jess studying him. She looked deep into his eyes and her expression was full of concern, of sympathy. He hadn't known what to expect. 'It's all pressure you know. I might have taken on a little bit too much — this negotiator thing. I didn't think it would bother me but it's had more of an impact than I expected.'

'There's no shame in something like that affecting you, Shaun. It can't be nice.'

'It isn't. You're off duty, supposed to be relaxing and the next thing you know your phone goes off and you're dragged into this world of someone else's misery. Can you imagine how someone can get to the point where they can throw themselves off a viaduct? I guess some of that has to rub off on you.'

'Of course it does. Bugger it, Shaun, just come off the rota. It doesn't have to be forever. You don't have to quit completely. Just tell them that you've had a rough couple of weeks and you need a break. There should be something in place for that. They should look after you when you have a bad call.'

'They should. I think they would if I asked.'

'Do that then. What are you on today? I saw the car, is that a police car?'

Shaun took a second, then remembered that he was in the Vectra. Jess must have seen him park on the cameras. The camera feed was on a monitor visible from her desk.

'Yeah. We're doing a bit of plain clothes stuff, a reccy for a warrant they want us to do at some point next week.

It's not far from here — I thought I would come down and have a cuppa if I could.'

'I can spare a teabag, I'm sure.'

Jess led the way back out into the office. They crossed the floor, Shaun was again aware that he seemed to be the centre of attention. He checked his watch — he didn't have much time. Jess led him through to a canteen area. There was an urn that brought itself noisily back to the boil as they approached.

'So, I reckon we should have a sit-down meeting. I can represent the police and maybe you and whoever is responsible for your intelligence down here.'

'Yeah, I guess that makes sense. I've always said we need to be more transparent. Bad guys are bad guys, right?'

'Can't argue with that. Who is that?'

Shaun had been speaking to Jess's back as she busied herself with making the tea.

'Who, the bad guys?'

Shaun smiled, he did his best to make it look natural. 'No, your intel officer down here?'

'Intel officer. You make it sound so grand. We're the poor relation down here, I'm afraid. The majority of the intelligence either comes from or goes through the counter terrorism unit, the police, the NCA or the French. We get fed the scraps, the stuff we might need to know, and that comes through at the last minute. Very much like the information from you yesterday. I have an admin clerk who sorts through what we get and what we can generate. She's been responsible for some pretty impressive stops recently though, she seems to have a real nose for a shitbag.'

'I remember you saying you'd had some good wins.'

'We have. Drugs seem to be her thing. If she marks it up, you can almost guarantee it'll have something on it. She's had very few misses.'

'Did she mark up the lorry I told you about?'

Jess didn't answer immediately. She seemed to be studying him again. He knew her well enough to know she was sharp and she was smart. He couldn't be direct, but he had to get the information he needed.

'Yeah, actually. But only because it stood out that it was travelling on its own. She had some stats that show they don't generally do that. I guess we missed another good drugs job then did we?'

'I think you probably did yeah. It doesn't count as a miss if you're asked to look the other way though does it!'

'I wouldn't do it again, Shaun. I take it you stopped it then?'

'No, actually. We didn't. That's the reason we need to be sorting this meeting out. Who is your intel officer? Is she here today? I can explain to her in person what went on.' Shaun would need her on her own. He didn't quite know how he was going to do that yet but, first things first, he needed to find out who she was.

Jess put two teas down on the table. Shaun scooped one straight up. Jess looked thoughtful. 'She's not here today. She called in sick for this afternoon — first time since she started.'

Shaun gritted his teeth, he hoped it was disguised behind his mug.

'I think she's got a bit of a family issue. Alice, her name is. She asked about you, actually, when she called in.'

'Me?' Shaun was still trying to force natural. His mind was in turmoil, the pressure threatening to drop him to his knees. He pulled at a chair to sit.

'Are you okay, Shaun?'

'I'm fine, Jess! Really. We haven't met, have we? Me and this Alice?'

'No. It's her sister, you see. She's dating this bloke. The way Alice talks about him he's a nasty piece of work. I think he's been regularly beating on her sister. Today she calls in sick, but I could tell something was up so I pushed her a little bit and she broke pretty easy. Basically, her sister turned up all bruised and upset — out of the blue I think. They hadn't spoken for a while.'

'And she wants me to help? I might be able to.'

'Yeah. Sort of. I wasn't sure whether I should talk to you about it or not, but seeing as you turn up a couple of minutes after I put the phone down . . . well maybe it's some sort of sign, right? She's a good kid. I imagine her sister's the same.'

'Does she want me to pop up and see her? Maybe get this arsehole in custody? I could spare a couple of the lads to take him in.'

'No! Sorry, no, that wasn't the idea at all. Her sister was really adamant that she didn't want the police involved. She's desperate, she just wanted advice on what she could do. It was me that suggested talking to you actually — then I changed my mind. I reckoned that once you knew about it you might have to do something. The last thing I want is you going up there and hauling the boyfriend in and me causing more grief.'

'Sounds like something needs to happen.'

'I agree.'

'Are they in danger?'

'No. That's why Alice is staying off. Her sister is staying with her. I don't think this boyfriend will know where she lives.'

'Okay. You know, thinking on it, this sort of thing happens a lot. We have specially trained officers, they go out in plain clothes and they act just like a mate if the bloke is around or turns up. They sort of insert themselves into the victim's life a little bit, but not so anyone would know they were police. Then, over time, they build evidence, give advice to the victim and come up with an exit strategy. It works really well. Sounds like it might be perfect for your mate.'

Jess nodded, with a pinch of enthusiasm. 'That does sound like it might be of benefit.'

'Okay. Well, listen, I've got to get back to work but scribble down her details, where she's staying and that, and I'll pass it on to the relevant team. I'll get someone up there as soon as possible.'

'I don't know, Shaun, she was pretty insistent that I didn't tell you.'

'These officers, they're used to a bit of resistance. She'll thank you in the long run.'

Jess had to leave the room for a pen and paper. Shaun exhaled long and loud. He felt so weak, so exhausted. He could hardly remember a time before he didn't have this nervous tension that was draining every ounce of energy. He didn't like lying to Jess either. He'd have to make it right.

She came back with a handwritten name, address and telephone number on a piece of paper.

'Thanks, Shaun,' she said. She leant in for a kiss and her hand moved round to the back of his head. She pulled it away quickly.

'Jeez, Shaun, you're absolutely covered in sweat! You're not okay. You need to get yourself home.'

'I know that, Jess. I think it's just a bit of shock coming out late. Seeing that bloke go over the edge. I'll head back in, I think, and get home for some rest. I can make my excuses — the boys can handle a reccy without me.'

Jess nodded. She held him by the shoulder, leaning forward to look deep into his eyes. 'Promise me you'll do that. I'll come up and see you tonight after work, yeah?' She smiled. 'See if I can't make you forget about the last few days.'

Even in a moment when his body was nearly consumed by stress, he still wanted her badly. He smiled back, and this time it was more natural. That did sound good. God, he hoped this was all over by then.

Shaun made it back to the car. The nervous tension returned in a deluge and he fumbled to unlock his smartphone. He pulled the folded-up piece of paper out of his pocket and squinted at the handwritten address. Struggling to hold the phone still enough, he typed it into MAPS. The phone found the location instantly.

It was eighteen minutes away.

Chapter 23

'Are you sure you don't mind?' Becks peered at the façade of the house her sister had been renting with her fiancé for the last two months. It was a bungalow, drastically modernised to the point where it had a gleaming white front, a new grey roof that sat on top like in a perfect pyramid and a newly laid driveway with stainless steel lights along its edge. Small, but perfectly formed. It was tucked out of the way in the village of St Margaret's between Dover and Deal. A largely desirable place to live, it was mainly occupied by the older generation, the only group of people that could afford the premium prices.

'Of course I don't mind. We have a spare room and Dean will be cool. He knows that you've been having issues, he said you could stay here if you ever needed to.'

'Seems like everyone saw this coming but me.'

'Don't beat yourself up, Becks. I think you've had enough of that. We'll have a cup of tea and then I'll need to move some stuff out of your room. But it's good to go. Just stuff we haven't had the chance to unpack yet.'

'Great. But talk to Dean first. Make sure you tell him that this is a choice, I'm not imposing on anyone.'

'You're right, you're not! There is an alternative of course. You can go back home to mum's. And with that face! If you want all those questions and told-you-sos, you be my guest.'

'No offence taken! You make a good point. Right then, if Dean says I can't stay I'll kick his arse!'

'Sorted. We'll soon see him anyway. He's on a day off today.'

Becks pushed the car door open but she turned back to Alice and lingered.

'What?' Alice said.

'Thanks, sis. For this I mean. For all this. I should have listened to you — I feel like such an idiot.'

Alice smiled warmly. 'Yeah you should, but that doesn't mean you've done anything wrong. You don't deserve this, Becks. We'll make it all better.' Becks leant over and the girls hugged each other tight.

'Let's get you settled in.'

The girls stepped out of the car. Alice had her key out, she levelled it at the front door lock and froze.

'What's up?' Becks said. She was a couple of paces back and watched her sister push the front door. It swung open and Alice scowled in confusion back at Becks before stepping in.

'Dean?' Alice called out. 'Dean! You home?'

The only answer was silence.

The front door led into a tight hallway where there were doors off to the left and one directly in front — all were closed. Becks followed her sister in, stepping over trainers she assumed were Dean's.

'Maybe he's asleep?

'He'd better not be!' Alice smiled back tensely. She moved further into the hall and pushed the first door open on the left side. She leant in, then re-emerged shaking her head to continue down the hallway. She left the door open. Becks walked past. It was a bedroom — very neat and tidy, the pillows arranged just so. And undisturbed.

'DEAN?' Alice called out again. She was stood at the door at the end of the corridor that Becks reckoned was the bathroom. No response. She turned right, to where the house opened up — then she stopped. Becks could tell there was something wrong.

'What's the matter?' She bustled forward, pushed past her sister, into the open-plan kitchen. The units were a modern white finish, but the tall one directly in front of her was smeared with red. The floor had red stains too, some of it in a fan-like pattern as if someone had slipped in the mess. There was a small island that stood in the middle and the red was pooled thick at its base. Becks knew it was blood — a lot of it — and not just from what she could see; the metallic scent of blood hung in the air, unmistakable. She could almost taste it. She took a sharp intake of breath and she could feel her sister pushing lightly into her back.

'Dean?' Her sister said, almost whispered. 'Where's Dean?'

Becks had a feeling she knew where he might be. She stepped forward slowly, holding her breath as she was able to see more of what was behind the island. A hand, palm up on the white tiles, blood on the fingers, darker under the nails. She moved a little more, the arm that it was attached to hung limp next to a body propped up against the island, facing directly away.

Becks stepped back, colliding with her sister. 'Alice, call the ambulance. Don't look, love — there's no need. Just call the police!'

'What, Becks? *What?*' Alice pushed past. Becks made a half-hearted grab at her hips to stop her but her sister brushed it off. Alice's face contorted, a picture of anguish. Her hands rose to her face. Her scream was long, and ended with inconsolable sobs. She dropped to her knees, Dean's unmoving eyes seemed to look beyond her as she slapped his face and shook him by his shoulders.

'Dean! DEAN! WAKE UP DEAN!' Becks tried to get hold of Alice under her shoulders to pull her away. She shook her off. 'No, No, No, NO!' Becks gave up, she backed away, her own tears starting as she took in her distraught sister with her dead fiancé in the blood-soaked kitchen.

Movement. Her periphery and to her left. There was no time to turn before the first blow struck. Hard and to her left side. Becks stumbled — she felt like she had been punched, the wind forced from her body. She couldn't catch her breath. Another punch. Her legs buckled and she was on the floor, she put her hands up, a dark blur loomed over her. Another blow, her hands took some of the impact but she felt a sharp pain in her neck. Her hands suddenly dripped blood, her side now excruciating. She could hear Alice calling her name over and over. She sounded upset but it was getting quieter, just like the pain was going, drifting away. She felt a blow to her chest but it was distant, like it might have been happening to someone else. She needed to rest now. It was overwhelming.

She closed her eyes to the chaos.

* * *

George had killed the sirens but the grill lights still flashed an urgent blue. He pulled the car up in a service bay opposite the immigration building at Dover's port. A line of HGVs rumbled past and he had to wait for a gap to cross. A woman in an immigration officer's uniform stepped out of the office to meet him. She wore her brown hair tied back in a long ponytail and her eyes were wide and questioning. George guessed this was Jess.

'Hey. I'm Detective Sergeant George Elms. I spoke to Shaun Carter earlier. He asked me to meet him here.'

She looked him up and down. 'He left. Maybe ten minutes ago.'

'Did he say where he was going?'

'I assume he would have told you that. Seeing as he was planning to meet you.'

'Can we have a quick chat? Maybe somewhere a little quieter. There may be some things you need to be aware of.'

The door closed behind him as he walked into the immigration office and the roar of the busy port was replaced by low conversations on phones and the tapping of keyboards. A few people turned around to look at him. Most didn't. Jess led him across the floor to an office. She showed him in, then pushed the door shut behind him. He was invited to sit.

'What's going on? Is Shaun in trouble?'

'Of sorts. I think he has been targeted by criminals. Shaun has been seen as someone that can help them out in some way. I think you're part of that.'

'What?' Jess gaped and looked incredulous. 'Me? How?'

'Shaun called you yesterday and asked you to assist with a lorry getting through your checks.'

'He did yeah. You lot had some intelligence around it and he was concerned that we didn't have enough people down here to deal with it if we did stop it. He didn't say what the intelligence was.'

'From what I can tell, Jess, there was no intelligence. That was a lie so you would let the lorry through without asking him too many questions.'

Jess flopped in a chair opposite to where he himself had sat. 'Jesus Christ! What . . . you think someone has got to him? I know Shaun. He wouldn't work with criminals — not for anything. Are you sure about all this?'

'Pretty sure, yeah. We all have our weaknesses, Jess — that something in our lives that we would do anything to protect. Have you any idea what they might be in Shaun's case?'

'He has a son.' Jess looked at him with frightened eyes. 'You don't think his son's in any danger do you?'

George shook his head. 'I don't think so Jess. But until I've been able to find out exactly what's going on we shouldn't rule out people close to him being threatened with harm. That includes you, Jess.'

'Me? We hardly know each other. I mean in the grand scheme of things . . . It's a casual thing, you know? He's quite a distant bloke. I don't see him helping out criminals for my sake.'

'That may be true, Jess, but just be aware. These criminals . . . It's likely that they know about you. They knew that Shaun would be able to get that lorry through, so they must know about his link with you.'

'We're no secret. Never had to be. My picture on Facebook is me and him dicking around on a canal boat.'

'And why not? You've not done anything wrong. I don't know too much more. I'm trying to piece it together and I'm trying to keep Shaun out of trouble as best I can. You're sure he didn't say where he was going?'

'No. I got the impression he was going to call it a day, knock off work and go home.'

'He's not going home Jess. So where do you think he was going?'

'I don't know! I really don't know. This is all out of the blue. I could tell he was upset. I should have asked him more about it all.'

'Not at all. How could you have known? What did you talk about?'

'He was here just a few minutes. We talked about his weekend. Then he talked about the phone call he made to me about this lorry. He knew that he had pissed me off, I don't like being kept out of the picture and I thought he was holding back intelligence. I know why now.'

'I guess so. What else? You said you could tell he was upset. What made you think that?'

'He was odd. When you're with someone — even after just nine months — you know them, right? I know Shaun. He looked pale, he was clammy and it was like he was really nervous. He started talking about arranging a meeting with me and my intel officer so that this didn't happen again — so we were better at sharing information. That was odd. One minute he was talking about a horrible weekend, sweating and talking about knocking off early, then we were arranging a work meeting like it was any other day.'

'Meeting with who?'

'My intel officer down here. Alice Young.'

'Does Shaun know Alice?'

'They've never met.'

'Did Shaun speak to Alice when he was down here? Which one is she? He might have told her something significant.'

Jess shook her head, her hair shuffled against her back. 'She called in sick today. She's not coming in. That's something else we talked about and he gave me sound advice. He was all over the place and anxious and then he was suddenly giving out domestic violence advice.'

'Domestic violence?'

'Yeah. Alice's sister is getting knocked about — it hardly matters right now, though, does it?'

'Tell me about it. What was said?'

'It's nothing to do with Shaun. She's told me about it before but it's never been too bad. Today I get a call from Alice saying she's not coming in. Her sister has turned up at her house and she's been badly beaten. She wants her sister to report it to you lot but she flat out refuses. She asked me to mention it to Shaun as a purely hypothetical issue to see what he would advise.'

'And you spoke to Shaun about it?'

'Yeah. I missed out the purely hypothetical part. I said that Alice had been having some issues.'

'And he gave you advice?'

'Yeah. He told me about the officers that you lot send out, specially trained domestic violence officers who go out in plain clothes and become mates with victims so they can give advice off the record — capture evidence, that sort of thing. It was good advice, it was weird that he was now thinking straight.'

'Good advice indeed.'

'He took her number and address and he said he would sort it out.'

'And that was all you talked about? There was nothing else that might give us a clue on where he was planning on going next?'

'Nothing else I can think of. Like I said, he wasn't himself.'

'Well then, thanks for your time. Do you mind if I take a contact number? I'll let you know then when we've spoken to him.'

'Yes, please do. I'm more than a little worried about him.' Jess found a scrap of paper. She scrawled her number. George took it. He scribbled his own number underneath and tore it off for Jess. He walked towards the door. He suddenly snapped his fingers and turned on his heels.

'Do you think it's worth me taking those referral details for your friend? I'm a little worried that Shaun might not put that through any time soon. He clearly isn't thinking straight. If he does then she gets referred twice — no harm done.'

'Er . . . yeah, I suppose that makes sense. You just need her phone number?'

'And Alice's address. It would make sense for the officer to visit Alice first. They can sort a joint approach on the sister that way.'

'Oh right. I'll just bring her personnel file back up.'

Jess took back her piece of paper to write Alice's details. George scooped it back up. 'Do you know the boyfriend's details? In case he's known to us?

'It's the sister's boyfriend, so I don't, really. I know his first name is Jake — that's all I know. Alice seems to think he's into something dodgy.'

'Aren't they all,' George said. 'Thanks for your help, I'll be in touch,'

'When you find Shaun, can you tell him to give me a call please. I'm worried about him.'

'I will do. I'm sure there's nothing to be worried about. Please be a little more aware yourself, though, Jess — just until we know what's going on with Shaun. Try not to be the person who comes out and greets visitors. Common sense stuff, you know?'

Jess crossed her arms. George could tell that she didn't appreciate the advice. 'I'll bear that in mind.'

George negotiated the busy traffic once again to get back into his car. He suckered his phone to the windscreen and immediately dialled Ryker. The car ticked over and the ringtone came through the speakers.

'George.'

'How you getting on, Ryker?'

'I've found Carol's address. I was going to take a ride out there, see what I can see. You know, basic detective stuff.'

'Are you still in the office?'

'Well, no. Actually, when I say I'm *going to*, I'm just about there.'

'Can you run a couple of names and an address through for intel please. Urgent. I'll need all systems checked.'

'I can phone it through. What have you got?'

'I missed Shaun at the port, but he came down here and spoke to his girlfriend. She said he was acting weird. He put it down to a traumatic weekend but he got some information about the intelligence officer down here.'

'Okay. Who is that?'

'Someone called Alice Young.'

'Not someone I know. We don't really have a good link with the ports, there are a few layers to go through, so the intel departments don't really speak to each other direct. What does it all mean?'

'She's called in sick today. Some emergency at home involving her sister getting beaten up by her fella. Shaun recommended sending out a specially trained domestic officer who can act as the victim's mate and help her out. He took her address for a referral.'

'Is that what we're doing now? What a service, eh?'

'No, Ryker. We don't do that — it's a load of shit. He used it as a way of getting what he needed. It worked too, he left with an address for where this Alice is staying.'

'Oh shit. I think I see what you're getting at.'

'Yeah, Shaun's got another task. I think this intelligence officer is how he gets his family back.'

'That isn't good for her, is it?'

'I can't see how it could be, no.'

'Send the address through.'

'Do what you can and text me anything you get. It's about fifteen minutes from here.' The blue lights flickered through the grill again. George put his foot down.

Chapter 24

Shaun turned off the High Street in St Margaret's Bay. The road narrowed and meandered through ancient looking cottages built in a higgledy-piggledy formation before roads and cars were a concern. A pleasant-looking tearoom drifted past on the left, the entrance to a primary school on the right. The road straightened out enough to see a small, whitewashed bungalow stood in the middle of a neat lawn. A Renault Clio was parked on the front drive. The front door was dead centre. It hung open.

Shaun parked slightly past the entrance. He walked up the drive, stopping at the open door. He knocked anyway and stood his ground, peering into the house as best he could. The door swung fully open.

'Hello!' Shaun called out. 'Alice, are you here?' He stepped back. There were windows to the left and the right. He could see through the left window, it was a bedroom with a picture-perfect pillow arrangement covering the top half of the bed. The right window had pulled curtains, he couldn't see in at all.

'Alice!' he called out again. 'Everything okay?'

Still no answer. He stepped over the threshold and the hallway opened up in front of him. It was simply decorated, a few pictures breaking up an otherwise plain white interior. He heard movement from within the house, a scuffle at the end of the hall. A woman stepped into view.

'Can I help you?' She didn't come any closer, just stayed rigidly still at the end of the hall. It struck him as odd.

'Sorry. I saw the door was open and no one answered. Are you Alice?'

'Yes. But it's a bad time.' The light at the end of the hall was dim, but good enough for him to see her bite down on a bottom lip that quivered for just a second.

'Oh. Well, I don't mean to disturb you. Jess asked me to pop up and see you. I'm Shaun. She said you might want to talk to me?'

'Oh okay. I will. It's not a good time.' She was still rigid, unmoving.

'Are you okay?' Shaun stepped forward a pace.

'You can't come in! I'm fine!' she snapped.

'Sorry. I don't need to come in. It's okay. I'll stand on the doorstep if you want a quick chat?'

'This isn't a good time.' Her eyes flicked left then immediately back to centre. Shaun was a little closer now, close enough to see that her eyes were a little puffy, her makeup not quite right, perhaps disturbed by tears.

'No problem. Sorry to bother you.' He stepped back to the door. 'You can get my number from Jess if you need to call. I'm happy to pop up.'

'Thanks.'

He turned back to Alice for a last look. She remained staring down the hall at him. 'Can you close that door on the way out, too, please? I must have left it open.'

'Sure.' Shaun pulled the door shut behind him. He walked down the drive and got to the road without looking back. He guessed he was being watched, someone making sure he left. Jake had been there — he had known from her very first reaction. He'd told her to get rid of him, he must have been stood just behind the wall. That gave him a real problem. The perpetrators of domestic violence were all obsessed with the same thing — control. There was no way he was going to let anyone leave with him. Certainly not with a police officer.

Shaun's car was to the right but he turned left at the end of the drive towards where he had seen the entrance to the school. He tried to walk casually, until he got around the corner a little way and then he broke into a jog as far as the school gates. They were closed but were easy to climb. From the top of the gate he could see the school fields behind the main building. They were positioned away to the left and he was pretty certain they would provide access to the rear of Alice's property. Shaun jogged through the grounds to an old, waist-high stone wall that made up the perimeter and followed it along until the rear gardens of the houses came into view. The wall continued along the back of the gardens but a more modern fence had been built on top after the first garden, making it around eight feet tall. He would need to jump the wall into the first garden. He reckoned there were two more gardens before Alice's.

He took in the first house. The back lawn looked freshly mowed, a patio door was open at the rear with a net curtain billowing out through it. A tree was central to the garden and from the thickest branch hung an egg-shaped chair that spun in the breeze. An elderly lady occupant engrossed in a novel spun to face him. He ducked quickly behind the thick stone. He waited a few seconds and swore silently. When he peeked back over the wall the egg seat had swung so it was side on, just a pair of ankles were visible. He looked to the right. The dividing fence between the neighbours was low enough to take with a run-up if he got it spot on. He couldn't see if there was anyone in the next garden. He would just have to hope he got lucky. The seat swung back around and Shaun ducked again. A few more seconds and his head lifted above the wall — the seat faced away. He scaled the wall easily and sprinted across the lawn, his footfalls almost silent on the grass. The chair started to move back around and he ran straight for the fence. Bringing his foot up to meet it at its middle, he grabbed the top with both hands and yanked his body over. He landed hard on the other side, his fall broken by a thick bush with branches that ripped at his shins and forearms. He gritted his teeth. It had been noisy, so he stayed still, listening for any reaction. There was none.

The back of this house was shut up, the garden not in use. The fence on the other side of the lawn was the same height as the one he had just jumped. He moved to squat against the bungalow. He stayed low, moving as quickly as he could along the house, keeping under the windows. He reached the other end where there was a six-foot gap to the fence. The next house was surely Alice's. He started another run-up.

He dropped to the other side and flattened himself against the wall of the house. There was a window to his left, through which he might have been seen if he was unlucky. Nothing he could do about that. He leant round to take in the back. The patio doors were open, they opened outwards, secured by metal clips protruding from the wall. He could hear voices — including a male voice, raised and angry. Shaun moved quietly along the wall until he got to the door. He could make out words now, the voice was slurred.

'You did, didn't you? You talked to the devil!'

Shaun couldn't make out the reply, but it was Alice.

'BullSHIT!' The male voice again — then Alice, clearly in pain. Her voice dropped to a whimper.

Suddenly the male was at the door, projecting the voice outwards. 'We'll see!'

Shaun dodged back around the corner, just in time. He heard footfalls on the patio, a metallic sound as the doors were released from the wall and then slammed shut. Jake — if it was him — obviously didn't want to disturb the neighbours.

Shaun moved back along the wall until he could just see in at an angle. The reflection from the front of a microwave gave him a restricted view — but a view nonetheless. He saw the back of a man who was gesturing angrily, his right arm lifted. Then came the flash of a blade. Shaun made a decision. He yanked at the door.

He had the element of surprise. The man had his back to him, a blade in his right hand and he started to turn. Shaun knew that the only way to deal with a knife was to get a hold of it. He grabbed the man by the right wrist with both hands, at the same time he kicked him as hard as he could in the legs. It was frenzied — five, ten kicks, some hitting their mark, some missing. He pulled the man towards him and threw his head forward in a head butt. The man grunted but kept pulling back. He swung Shaun around and his hip collided with a kitchen unit. He steadied himself and kicked out again, his foot meeting with the man's knee. He felt it give, bending the wrong way.

The man didn't react. He still tried to yank his arm free, he growled like an animal and Shaun kicked him again. This time the blow was square to his shin. This gave too, the bone snapping and forcing the man to his knees. Still he didn't cry out in pain; still he wrenched back. Shaun's hands were slippery with sweat and he was starting to lose his grip. He kicked out again and again, his forearms bled freely as the blade slashed at his skin until finally he heard the clang of a metal knife hitting the tiled floor. In a sudden blur of movement, Alice kicked the knife away. Shaun let go of the man's wrist and threw punches downwards until he was on the floor and stopped trying to get up. Breathless and exhausted Shaun quickly scanned the kitchen. A knife block with one missing sat to his right. He reached for the next biggest.

'Move and it's my turn with the knife,' he managed between breaths. 'You Jake?'

The man smiled and nodded, his mouth leaked blood, his leg was at a sickening angle beneath him. 'He did this. He did all this and he will do it to me too. We can't stop him.' Jake's eyes then lit up then moved away from Shaun as if he was searching for something. Sean saw a puddle of congealed blood at the foot of a kitchen island. Jake pushed his hand through it and lifted it up towards Shaun. 'This is what he deals in. This is what he sells.' His eyes were wild, his face still lit up by a smile of childlike wonder. Shaun had seen it before from someone suffering chemically induced psychosis. He kicked out again, the blow pushed Jake's head hard into the wall behind and he slumped to the floor.

Shaun turned to Alice. 'We need to get you out of here.'

'You're police, right? Jess's bloke?'

'Yeah. We need to get you away from here.'

'I can't leave them here. I can't—'

'Who?'

Alice pointed. Two sets of legs stuck out of doorway. The kitchen floor was streaked red where they had been dragged.

'Stay away from him,' Shaun said, gesturing at Jake, who was murmuring softly on the floor and starting to come around.

Shaun moved towards the utility room. 'Fuck! Alice, there's nothing we can do for them. We need to get out of here. Lock it up and call in the cavalry. Do you have keys?'

'I can't leave them here. This is all my fault.' Alice's eyes were glazed and downwards. Shaun took hold of her firmly by the shoulders.

'This isn't over, Alice. I've seen this before, he's not responding to pain. If his leg wasn't damaged he'd still be going. You're not safe. We lock him in and drive up the road, then we can call the police. They're dead, Alice, taking them with us doesn't change that.'

Alice wept behind her hand. 'I'll come back for you,' she whispered, her eyes locked on the two bodies. Shaun took a quick glance over to where Jake was attempting to support his weight on his elbows before walking around him to lock the back door. He then led the way to the front door and Alice followed him out.

* * *

George ignored the flashing of the speed camera in his rear-view mirror. He had to brake hard for the right-hand turn that would take him off the Dover to Deal road and into the village of St Margaret's. He picked up speed, the route into the village was twisty and the tyres squealed as they held onto the tarmac in the corners. His phone rang and the screen read as *Ryker.*

'Ryker, what do you know?' George killed the siren but kept the lights going. The car slowed a little.

'Not much. There's a package sat on my email from the MET about our Polish friend. I can't open it out here on my phone, the file's too big.'

'Sounds ominous.'

'Yeah. The address you gave me is no good neither. The last known occupant was a builder who had some tenuous links to drugs money. He was allegedly washing the money through his firm. That address apparently is one of the places he was doing up at the time. There's no suggestion he actually lived there so he might have sold it straight off or he's still the landlord. His name is Frank Nicholl. Never been convicted of anything, there's just that intel from eighteen months ago.'

'What about Alice and her sister?'

'No hits. I didn't expect there would be. In relation to Alice, immigration have a similar vetting process to us — it's all very strict. I can't find a sister or a Jake linked to her either. From the other databases I can tell you that Alice is registered to vote at a previous address and the DVLA believe her to be driving a Renault Clio.'

'Understood. I'll have to see what I can find out when I get there.'

'You will. Basic detective work I call it,' Ryker chuckled.

'You've taken that to heart, haven't you?'

'Not at all, George. I'm just happy you chose to let me in on the secret.'

'Let me know when you get back to the office with regard to this MET intel, if there's anything of interest there about our Polish friend.'

'Will do. I'm still sat outside Shaun's ex-wife's house. This shouldn't take long.'

'Speak soon.'

George came to a full stop at a junction then he took a right, followed by a sharp left at The Smugglers pub. He then had to take it slowly to manipulate the winding road through ancient looking cottages. Alice's address had to be just around the corner. He killed the lights.

* * *

Nackington Road was on the outskirts of Canterbury. A good area. Big family homes within walking distance of the city centre. These would cost a pretty penny. The drive on Shaun Carter's long-time family home was steep and it swung around a palm tree bedded into white stones. All very classy. It was a big place, detached with a double garage jutting out of its side. A brand-new Volkswagen Golf sat on the drive. Emily checked and the registration matched the car that was registered to Carol Carter. She stepped into an open porch and rang the bell.

No sign of movement.

She walked around the ground floor at the front as best she could. Every visible window had horizontal blinds, all were turned at the same slight angle. Enough to see into the house but only if you wanted to study the flooring. It was all very frustrating. She continued her walk. the Volkswagen was locked and there was nothing visible on the seats or in the boot. The garage was also locked. A gate connecting the garage to the house didn't budge and Emily found herself back at the front door, again ringing the bell. She lifted the post box but could see nothing through the thick, black bristles.

'Fuck it.' She looked around. The front of the house was completely shrouded from the neighbours. The road out the front was busy but the traffic was fast moving. No one was taking any notice of her.

'You're not the only one who can get things done, George Elms.' Emily often talked to herself when she was solving problems. The solution today involved dragging one of the wheelie bins over to the gate and standing up on top of it. It was a little unsteady but she managed to pull herself up onto the flat roof of the garage where she could drop down the other side.

The rear garden was in keeping with the property as a whole. It was large, neat and perfectly maintained. She walked past a rock garden with water slithering through it. There were two back doors, one was a long bi-fold style door that ran half the width of the rear and the other was a more standard back door on the side of the house. Emily faced another problem. Once again, she talked herself through it.

'I call this the George Elms key.' With that she threw the largest rock she could manage at the glass panel of the back door. It cracked the outer pane and bounced off. Emily swore. She picked it back up and tried again. The glass took another few blows before she was able to push through and spin the key from inside to unlock it.

The perfection of the house continued on the inside. Emily felt like she was walking through a show home. She did a quick tour. She wanted to be sure there was no one in the house first — and no nasty secrets. Then she started looking more for things that might assist, without really knowing what they might be. She found herself searching the kitchen first. Always the heart of any home, she noted the calendar, it was busy with handwritten notes including one for yesterday that said simply: *football.* The work surfaces were tidy, the cupboards containing nothing more than neatly stacked cutlery and cooking implements. Emily stopped to think.

'What sort of a freak doesn't have the standard bung-everything-in kitchen drawer?' No paperwork, no nothing. She paced through to the hall; there was a telephone table on the left side, against the stairs. 'Who still has one of these!' she said. She pulled out one of the drawers, a leather-bound address book lay on top. She opened the cover. The front pages were labelled *emergency contacts* and an address was handwritten with *mum and dad* next to it. Even the handwriting was neat.

'Some people have got too much time on their hands.' Emily read out the address as she noted it — *'Marybee, Crete Road, Langthorne'*.

She did a second spin of the property and made her way out of the front door. The house had revealed next to nothing. Maybe the parents would be able to provide something more useful.

Chapter 25

George made it to the address and noted the Renault Clio on the drive. He pulled the car up hurriedly out on the road, jogged the distance to the front door and knocked firmly — then backed away to take in the frontage. He took a few paces to the left and peered through a window into a bedroom. He moved back to the front door and banged again, harder still. He tried the handle on the door, it was unyielding, as if it was double locked. He moved to the window to the right of the door but thick curtains were pulled across and he couldn't see in.

Still no movement at the front door. He moved to the right side of the house. There was a six-foot gap around the bungalow, a wooden fence separating the plot and a gate that cut across half way up. It was locked too, but easy enough to scale. He dropped down the other side where he found himself in front of a side window that was high up in the wall and circular — more for show than for purpose. He peered in. He could see into the kitchen but the angle was restrictive. He moved around to the back, where he cupped his hands against the patio doors so he could cut out the reflected light.

He saw the blood first: smeared on the floor and the cupboards, thick and crimson around the island in the middle; a fiery red on the white units. Then he saw the movement, low down and on the right side. He stepped back as something threw itself hard against the back door. George stepped back and peered in. He could see a wide-eyed male lying on the floor and facing out, his legs stretching away. One of them was damaged, his ankle twisted at an absurd angle. The man frothed at the mouth and his hands were covered in blood. George watched as he scooped more gore from the floor and wiped it across his forehead. His lips were moving as he mumbled something indiscernible, then he threw his head firmly against the door. His face opened up — a split above his left eye that bled instantly.

What the fuck was going on? George backed away from the door and looked around for another way in — other windows, perhaps. Then there was another thud from inside. As George turned, he saw that the man's wild eyes were still fixed on him, his mouth still moving as he babbled incessantly. George stepped back to the door and got close to the glass.

'What's your name?' he shouted. 'You're hurt! I can help you!'

The man smiled then he turned his back suddenly. He dragged himself off to the other side of the room and crawled out of sight into a room off the kitchen, maybe a utility room. George tried the door handle again but it wouldn't budge. The man's legs reappeared. He seemed to be crawling slowly backwards as if he was dragging something — something heavy. He had a handful of something that looked like straw. George flattened himself against the glass to see more clearly. The straw was blonde hair and the man had a big handful. George watched as he yanked it hard. A girl's face came into sight. Her eyes were opaque and lifeless.

Fuck! George recoiled from the door and stumbled off the step. Then he leaned forward again immediately; he wanted to be sure what he was seeing. He rattled the door again, hopelessly, and the man reacted to the sound. He let go of the girl's head as if it were a piece of meat. He turned to George, his lips moving quickly, his face a gleeful smile.

George turned to see what was around — anything he might use. There was a small shed directly behind him. The clasp was held shut by a large screw pushed through it. The shed's contents were sparse: some flower pots of differing sizes and materials, some old deck chairs, an old metal fence post with an untidy mass of concrete clinging to its base and a rusty gardening fork. He grabbed the fork and threw it towards the door of the house. Then he picked up the post. The concrete made it heavy and cumbersome but he was able to lift it so it rested on his shoulder, the mass of concrete just behind his ear. He lugged it to the back door. The man was still lying down. He was caressing the girl's face, mopping up blood from the floor and painting it on her.

George swung the pole forward as hard as he could, keeping hold of the metal pole as the concrete lump crashed into the glass, opening up a wide hole. The man stopped what he was doing, he looked over as if he was mildly curious. George swung again. There was no key in the lock and he had to make a hole big enough to step through. He threw the post away and it ploughed into the garden. Then he scooped up the garden fork and stepped into the kitchen.

'You can't beat the devil!' the man growled, his face contoured in fear, his eyes focused, unblinking, on George. He got to his knees, his right leg still flapping useless from the shin down He tried to put weight on it and fell back to the floor. He couldn't get up for now, seemingly oblivious to any pain. George stepped in and moved closer, keeping the fork held out in readiness.

'You don't know the devil!' It was more of a screech this time. The man blew bubbles in the white froth gathered around his mouth. 'He's coming for me!'

George stepped closer. The girl was clearly dead. Her left side was coated with dried blood, her skin waxy and washed out, her lifeless eyes staring up at him. Another body was visible: a young man lying on his side and facing George from the utility room. There were puncture wounds on his bare chest. The blood made it difficult to see how many wounds, but there were a lot. The attack must have been frenzied. George could still hear the madman screeching as he persisted in trying to stand. He knocked over a kitchen stool, which crashed to the floor. George checked the rest of the house. He had to open doors to do it. Everywhere else was pristine. No sign of any disturbance. He returned quickly to the kitchen. There was no one left to save.

He pointed the rusty fingers of the fork downwards as he entered; his grip was one of readiness. Somehow the man had managed to stand, his left hand smeared blood on the kitchen top, his right foot twisted underneath him, forming an awkward base. He'd picked up a kitchen knife, small but sharp-looking. He held it firm in his right hand.

'I won't let him,' the man whispered, his teary eyes fixed on George.

George stayed far enough away. 'I can help you. Let me help you,' he soothed.

'I won't let him. Not like that!' Then the man screamed, a guttural scream from deep in his soul as he turned the knife on himself and forced it hard into his chest.

'No!' George shouted. He stepped forward, but the man pulled the knife back out and blood spurted from the wound. He roared as he brought the knife back into his chest again and started to rock. George stepped back to let him fall as the shouting was replaced by a rattle from the man's chest. He fell forwards, his head sideways at

George's feet. He blew a crimson bubble from his mouth. Then all the noise stopped.

Chapter 26

'Do you want the good news or the bad news?' Emily sang. She was happy with herself.

'Bad time, Ryker,' George responded, morosely.

She knew straight away something was very wrong. 'What's happened, George?'

Emily had practically needed to pass the police station to get to Carol's parents' house. She had taken the opportunity to swing in to read the intelligence the MET had provide about Nowak. She had been excited at the result, but now that had been swept away in an instant.

'Three dead up here, Ryker. I fucked up.' The shock in George's voice was clear. 'I should have called this in earlier. It's like hell on earth up here.'

'Fucking hell, George! Shaun?'

George took his time. She could hear him sniffing over the phone and his voice cracked as it came back. 'No. Shaun wasn't here. He must have left before I got here. I think he took Alice. But her sister and boyfriend are dead. I think it's her sister at least. There's pictures of Alice and her guy on the wall. Jesus, Ryker, they look so happy.'

'Fuck, George. What happened? Do you want me to come up?'

'No. I've called Whittaker.' George's voice sounded more composed. 'I brought him up to date. The whole world is on its way up here.'

'Three dead? Who else if it isn't Shaun?'

'I think it's Jake — Alice's sister's boyfriend. He was hurt when I got here, Ryker, but he was on something. His head was absolutely gone — I've never seen anything like it. He was like a wild animal. But terrified, absolutely terrified. I don't know what's going on. I think Jake did all this. He stabbed himself in the chest right in front of me.'

'I'll head up. I can pick you up.'

'Don't. I have a car. I'll come away as soon as uniform get here. What's your news? We need to find Shaun, before this gets any worse.'

'I've got a little more on Nowak. I'm not sure it helps us find Shaun in the short term. It just gives us more of an idea of what we're up against overall. The MET sent me what they have on him and what's he involved in. He was on their watch list — he's part of an OCG that's being run as a Level Two concern.'

'Level Two? For big fish?'

'Yeah. It's what Intel call the "proper criminals." Level Twos don't get policed by the likes of you and me — all the intelligence around them is kept away from anyone with only standard clearance. They use undercover resources and grasses to help build a case over time so that when they take action they can get some serious custodial sentences.'

'So Nowak is a big fish?'

'No. Not at all, I don't think. But he's on the coattails of bigger fish. The man we know as "Tee" down in Lennokshire is Benjamin Tremaine. He's a legitimate businessman on the surface but he was arrested a couple of times with regard to some complicated frauds ten years ago. Nothing that stuck, but he made a lot of money it would seem. Now he runs a property company, but there are long held suspicions that he's controlling a drug empire. Covert teams have been on him and they have him in our county a lot over the last few months. The latest intelligence shows him linked to a white Transit van and a silver Mercedes S Class. I did some ANPR work. Specifically I ran a convoy analysis using the details for the Vectra and for these vehicles. What do you think I found?'

'That they're in convoy.'

'Not in convoy exactly, but the Vectra has hit six times in the last twenty-four hours — all in the Langthorne area. And on four of those occasions the Mercedes has hit within ten vehicles. And always heading in the right direction.'

'So this Tremaine has been following Shaun about?'

'Well, vehicles linked to him have. They're both hire cars. He may well have minions doing his dirty work for him. The hire car company is based in Dover — *Castle Hires.* This company has intelligence of its own linking it to Tremaine's drug supply and money laundering, according to the MET. They've not done many enquiries there for fear of spooking them, but they've been counting them in and out. There's a shit load of car registrations here. You can be sure they're both being used by this Tremaine. You can't easily leave the area without pinging ANPR at some point. The Transit van has far less hits but I reckon it's still in the area.'

'So we should assume one or both are going to be wherever Shaun is?'

'Yeah. Maybe the Transit with Shaun's wife and kid in the back — ready to hand them back when he does what he's asked?'

'Maybe. And what happens to Alice for that to happen?'

'I don't know.'

'I think I do,' George said.

'I've nominated them both on ANPR, with the same silent marker. If they hit, I'll get a call.'

'No, Ryker. We're past that now. Put it out on general. Let's have ANPR and marked units all looking out for them. We need that van. I reckon keeping that van and Shaun apart might be the only way of preventing anyone else getting hurt. That's assuming they haven't met already.'

'Understood. I'll get it broadcast out to everyone.'

'Do that. When Whittaker gets here I'll ask him to call up and put his weight behind it. We need to find that van, Ryker. It's all that's left.'

'Understood.'

'How did you get on at the ex's house?'

'All locked up. The car was on the drive, the house is immaculate. All I got was her parents' address and I intended on going up there to see them after checking in here. I figured they might be able to give some background that could be of use.'

'How do you intend to play it with the parents?'

'I was just going to ask them a few questions about Carol. See if she's in a new relationship, that sort of thing.'

'They don't even know she's missing, Ryker, don't forget that.'

'Shit! You're right, I'd forgotten.'

'It'll be a massive shock to them, too, Ryker. The parents will need to be managed carefully.'

'You reckon I should think again?'

George took a moment. 'Not at all, actually. Maybe you're the best person to go and speak to them. We just need to be telling them what we know at this stage — that their daughter was snatched by somebody trying to get to Shaun. That should get them talking at least.'

'I wonder how they'll take that?'

'You want me to come to you? I'm happy to talk to them.'

'No, you're right. I can do this.'

'Whittaker will send someone out to them as one of his first actions. If you don't want to do it, it will get done. But, like I said, I think you're the right person. If there's one thing you're good at it's getting information out of people. Whittaker will probably send uniform, once people that look like police officers turn up it all starts to become very real. They might clam up.'

'No problem. I'll head straight up there.'

'Great. And, Ryker . . . How did you get the parents' address from staring at the outside of a locked house?'

'You're not the only one who can get things done, George.'

George seemed to be trying to stifle a chuckle. 'Good girl. Follow that up. I'll do what I can to keep the heat on this van.'

'Okay. You sure you're okay up there?'

'Yeah. I'll be fine,' George said, although he then went quiet for a few seconds. 'You know, sometimes, Ryker, there's just so much hate in the world I feel like I just can't take it.'

'I think I know what you mean.'

'Goes with the job. I really wish you didn't.'

* * *

'This is all my fault. He killed them both! My poor Becky . . . My Dean!' Alice had been repeating the same thing over and over since Shaun had bundled her into his car. He had driven away from the bungalow as fast as he could. The cute cottages and Georgian manors of St Margaret's had quickly given way to the more modern houses on the outskirts of the town of Deal. He didn't know where he was going. Then he saw a track appear on his left, it led into woodland and he had to brake hard to make it.

'What are you doing? What are you doing!' Alice wailed. The car hit a rock sticking up from the track and she whacked her head on the car roof from the jolt. Shaun continued until he could pull round enough to be concealed from the road.

'Stop it!' Shaun bellowed at the sobbing Alice as she started going back over the same words again. He shocked her enough to stop her for just a second.

'You don't understand, you don't understand! This is all my fault. I did this. You don't understand.'

Shaun reached over, and grabbed her roughly by the head. He pulled her into his chest, wrapping her up in a firm hug.

'It's okay,' he said. 'It's okay now. There wasn't anything you could have done. You're safe. We can sort this out. We can sort it *all* out.'

He felt her head shake under his arm. 'It's my fault,' she sobbed. 'He was there for me.'

'Calm down, Alice. We'll talk it out.' He held onto her for a minute or more. Her sobbing calmed down so that it was little more than a sniff, though her head still twitched with rushed intakes of air. 'That's better Alice. None of this is your fault. That man back there, he killed those people. There was nothing you could have done, okay? Nothing.'

'Those people? I loved those people! They were everything to me . . . everything!' The wailing started again and he hugged her firmly, waiting until she calmed back down.

'Tell me what happened?' he said.

Alice sat back up. She moved her hair out of her eyes. 'Jake. He came round to see me. My sister doesn't know anything about it.'

'About what, Alice? What's going on?'

She turned to face him. Her face was flushed red, her cheeks marked with streaked mascara. She had smears of blood on her cheeks, but Shaun reckoned it was from his own bleeding forearms.

'I needed a job and Jake got me a job. He knows people and he said he could. Next thing I knew I get this job without really trying. Down the port, doing the intelligence admin. I was there like a week and Jake comes to my house when Dean's out. He tells me some stuff, about lorries and cars coming through. He said they would have gear on them. He tells me to make sure they get stopped.'

'And you did?'

'I stopped most of them, but missed a couple. I didn't realise it was such an issue. Jake went mad, he came back round again, got me on my own. He was so angry that I had let some through and he . . .' She was consumed by sobs again. Shaun let her compose herself until she could continue. 'He forced himself on me. We got a little way and then I pushed him off, I hit him as hard as I could and he just smiled! He said that I should do as I was told, that I had to do what he told me in the future *like a good little bitch*. He said if I didn't then he'd tell my sister about how I'd fucked him. I never did — I never did anything, but she was so into him. I tried to talk to her. I wanted her to know what sort of a bloke he was but she turned on me. I'd never seen her like that. She wouldn't have it, she said it was my fault. Said I'd led him on and I was a slut. We'd never argued — not like that.'

'So Jake asked you to do more for him down the port?'

'Lots more. I never saw him again though. He would just text or call. His information was good — I was getting loads of really good stops in at work. Jess thought I was great and life was good — it was great with Dean . . .' Her face scrunched up again. She covered her mouth with her hand. Shaun waited until she found her strength. 'I knew my sister was going through it, I knew what sort of a bloke Jake was. I couldn't get to see her, I knew he was stopping her going out, stopping her talking to me. I tried to be places I thought she might go so we could talk. But I couldn't get to her. Then she just turns up out of the blue and all beaten up by him. I thought she had finally seen him for what he is. My God, Shaun, she never stood a chance!'

'No she didn't, Alice. Neither of them did.'

'I saw it. He stabbed her. It was like she was a piece of meat — he just kept stabbing her. He wasn't human. I've never seen anything like it. Then he held the knife to me, but I saw that *he* was so scared! I could see it in his eyes! I tried to tell him everything was okay. I tried to tell him. He was so scared. He was shaking and talking about the devil. He kept saying that I hadn't seen what he had. He kept asking me over and over who knew about me, who knew about him telling me information about lorries to stop. But I'd told no one, Shaun. Not a soul. Why would I? I think I'm going to be sick!' Alice pushed her door open and bundled out of the car. She slammed the door shut and stumbled into the woodland. Shaun could hear her retching, bent double and out of sight.

He pulled the phone from his pocket. This was his chance. He pressed a button and the screen lit up, the only stored number across its centre. He hesitated, peering back through the window where Alice was stood facing away, her hands on her head, a picture of devastation. She didn't deserve any of this. But he had to stay strong — it wasn't about her. It was about him. And his son.

Shaun pressed the button to call.

Chapter 27

'You okay, George?' Whittaker surprised him with the question. He had anticipated Whittaker's fury when he arrived and especially when he brought him further up to date. It had been nothing like their usual exchanges: Whittaker stayed silent then walked with George round to the back of the property where he peered in through the hole in the rear patio door. Whittaker had kept his distance, obviously aware of the forensic work that needed to be done first, but he was close enough to see three sets of dead eyes and a whole load of blood. He still hadn't spoken to George when he walked back round to the front of the property and busied himself talking to other officers, making phone calls and barking out orders. George had slunk away to sit in the front seat of his car, the door hanging wide open. He was reflecting on everything he had seen and everything he had done leading up to that point. Oddly enough it was the silent treatment from an old friend that seemed to be on his mind the most.

Now the chief inspector was stood at the open door, asking him if he was okay, his expression softer, maybe even carrying some concern. George instantly felt a little better.

'Yes, Major, I know I fucked up. I should have been straight with you from the start.'

'Shaun Carter told you not to tell anyone. He trusted you with that and you didn't betray him. Part of me can understand that.'

'It wasn't just out of some loyalty. I was just trying to get his family back. I thought that was best done under the radar — to start with, at least.'

'You were wrong, George. I know you have little faith in this organisation but you should have had more faith in me.'

'I'm sorry. You're right. I should have.'

'I could have given you support, a few more eyes and ears out looking for Shaun might have made the difference.'

'I know.'

Whittaker stood in a black stab vest with a radio strapped to his chest. He cocked his head abruptly to an excited update — a female voice from the control room. George had the car set on, too. He turned it up.

'Confirm you have a sighting of the van? M20 coastbound?'

'Yes, yes. Lane One. No reaction to the marked vehicle at this time. We have not made any attempt to stop it. Can we have additional resources to assist please?'

'More eyes and ears, George.' Whittaker almost smiled. 'You see what they can do?'

'Yes, sir.' George took a long breath. 'Sir . . . I—'

Whittaker interrupted with a sigh that turned into words. 'Go ahead, George. And for fuck's sake, man, get this finished. And peacefully.'

George reached for his door. 'I'll do what I can.'

The Skoda fired up. George saw Whittaker step away in his side mirror and he raised his hand as he accelerated away.

His radio provided an update on the van's location. He pressed his radio button to transmit.

'Control, this is DS Elms. Can you show me en route to this van please?'

'All received, Sergeant Elms. I have marked you up.'

'Thank you. For all patrols monitoring this channel, can I just reiterate . . . it is highly possible that we have two civilian victims in that van.'

'You were on talk-through, Sergeant. We have already broadcast this and there are patrols getting ahead of the van with a stinger option among others. The marked unit is hanging back. The van has made no reaction at this time.'

'Understood, Control.'

George discarded his radio. He moved towards activating his lights and sirens just as his speakers were filled with the sound of a ringing phone. The screen read as *Jess.*

'Shit timing, Jess,' he said, his teeth clenched. Then he answered the call. 'Jess! No news I'm afraid.' George had to brake hard as he abandoned an overtake past some slow-moving traffic. 'Can I call you back when I have something more?'

'He's just called. He sounded really upset.' Jess was breathy, and hard to understand.

Traffic was now flowing steadily in the other direction and he couldn't see another opportunity to overtake. He cursed his luck. 'Sorry, Jess, who's upset?'

'Shaun. He just called me. I've never heard him like that before.'

'Shaun?' George now focused on the call. 'What did he say?'

'That he was sorry. That things just got out of control and he didn't mean for any of it to happen. He sounded so down. I asked him to come down and see me — or I would go and see him, but he wasn't interested. He wouldn't even let me speak, really. He just wanted to tell me he was sorry. He told me he couldn't make me understand and he had to go.'

'Okay. He didn't give you any idea where he was at all? Or where he might go?' The response vehicle slowed naturally.

'He said he was going back. He said he had to go back.' Jess said.

'Going back?'

'Yeah. What's going on, George? Go back where?'

'I'm not sure, Jess. Don't worry, I'll find him and I'll make sure he's okay.'

'Please do. And let me know when you do.'

The phone beeped confirmation that the call had finished. George once again pressed to transmit on his radio.

'Control, this is DS Elms. Can you confirm how many patrols you have making their way to this call please?'

'Yes, yes. We have eight patrols making way. Four traffic units are tracking just a few minutes out and we have the remaining patrols plotting ahead.'

'Received. I'm a little way off, Control, and there are enough making way. Can you show me cancelling please.'

'Received that, Sergeant.'

George moved back to his phone, it connected on the first ring.

'DCI John Whittaker.'

'Sir, George Elms.'

'Elms. You left me minutes ago. If you're ringing to tell me about another fucking mess already I will be shoving something long and robust up your arse, George. No lube.'

'Well, at least I know you're not angry at me anymore.'

'I'm angry at everyone right now. It's getting things done here.'

'Sir, can you get angry at Firearms. I need a plain car, preferably two, to go into Langthorne. Right away.'

'What have you got?'

'Well, a hunch really. Shaun has made contact with his girlfriend. He wasn't making much sense, but I think he's back in Langthorne. I'm going to have a look. Can you arrange for an unmarked firearms patrol to assist with an area search for the Mercedes hire car? I gave you the details. They *have* to be unmarked.'

'I can, George, but right now we have firearms resources responding to the van sighting. This hunch of yours . . . is it strong enough to start pulling resources away from that?'

'There are enough patrols to deal with that. I'd actually feel better if there were fewer guns there, to be honest.'

'Fine. But if you're wrong, George . . . No lube, old boy. You remember that.'

'Understood. When you speak to Firearms, can you ask them to use the viaduct where it crosses Foord Road as their starting point.'

'Will do.'

George cut the call and fired up the sirens.

Chapter 28

Shaun parked the Vectra on Bradstone Road in Langthorne. It was a quiet, residential street with a large gap in the housing filled by some wasteland on one side and the rear of a storage warehouse on the other. The viaduct loomed above him as he stood by one of its massive pillars. The base was more than two car lengths wide. Patches of the red brickwork had been replaced over the years; the brighter, newer bricks stood out from the Victorian structure like slash wounds. The car was level with steps that led up to where access to the viaduct was possible. It was a similar position to where he had parked to speak to Bobby Leonard.

He stood up out of the car, shut the door behind him and put the burn phone to his ear. Alice stayed in the passenger seat, still and silent. She looked totally lost, staring forward as if she had run out of tears. He had told her that he was driving her to the police station but that he had to pull over to make a call. If she'd been thinking straight, she would have questioned where they had stopped but, lucky for him, her thoughts were elsewhere.

'I'm where you said. Let's do this.'

There's a bin by the bottom of the steps. Put the wire and the gun in there. You won't be needing those anymore.' That same voice. So matter-of-fact, so arrogant. Shaun had never hated anyone so much.

'I can't just put a gun in a bin.'

'It won't be staying there. It will be cleaned up behind you, don't worry. You will need the gloves and the tape.'

'What for? Why can't you just meet me here? You can have the car with her in it — I'll just walk away with my son.'

'Because you're not in charge, Shaun. Because you're not quite finished.'

'Like fuck I'm not! I've done everything you asked, more than you asked in fact. You've had enough from me. Give me back my son and go fuck with someone else!' Shaun could feel his emotions getting the better of him, spilling over.

'You're close, Shaun. You've done well, but don't start thinking you've earned the right to piss me off. The gloves are for you. Put them on first. Then you will need to wipe the gun and the wire down with the cloth provided. Put them all in the bag and put that in the bin. Do it now.'

Shaun opened the boot. The shoebox was sat in the middle and towards the left and inside, in a clip seal bag, were the gloves. They had an odd softness, and a fine, white powder drifted from the cuffs as he pulled them on. It had been a while since he had come across the powdered type. He looked around him as he leant in to wipe down the gun before pushing it into the bag. He sensed that Alice was looking out at him as he passed her door and dropped the bag in the bin. He walked back to the rear of the car where the boot was still up. Only the Gorilla tape remained in the box.

Shaun picked up the phone. 'Done,' he growled.

'The tape is for Alice. You need to cover her mouth so she doesn't shout. If she attracts attention to you and you are challenged, this is all over. Do you understand?'

Shaun stepped away from the car and lowered his voice. 'For Alice? No, I don't understand! I think she's had enough shit for one day, don't you? I can walk away from the car and she's yours.

'The tape is for her. And Shaun, you will need to make sure she understands that she needs to do as you say or this will not work and she will fuck this up for you at the very last moment. You need to walk her up those steps and out onto the viaduct. Take her to the spot where you had your long conversation with Bobby Leonard.'

'Why would you have me walk her up there? If you think I'm going to—'

'I think you will do what you are asked when you remember the alternative, Shaun, and I think you are starting to piss me off! You do not want me to lose patience, Shaun, trust me on that. There are ways of speeding you up — of stopping you questioning me — but your son would not like it.'

'Jesus! She's had enough! Why up there?'

'Because it suits my needs. You may not have taken the time to enjoy the view the last time you were up there, but Bobby Leonard could be seen from any number of houses, cars or vantage points. I am watching, Shaun, just like I was watching Bobby Leonard. And he understood just how easy it would be for me to blend in and disappear, never to be seen again, if he didn't do what I instructed.'

'Who *are* you?'

'There are some things, Shaun, that you may never know. I appreciate that, as a police officer, this doesn't sit easy.'

'We'll see about that.'

'I guess we will. You're out of time. When I can see you are in position I will call you — a little demonstration, should you need it, that you are being watched. I am close, Shaun, and I have your son.' The line went silent.

Shaun slipped the phone back into his pocket, pushed the boot shut and lingered on it, leaning so it took his weight, his eyes moving around the rows of housing and parked cars in front of him. He turned to take in the view behind him; it was more of the same. Further in the distance was a Tesco Express and a Citroen Garage in front of a block of flats. The man was right: stood out on the top of that viaduct, someone watching him could be anywhere.

His focus moved back to the task at hand. His gloves had already turned transparent from his sweat. He looked through the rear window to the back of Alice's head. She still stared forward, no doubt still lost in the nightmares of her day. Shaun would like nothing more than to wrap her up and tell her everything was going to be all right, to take her to a police station and to make her safe. But he couldn't. Not now. He was so close to the end. There would be no fooling her now, he would have the element of surprise, it would give him a few seconds and he would have to be aggressive. He had the Gorilla tape in his hand. It was unravelled a little but it was still sticky. He checked around him for a final time, careful that there was no one else about. When he was satisfied he stepped forward.

He wrenched the door open and climbed in immediately. Alice turned to the noise and Shaun was ready with the tape, he pushed it firmly on her face, wrapping it swiftly over her mouth and around her head. She raised her hands to pull it off, but Shaun was ready for that too. He took hold of her wrists firmly and pulled her out of the car, twisting her round and snapping handcuffs expertly over both her wrists as he had done to so many deserving criminals. He cuffed her behind her back so she couldn't get at the tape. She tried to scream but it was a muffled noise, nothing that was going to travel any distance. He wrapped the tape round another couple of times to be sure, secretly relieved that she wouldn't be able to plead with him. He didn't think he could take that. He slammed the Vectra door shut and pushed Alice towards the steps.

'We're walking up,' he told her tersely.

The steps were steep and numerous. His head felt light half way up and he had to pause for just a moment. He'd barely eaten and hadn't slept for twenty-four hours and he was running purely on nervous energy. He had to keep pushing Alice in her lower back each time she stalled on the steps but at least she was making less noise. They got to the top and Shaun shoved her through the same gap in the fence he had used to approach Bobby Leonard.

The conditions were identical to when he had last stepped onto the top of Langthorne's viaduct: the same warming sun, the same breeze moving the few stoic weeds that had forced their way through the grey gravel. This time, however, the track was live, it buzzed and crackled and he pushed against the low wall, over which he could see the hundred-foot drop. His stomach twisted in a tense knot, a car passing underneath looked like a toy in the scale model of a town. He could see down at an angle where floral tributes lay against the brick base. He hadn't noticed them when on the ground. He stopped at the point where he was pretty sure Bobby had stood for his last moments on this earth. The brickwork carried black layers of grime, but the words scratched into it looked fresh: *where heaven ends.* Alice was still in front of him. He pushed her to the ground and she went with no resistance, seemingly on her way down already. She twisted to get her back against the wall, her legs splayed open and her head rocked to the side. He thought her breathing sounded quieter after the initial panic of being forcibly taped and cuffed. His phone rang.

'You made it.'

Shaun felt confused: the voice was the same but it sounded different somehow, distant maybe.

He had to concentrate to reply. He blinked a few times, his eyelids suddenly heavy. 'I made it. So what now?' He suddenly felt sick and folded to his right — away from Alice. Nothing came.

'I think you know, Shaun. This has to end now.'

'My . . . son . . .' Shaun struggled with the words. He could hardly breathe properly. He leant on the wall on his elbows, staring out through eyes that were quickly losing their sharpness. He tried to stand back up. Far below, a silver Mercedes slipped out from a row of parked cars and moved towards him, disappearing under the viaduct.

'Goodbye, Shaun.'

Shaun felt numb, he'd lost the feeling in his legs and he dropped to his knees. He heard the phone hit the gravel. He leaned over to Alice and struggled to pull the tape from her mouth. Her lips had drained of their colour, her eyes shut. He tugged one of the gloves off to feel for a pulse, a clump of the white powder mixed with sweat fell to the ground and he peered at it. *Fucking fentanyl!*

'Alice!' he said, unable to stop himself from sniggering inanely as if *fentanyl* was the punch line to one of the best jokes he'd heard. 'The bastard, eh?' Then his eyes blurred further at the same time as a rumble in his head built like thunder. It had come on swiftly and it was getting closer. He tried to turn towards it but realised that he was falling forward and then his head met with something solid that was vaguely cold on his forehead and vibrated quickly against his cheek bone. And then everything was dark.

Chapter 29

Emily Ryker took a second before she knocked the door, a second to turn and take in the view from the very top of the North Downs. The green hills rolled away into the distance with the town of Langthorne some distance below, a grey square, like a scab, over an area of outstanding natural beauty.

'Mrs Pato?' Emily smiled and held up her warrant card for the woman to see.

'Yes.' Anna Pato stood in her doorway and seemed to be looking beyond Emily's shoulder as if she might be expecting someone else.

'Sorry to turn up out of the blue like this. Do you mind if I pop in for a quick chat?'

Mrs Pato backed into her own house, her face a clear expression of shock. She had long, dark hair that fell in ringlets, and attractive brown eyes that were deep and surrounded by laughter lines. A number of wooden bangles clacked on her wrist as she gestured to her left. Emily walked into a large kitchen that also had a seating area. Mrs Pato leant on the benches and crossed her arms.

'I'm, err, sorry if I took a while to answer the door. I was up the garden.'

Emily could see the garden through the kitchen window. It was a long area of turf, broken up by a summerhouse half way up and flowerbeds that cut in from both sides in imaginative patterns. In the bright sunshine it was a blur of colour. 'It's a beautiful garden.'

'What did you need to speak to me about? We don't usually have the police up here.'

'No, I can imagine. It's about your daughter, Carol. When was the last time you spoke to her?'

'Carol? Oh, about twenty minutes ago. Is there a problem?'

Emily could do nothing to hide her surprise. 'Twenty minutes ago?'

'Yes, she was just making sure I was in. She's on her way. I thought it was her at the door and that maybe she had lost her key. What is this all about? Is she in trouble?'

'No!' Emily stumbled a little, thinking fast. 'She's not in any trouble at all. She was reported missing is all — to us I mean. To the police. I err . . . I was coming up here to see what you might know about it. Seems you know a lot more than I anticipated! Are you sure it was Carol you spoke to?'

'Well, yes.' Mrs Pato clicked her fingers, her face contorting to a sort of half smile. 'I bet it was Shaun. I bet he reported her missing. Am I right? She did tell me that something like this might happen.'

'Shaun? I'm not sure who made the report, Mrs Pato. Who is Shaun and why would he report her missing?'

Mrs Pato waved her hand dismissively. 'Please, call me Anna. My daughter was married to a police officer — Shaun Carter. Do you know him?'

'Shaun Carter . . . The name rings a bell.'

'Well, anyway, their marriage went through a very bad patch — one they never recovered from. It seems Shaun felt the grass was greener elsewhere and he was having relations with another woman. Well, it all came out, as it always does, and Carol quite rightly threw him out on the street. He was all very sorry of course, and for a period I did think she might be softening to him — but it hasn't happened. Well, Shaun, you see, he became a bit of a pain. He would turn up here as well as at her house saying that he wanted to talk to her, playing on the guilt of not living together as a family anymore and how it was damaging Tyler. I mean, the cheek of the man!'

'How long ago was this?'

'Well, ongoing really. He's been giving her hell for a few months, she's been under real pressure just trying to keep everyone happy and I think it was really starting to get to her. Then she met someone new. Nothing serious or anything, but just someone that she can spend some time with and maybe start enjoying her life again.' Anna smiled warmly. 'This new man runs his own business, he's wealthy it would seem, very wealthy, and he's been treating Carol very well. It was just a few dinners out to start with, a show or two, and he always liked to include Tyler. But this weekend he asked to take them away for a mini holiday. Well, Tyler you see, he's a big football fan — loves Tottenham Hotspur and so Terry, well he got them all tickets for the game on Sunday afternoon. They made a bit of a weekend of it, went up on Friday.'

'Terry? That's the new man, is it?'

'That's right. He picked them up on Friday — from here, actually. Handsome man, genuine smile. Good teeth. I only said hello, but my Carol seems very happy and she's not a bad judge — well, not generally.'

'Do you know anything more about Terry? A surname or a contact number?'

'I have a contact number. Their weekend didn't get off to a very good start it would seem! Carol called me Friday evening on a number I didn't recognise. Her phone had been stolen — she thinks she was pickpocketed on the train on the way up. I don't think it made too much of a difference. I think she was actually quite relieved she wouldn't have to lie if Shaun called. I don't think she was looking forward to lying to him.'

'Lying?'

'Yes. You see football and Tottenham Hotspur, that's something Tyler and his dad do. That's kind of *their thing* and Shaun would be furious if he knew that the new man was taking Tyler up to watch a game. Obviously she will need to tell him about what's going on — none of us want him to hear it from Tyler. But at least the weekend would have been uninterrupted. She wasn't going to go, but I think she's been so unhappy recently and under so much pressure that she just thought well, why not, you know? So I assume that Shaun has been his usual dramatic self, called Carol to find her mobile isn't answering or is switched off or whatever and has called to report her missing.'

'So Tyler is with her?'

'Yes. I spoke to him on the phone too. He was quite insistent on telling me how Tottenham Hotspurs won and what the score was. It means nothing to me, you understand, but I try and act delighted for him. He's only ten!'

'And they are both on their way here now?'

'Yes. I believe Terry is dropping them off. So you can have it from all three of them if you need to. There really is no need for any police concern. I'm just sorry you appear to have wasted your time coming out today.'

'Terry's coming here too?'

'Yes, they were getting in a taxi at the station.' There was a knock at the door. Emily snapped her head towards it. Anna smiled. 'Talk of the devil!'

'Er . . . Anna . . .' Emily wasn't sure what she intended to say, but it didn't matter anyway, Anna was already at the door. Soon she was pulling it open and explaining that the police were here. 'You'll never guess what that idiot Shaun has gone and done now!'

A well-built man with shocking blue eyes against dark stubble was already stepping over the threshold. His gaze locked onto Emily as she stood in the kitchen. He wasn't smiling. A young boy with dark hair squirmed to get past him.

'Talk of the devil,' Emily whispered to herself as she slipped her phone out of her pocket. She selected George Elms's number and held the phone to her ear. The man brushed the other two women lightly aside. Three steps and he was on her. Emily backed away until she collided with a kitchen unit behind her.

'George! They're all here! Him too! Marybee, Crete Road—' It was all she could manage before the phone was snatched from her hand.

Chapter 30

George pulled into Bradstow Road and saw the Vectra straight away. He accelerated towards it, parking across its front to block it in as best he could. It turned out there was no need — now he was close, he could see there was no one in it. The steps up to the viaduct were on the other side of the Vectra. He took them two at a time. At the top, a concrete path split two ways: one led into a housing estate and the other ran parallel with the viaduct. He jogged the path, back on himself until it ended at a steep bank that led up to the viaduct where a section of fence was damaged. He scrambled through and out onto the grey gravel. Straight off, he could see somebody. He thought it had to be Shaun. He was lying on his front, his head turned away and over the outside track, his arms by his side. George could hear the inside live rail buzzing. He had called up to ask for it to be turned off but they obviously hadn't managed it yet. Sometimes it could take a while for messages to be passed through to the British Transport Police.

'Shaun!' George shouted. There was no movement. 'Shaun! We need to talk.' George considered the risks of both the live rail and the live trains and started making his way towards the prone figure. He checked his watch. It was thirty seconds to 4 p.m. He didn't know the timetables well and couldn't remember if the high-speed link to London was on the half hour or on the hour. The viaduct wasn't as wide as he had imagined from the ground: two tracks — enough distance for two trains to pass, but the track looked close to the brick wall on both sides. If the viaduct had been built today, it would have been twice as wide. The track sat on grey shingle, which cambered away on each side to the blackened wall. He reckoned the side of the train must pass pretty damned close to that wall. He didn't want to find out how close.

George got nearer. 'Shaun!' Still no movement at all. Something was wrong. He was half way to Shaun and now he could see a second pair of legs, pointing directly out, finishing almost against the rail. These were attached to a girl, who was sitting up and likewise motionless. From the pictures he'd seen at her home, the girl was clearly Alice. There wasn't a flicker from either of them. George heard a sound like a distant wind. The sound built and the ground started to agitate the gravel beneath his feet.

Shit!

George ran at the two figures. The noise was building and he didn't have much time. He got to Shaun and grabbed him by the shoulders, his head was heavy, he leaked blood from above his eye. George heaved and Shaun's torso fell awkwardly into Alice's lap. She was still sat up behind him, her head slumped to the side. He grabbed her legs by the ankles as the gathering wind became a roar. A horn blared so loudly that it seemed to surge through his body like an electric shock. He pushed Alice's legs flat against the wall and threw himself on top of both Shaun and Alice, hooking his right arm under Shaun's torso and hanging his left arm over the low wall. The wind struck first; the train was moving so fast it was pushing a huge pocket of air with it that hit George in the back like a sucker punch and slammed his legs into the wall, his knees banging off the girl's head. A split second later, the wind direction reversed like a rolling wave crashing on a beach and an invisible force nipped and tugged at him, beckoning him towards the gigantic wheels and the irresistible force of the train. The noise was terrific, the deep *woomph* as it passed now replaced by the squeal of metal wheels gripping metal rails. George had his eyes scrunched tightly shut but he could feel the beast passing inches from his head, each carriage taking its turn to roar in his ear. He could feel the heat as electricity sparked and fizzled and the air stank of scorched metal and fumes.

And then it was gone.

George pushed himself into a sitting position and groaned as panic was replaced by relief. He watched the rear end of the train shrink away and disappear, the mechanical clamour yielding gradually to the buzz of the live rail once more. He turned to Alice and felt hurriedly for a pulse. He couldn't find one, but then his hands were shaking and his fingers numb. He put his cheek to her mouth; there was perhaps a light breath. A quick survey of Shaun revealed the same. He picked up his police radio and pressed the raised panic button. That would give him ten seconds of air time across the network. He tried to speak. He could only manage a moan and a feeble cry but he knew that would be enough. They would find him. He crawled a few yards to vomit.

Chapter 31

The firearms team had been nearby. Alice and Shaun were slipping into respiratory arrest and George watched as they were treated the only way they could be in the field. Both were stabbed in the outside quarter of the thigh with a Naloxone pen. It was essentially a very concentrated and very sudden dose of adrenalin and it was often very effective. Alice had taken two doses before they had seen any sign of recovery. But it had come. In Alice's case it had improved her condition but she was far from out of the woods and George was glad to see the green overalls of two paramedics arriving at the top of the viaduct. Shaun was starting to respond to vocal instructions from the officers. Shaun managed a few words, one of them being 'fentanyl' and the medical men reacted by putting on additional masks and gloves and ordering the police officers away. The officers walked over to George.

'You okay? You feel okay?'

'I feel like I nearly got hit by a train.' George managed a grin. 'I'm okay.'

'Did you touch them?'

'I laid on top of them. It's not how it sounds.'

The officers didn't smile back. 'You need to get checked out. Looks like fentanyl poisoning. It's normally fast acting but it doesn't have to be. Do you feel lightheaded? Anything unusual?'

'I feel fine. I'm okay.'

'There's another ambulance on its way. We'll take you down to it and get you checked out, Sarge. This is some serious shit. Your man's got some powder in his gloves and the paramedics reckon the girl got a hit from the tape that was on her mouth. She's probably absorbed it through her gums. They're very concerned about her.'

'Good God, it'll be enough to kill them. He needs them dead'

'Who?'

'I don't know for sure. But I bet these two do. Can I talk to them? From a distance of course?'

'They're not making much sense. We'll walk you down to the ambulance. They're going to bring them down shortly. You might be able to talk to them then.'

George could see that both Alice and Shaun had oxygen masks strapped to their faces. Shaun was sitting up but his eyes were glazed, his head rolling on his neck as if he was drunk. Alice was still lying flat, her eyes closed. He wouldn't get anything out of them — for now, at least. He stood and walked with one of the officers, the other stayed to maintain the scene. George lifted his radio, turned the dial to turn up the local channel — and swore at the excited update coming through.

* * *

'Control, the van has now reacted and is making off! It was in Lane One, passing the slip for Capel and has made a last second manoeuvre. The van is now increasing speed towards the roundabout at the end of the slip. Stand by for direction of travel!' PC Pete Hemingway released the button on the radio but kept it clamped to his mouth. PC Ellie Missen was at the wheel. The van suddenly showed brake lights and Ellie had to be evasive to prevent the marked BMW crashing into its rear.

'The white van takes the first. We are now in the general direction of Dover.'

'Received that, Tango One. Vehicle is now making off. You are authorised Phase One pursuit. Confirm you have activated lights and sirens.'

Pete tutted. 'Yes! Yes, Control. Speed eight zero. Passing The Plough Inn public house on the nearside. Speed increasing, now nine zero. Will be held up by slow-moving traffic ahead.'

'They want us to keep up its chuff or what?' Ellie said, her voice strained. 'I thought there was a kid in there?'

'We've not been cancelled. We can't lose them.'

'It's heading into the town — it'll be slowed up in the traffic. Is there anyone plotted ahead or are they all up on the motorway?'

Pete peered ahead. The van was caught up in a stream of traffic in front. There was traffic in the opposite direction too. The van moved out and a cloud of dust trailed out from behind it as it met with the loose gravel and stones. The first two cars in the opposite direction swerved to avoid it, the second swerve was particularly tight, but a third car didn't see it in time. The van tried to swerve back in, its speed still more than eighty miles per hour. Its fate was inevitable. Its rear quarter struck the car behind and the van was spun enough for its wheels to be out of line. It hopped once then flipped almost instantly. The first flip was so severe the roof just kissed the tarmac. The axle hit hard on the second rotation. Now all Pete was aware of was a lot more dust, a terrific noise and a white blur disappearing up into a grass bank and a row of trees.

Ellie braked hard. Pete was out while it still rolled. He sprinted up the bank. The van was the wrong way around and on its side, its front towards him as he ran forward. The windscreen was almost completely gone and there was no sign of the driver. Pete made it to the front door and peered in. The cab was empty. The seatbelt still hung beside the driver's seat. A wooden partition made it impossible to see into the back. The bank got steeper and the back of the van had dug into the mud, jamming a rear door open. Pete braced himself. He heard footfalls as someone else ran up the other side. He looked in.

Empty.

'What you got?' Ellie said.

Pete unclipped a torch from his belt and shone it in to be sure. No sign of anyone — just a push bike lying on its side — professional looking, its front wheel spinning slowly. No blood, no sign of anyone thrown from the van. Nothing.

'Pete!' Ellie called out.

He turned and looked further up the bank. Ellie was stood over something. He caught up with her. It was a male, his head at an angle, clear trauma to the neck and head. His eyes lifeless.

Pete exhaled heavily. Ellie was already giving the update over the radio.

Chapter 31

'Empty?' George said out loud. *The van was fucking empty!*

'What's that?' said the firearms officer walking down the steps behind him.

George ignored him and tugged his phone from his pocket. He needed to speak to Ryker. He saw that he already had a missed call from her and he pressed to listen to the message.

They had made it to the bottom of the steps. The firearms officer was talking to the paramedic and saw them both looking in his direction. Ryker's voice came through: *'George! They're all here! Him too! Marybee, Crete Road!'*

George sprinted for his car. He fumbled with the keys, yanked at the handle and started the engine before he had even pulled the door shut. He knew Ryker, he knew her better than he knew most people in the world. And he knew when she was genuinely scared.

The radio was busy with updates from the van crash. He had to calm his hands to switch to another channel. 'Control, this is Sergeant Elms. Can you run an address through for me, please? Urgent.'

'Go ahead.'

'Marybee, Crete Road, Langthorne. Run it local, see if we know anything.'

'Stand by.' It seemed like an age. George wasn't good at *standing by*. The controller came back. *'Marybee, Crete Road, Langthorne. Last linked to a Mrs Anna Pato. She was the informant for a domestic abuse incident involving her daughter, Carol Carter in January of this year. It was recorded as a secondary incident only. No crime. She's the only person we have listed. She shows as the mother of the victim.'*

George beat the steering wheel as he turned onto a main road and suddenly came into rush hour traffic. Bumper to bumper. He killed the sirens so he didn't panic anyone into closing the gaps even more. His attention moved back to his phone. When his call got through, John Whittaker sounded harassed.

'George.'

'Sir. I need some more of your eyes and ears.'

'I'm very quickly running out of anything here, George, as you can imagine. I'm holding a scene with three bodies, we now have a crashed van and of all the times, a burnt-out car's just been found near Sandwich with what looks like human remains in it.'

'Sandwich? The missing Polish guy?'

'Yeah. Some dog walker's stood with it for now. He's ex job. I might have to ask him to come out of retirement to man the scene at this rate.'

'Sorry, sir. This is urgent, too.'

'What is?'

'Ryker's been sniffing around Shaun's ex. She was on her way to her mum's address at the top of Langthorne — Crete Road. I think she's got some answers up there.'

'I got copied into some intelligence for her from the Met. More around this Nowak character.'

'She called me, around quarter of an hour ago. She sounded rattled. Ryker isn't the sort to sound rattled. The call was cut all too sudden and she said something about them all being there. *Him too.* We have to assume she means this Benjamin Tremaine, right?'

'That's all she said?'

'It sounds like the phone was snatched. I'm on my way but I'm stuck in fucking traffic. Can you see if there's anyone closer?'

'You want me to send someone right to the door? What sort of threat do we have?'

'I have no idea. I think they might be expecting someone to the door too, if she was found on her phone. The Mercedes . . . if you're back at your desk, can you spin it through the ANPR system?' George's car squirmed free from the stationary traffic. He pressed the horn to activate the siren again as the road opened up a little.

'That's odd, George. The ANPR camera at the top of Langthorne — it shows as inbound at 16:06 hours. Then it's outbound at 16:09.'

'It doubles back?'

'That's the last hit.'

I think Ryker's spooked them, boss. If she stumbled on them at a house they will know we're closer to them than they thought. The Mercedes will be out of play.'

'The van's out too,' Whittaker said.

'Crete Road is the one that overlooks the whole town, right up in the hills. You couldn't be there without transport. But you need to stay off the grid.'

'Taxis?'

'Maybe.'

'I'll get one of the tribe here to make a few calls to the local firms — see if anyone's had a drop up there in the last hour or so.'

'That's assuming he got there in the last hour. He might have been there the whole weekend.'

'Yeah, he might. I can start the ball rolling on an emergency warrant, George, but that might not be ready for at least an hour.'

'I'm heading up there, sir. I won't be needing a warrant. I'm fifteen minutes in this traffic.'

George killed the siren again at a red traffic light. The traffic was gridlocked in both directions. The cars did their best to shuffle forward but they were getting nowhere. He beat the steering wheel again. He tried Ryker's number again and got the expected engaged tone — again. Then his phone rang. It was Whittaker — back within two minutes.

'First call we made, George! Langthorne Taxis dropped an adult male, an adult female and a juvenile male at Marybee, Crete Road just before four this afternoon. We were put through to the driver himself. He said he had the hump as the bloke had him waiting and then cancelled him.'

'I bet he did. Change of plan.'

'I'll get some firearms together. We'll hit the door hard. I'm done fucking around with this guy now.'

George was silent long enough for Whittaker to prompt him.

'You don't think that's a good idea?'

'I'm not sure it's the best idea, boss.'

'What have you got?'

'Have you read the intel from the Met yet? Around the car hire company?'

'Skimmed it.'

'I'm sure Ryker said the Met had paid this place some attention. They supplied some registration numbers for the vehicles. They're based in Dover. They can't get here without pinging ANPR if they go the major routes.'

'You think he's made a call for them to turn out to pick him up?'

'To pick them *all* up. He cancelled the taxi because he couldn't take the rest of them in it with him.'

'Christ almighty, George. I'm looking at the intelligence around this place. There's a lot of it!'

'Any vans or lorries?'

'Yeah, a lot fewer.'

'Focus on them. Run them through, see if any of them are moving.'

'Far better to stick hostages in the back of a lorry,' Whittaker boomed.

'I reckon so. I'm ten minutes out now. See if you can get a firearms patrol there. Anyone really. If any of these hire vans are moving in this direction we need to know about it.'

Whittaker cut the call again and George turned up the police radio in the car. The officers at the scene of the van crash confirmed the driver was dead. He had ID on him — Nathaniel Soanes. He was known on the police system and recent intelligence linked him to the movement of drugs through the ports. The controller maintained a dry tone as she explained that he was also thought to be driving for Castle Hire Cars. Of course he fucking was.

Whittaker's name flashed up for a third time. 'I want good news, boss.'

'We have a box van on the move. Pinged out near Hougham — direction of Langthorne. It's pinged a mobile camera. A marked unit has a vehicle stopped out there and it must have drifted right past them. I got hold of them on the phone and they're trying to make ground. I also have the unmarked firearms patrol that assisted you earlier. They're not far behind you.'

'Ideal. Major, cancel the marked car. Tell them to let the van run. I'll talk to the firearms patrol, they can do the stop when it's committed to Crete Road. I think I might know a way of getting you a resolution without making a mess.'

'That doesn't sound like the George Elms I know and love.'

'Unless Ryker's hurt, Major. Then you'll be cleaning up for days.' George ended the call and called up on his radio for a talk-through with the firearms patrol. He was a few minutes short of Crete Road. He cancelled lights and sirens just as he crossed a bridge over the M20 motorway. There was a pull-in on the left where a bored looking woman leant on the counter of her hot-dog van, flicking through the morning paper. George bounced up onto the hard standing to wait.

Chapter 32

Emily flinched as the big man threw her phone to the floor and stamped on it. His veins stood out on his neck with the exertion and he was smiling as he straightened back up.

'What's going on, Terry?' Carol's face was a picture of surprise and horror. 'What is this all about?' the woman had a wailing voice.

'Stay out of this, Carol!' his smile had given way as he growled his instruction.

'Terry! Don't talk to me like that!'

The man spun. He moved away from Emily and he was on Carol in an instant. She was still by the front door and it swung open behind her. He threw his hand and she flinched. It missed her face, collided hard with the door and it slammed shut. The noise made the boy jump, then his face broke as if he might cry.

'*You*, don't talk to *me* like that!'

'It's not Terry, is it?' Emily called out. The man was sideways on to Emily. He had intent in his eye as he stared at Carol. The boy stood between them. Emily wanted his attention away from them.

It worked. 'What did you say?' He rounded on Emily, his face flushed red, his eyes intense — a brilliant blue surround with a black centre. He snorted like a bull.

'Benjamin, right?' Emily said. 'The conman.'

'Conman?' Carol's voice was little more than a whimper.

The man turned his attention back to her and he grabbed her by the hair.

'This has got nothing to do with you!' Carol was dragged into the living room and her mother followed them in. Carol was hitting him on the back all the way. He gave no sign that he'd felt a single blow. 'Sit the fuck down and shut up while I work out what we do here.' He flung her by her hair into the chair and she squealed in pain. The boy ran over to her. The man ducked back to the front door and twisted the key that was sticking out of the lock.

Emily saw her opportunity and she dipped into the kitchen. She re-emerged holding a bread knife. The man gave her that same smile.

'What are you going do with that, sweetheart?'

Emily wasn't sure. She was gripping it as hard as she could but it still trembled. 'Just get out. Fuck off and don't come back. This is all over. We know who you are. We know what you do. The best thing you can do is get as far away from here as you can.'

'You're right,' he said. 'But maybe I want to give myself up. I'll call the old bill right now, yeah?' He pressed three digits on his phone, then stepped towards Emily with it stretched in front of him. He spun the screen — the phone was dealing *999*. 'You talk to them,' he said. He threw the phone and Emily watched it arc towards her.

She felt the blow in her stomach without ever seeing it coming. It was a punch, but it felt like she'd been hit by a car. The force lifted her off her feet and she hit the floor, scattering a rack of wine bottles. She found herself breathless; the combination of panic, excruciating pain and the lack of oxygen had her reeling on the floor. The man had retrieved his phone and was already making a call.

'Yeah, I need a clean-up. Now!' he said.

Emily managed to get in a strained breath, which rasped in her throat.

'I don't know . . . Hang on . . .' He stepped over Emily into the kitchen, stooping to pick up the knife on his way. She must have dropped it. He turned over an envelope on the kitchen table and read from it. '*Marybee, Crete Road, Langthorne*. Yeah. Soon as.' His call ended and he looked down to where Emily was still struggling. 'Get over on the fucking sofa!' He kicked out at her and it stung against the backs of her legs. Emily got to her feet. She clutched at her stomach and stumbled across the room to the large sofa. Carol, her mum and the young boy were already sitting there obediently. The man's attention turned to his phone again and seemed to be sending a text.

'What's going on, Terry?' Carol persisted, sheepishly.

'He's not Terry.' Emily grunted, her breathing returning gradually. 'He's Benjamin Tremaine.'

He turned to them and smiled. 'The very same. And I'm no conman.'

'That's how you started out, though, right? And this whole thing's been a con from the very start.'

'What thing's that?'

'Convincing Shaun that his family got kidnapped when all you did was take them to London and pay off another family to be your stooges.'

'I just took my girlfriend to London, love. That's against the law now, is it?'

'You normally steal your girlfriend's phone when you take her away?'

'My phone? I was pickpocketed on the train.' Carol looked quickly from Emily to Benjamin. 'What is going on?'

'Seems you've got some explaining to do, mate.' Emily said. Her stomach still shot with pain, her breathing only just returning to normal.

'You know nothing.'

'I know you got desperate. Enough to convince Shaun that Carol and his son had been abducted and were in danger, just so Shaun would do your dirty work.'

'Shaun?' Carol exclaimed.

Tremaine ignored her and continued speaking to Emily. 'They weren't in any danger. Not until you knocked on the door — you think about that, copper! And I hope you've got a lot of evidence to back up what you're saying. I was in London, love. The whole weekend. Now . . . Nobody fucking moves or speaks. I've got some messages to send so I can get this shit all sorted out. You make a noise and I start getting angry — and I take it out on the boy. You understand?'

No one spoke.

'Good,' he said.

It was twenty-five minutes later when Tremaine suddenly became animated. He stood up and produced the door key from his pocket. He opened the door to reveal a big box van, its diesel engine revving and its reversing alarm beeping as it backed up the drive.

'Your lift.' He smiled at them all in turn, seeming to enjoy the scared expressions looking back. Emily was determined to deny him the satisfaction and did her best to look disinterested.

'I'm not going anywhere!' Anna spoke for the first time. Tremaine strode directly at her but she held her ground. He turned at the last so he was facing the boy and slapped him hard across the face with the back of his hand. It made a loud sound, the boy yelped in surprise and pain, the two women folded around him. Emily got to her feet.

'What the fuck!' She tried to push him but he deflected her wrists, knocked her off balance and punched her hard in the side of the head. Her vision was instantly a blur. When it began to clear, she realised she was down on one knee.

'Your fucking *lift!*' he spat. 'Anyone got a problem and I start on the boy again.' The force of the blow had pushed Tyler back into the sofa. He got to his feet, supported by his mother and his nan. They shuffled past Emily. She locked eyes with Tremaine again and walked out behind, wiping her face. The box van was parked as close to the door as the porch overhang would allow, the rear door already slid open. It was empty. Emily climbed in behind the other three and the door was slammed shut behind her. She felt it graze against her heel.

* * *

The passenger door was tugged open and a heavyset man threw himself up into the cab. 'We've got to get going,' he said, then, 'who the fuck are you?'

George Elms did his best to grimace over the collar of his borrowed polo shirt. It had *Castle Hire* stitched on the chest. 'You call like that in a fucking panic, telling us we got to get over here and dig you of the shit — you get whoever's available.'

'Just get going.'

George selected first, the gearbox crunched as he edged forward. 'Did they give you any shit?'

'Who?'

'Cunts in the back. Did they give you any shit?' George said.

'Only to start with,' the passenger grinned. 'I had to slap the fucking copper about a bit. Mouthy bitch.'

The van swung left and straightened up. It travelled along the road just a few metres, the roadblock ahead clearly visible, made up of police cars fended off at an angle across the road, their blue lights shimmering a disjointed pattern. John Whittaker stood out the front, his hat pulled down firmly on his head, the rim just above his eyes in a perfect line, his hands thrust behind his back. He looked every bit the Major.

'Fuck! Turn this shit . . .' Tremaine realised that George had a bright yellow Taser pointed at his chest. George watched as the Tremaine's eyes were fixed on the tiny red dot.

'I'm Detective Sergeant George Elms and you're under arrest for a whole host of shit. You do not have to say anything, and if you do, you will be Tasered.'

'What the f—'

The barbs burst from the end of the weapon, lodged firmly in Tremaine's chest and 20,000 volts of electricity surged between them. Instantly paralysed, he gulped in pain and slumped into the window.

'What did I just say?' George exclaimed.

The man moaned, but he had started to make a recovery and his hands moved towards the source of the pain on his chest.

'And this is from the mouthy bitch in the back.'

George pulled the trigger again.

Chapter 33

George's back was against one of the front wheels of the van, his legs straight out in front of him. Ryker sat next to him and he could feel her pushed in against his hip. Benjamin Tremaine had been conveyed away to custody in Langthorne and someone needed to sit with the van until it could be lifted and seized as part of the evidence.

'He hit me, George.'

'You said.'

'I got hit.

'You mentioned it, Ryker. I'm sorry you got hit. I got him back.'

'Do you reckon I could borrow your Taser and pop down to custody when I get back?'

'I certainly don't mind. I don't reckon Whittaker would either.'

'My name in vain?' Whittaker's booming voice came first, then his determined march as he stepped out from the side of the lorry, his hands still clasped behind his back. George looked up.

'Ryker here, Major sir, would like permission to attend custody, in order to Taser Benjamin Tremaine in the testicles, Major, sir. I was merely suggesting that you might grant permission to do so, sir.'

'I might indeed,' Whittaker said. 'I thought you two giggling school children would appreciate an early heads up. The search teams are in at Castle Car Hire. We're done rounding up the sorry looking staff down there and we're already getting reports of finds. Nothing confirmed of course, but bags of white powder in a hire car centre are always going to look a little out of place.'

'I'm sure there's a perfectly reasonable explanation.'

'I fucking hope not, George. For the amount of shit I've caused this weekend, the powers that be are going to want the seize of the century.'

'I fancy your chances there, sir.'

'So do I, George! So do I. The Mercedes has now been stopped by our friends at the Dartford Crossing. Two occupants, both under arrest. Seems they were running home.'

'Wish they'd stayed there, sir.' Ryker mused.

'I assume you kids are going off duty shortly. Lord knows it's been a long day.'

'George is taking me out to dinner, sir.' Ryker nudged George playfully in the side.

'That's right. I think I might have won a bet, sir. Which somehow means I get to pay for dinner.'

Whittaker stared down at him. He lingered a little too long, a knowing smile on his face. 'Well, you have a lovely time. And Emily, my advice if you're going out with George is to get into one of those places where they can supply something he can colour in.' Whittaker boomed his laugh out across the elevated view of Langthorne.

George's attention was then drawn to the arrival of an ambulance. It pulled past the van and swung onto the drive where Carol, her mum and son were standing with sympathetic detectives. George stood to get a better view and he felt Ryker stand next to him.

'Is someone hurt?' George said.

The rear doors opened. Carol and her son swept down the drive as Shaun Carter emerged. A uniformed officer stepped out right behind him. The family embraced, and George could hear the screams of delight from where he stood.

Whittaker made his way over to the scene. 'Just five minutes, Shaun,' he said.

Shaun pulled away from the huddle, wiped tears from his eyes and took up Whittaker's hand in an enthusiastic shake. 'Thanks so much, sir. I really appreciate it. Five minutes.'

George walked over, too. Shaun saw him coming and offered a pained smile. He stretched out his hand and George took it warmly.

'Sorry, George. I should have kept you informed. But it all got out of hand so quickly.'

'Forget about it. I'm pretty sure I understand.'

'I thought Carol . . . I thought she was dead. He told me he had thrown her off a bridge into traffic. Made me listen to it on the radio . . .' Shaun broke down, the sobs wracking his body. His son was still wrapped around his waist; he seemed to grip tighter. 'It looks like it was just some woman — some passing cyclist he must have just grabbed. Someone's mother.'

'It makes no sense, Shaun. Not to a good man like you.'

Shaun broke into a tense smile. 'I've got a difficult time ahead, George. I made some bad decisions. People got hurt.'

'You're allowed to be wrong, as long as it comes from the right place. You're going to be okay, Shaun. In time.'

The five minutes were strictly enforced. Shaun was shepherded back down into the rear of the ambulance and driven away. George looked on as his son and ex-wife still embraced tearfully.

'I'll let you off dinner.' Ryker's voice was close to his ear. George turned to her. 'Go call your wife, George.'

‘I tried that, remember? Calling out the blue? I need a pretty good reason these days.’

Ryker thrust her hands into her pockets. She looked back over at Carol and her son. ‘That’s your reason, George. That’s all that matters to you.’

‘There’s a lot that matters to me.’ George said. He thought he heard a chuckle from Ryker as she walked towards her car.

THE END

Thank you for reading this book. If you enjoyed it please leave feedback on Amazon, and if there is anything we missed or you have a question about then please get in touch. The author and publishing team appreciate your feedback and time reading this book.

Our email is office@joffebooks.com

www.joffebooks.com

ALSO BY CHARLIE GALLAGHER

BODILY HARM

PANIC BUTTON

BLOOD MONEY

END GAME

Made in the USA
Lexington, KY
26 September 2017